COMMON GIRL

FAÎTE FALLING
BOOK EIGHT

MARY E. TWOMEY

MARY E. TWOMEY

Common Girl
Book Eight in the Faîte Falling Series

By

Mary E. Twomey

COPYRIGHT

Copyright © 2017 Tuesday Androsian
Cover Art by Emcat Designs

All rights reserved.
First Edition: July 2017

This is a work of fiction. Any resemblance of characters to actual persons, living or dead, is purely coincidental. The author holds exclusive rights to this work. Unauthorized duplication is prohibited.

This book is licensed for your personal enjoyment only. If you would like to share this book with another person, please purchase an additional copy for each reader. Thank you for respecting the hard work of this author.

For information:
http://www.maryetwomey.com

DEDICATION

For my Aunt Irene,
who is simply and utterly magical

1

MY NAME IS ROSE

"My name is Rosie, and I'm an alcoholic," I said, holding onto the podium with white knuckles. A few strands of brown hair fell loose from the messy bun atop my head, but I couldn't let go of the podium to brush them from my face. I waited for the obligatory, "Hi, Rosie," before I continued. "It's been three days since my last drink."

I'd said the same thing for the last six months with literally no change in my status. At every single one of the weekly AA meetings, it was never more than three days since my last hit of blood from Bastien. Sometimes it was that morning I'd broken my fast and meandered glumly into the bedroom to ask for a little snack.

Bastien never minded. In fact, he looked forward to my meals. He loved the fact that I was the *Attelage* kind of Vampire, which meant I could only feed from him. Usually we got so worked up during my meals that we made love right after I drank. He was never reticent to give me as much blood as I wanted, and loved every second of it. He relished being the only one who could sustain me, and drive me as crazy with lust as we did. We'd developed a sort of unquenchable hunger for each other, not wanting to be apart for more than an hour or so. We'd spent too much time trying (and failing) to get together; we didn't waste the gift we'd been granted.

The thing about it was that I didn't want to need blood. It had been a total accident that I'd been infected with Éireland's lost magic. I hadn't even been in Éireland, but was at my mother's castle in Avalon when it all went down, and the lost magic was released back into Faîte. Now I was part Vampire, and part some second benign thing that hadn't shown any symptoms. Bastien's guess was that the second black snake-like strand of magic that had flowed into me after I'd killed my mother and accidentally set all the lost magic loose, was just more Vampire mojo. He reasoned this as the guess why I couldn't go more than three days without gnawing on my own fingers for a hit of my husband's blood. I wanted to be a normal wife. I wanted my stinking 30-day chip.

A middle-aged woman named Marianne had hers now. It was her first one, and she was showing it to everyone like the coveted prize it was. I was proud of her, but part of me wished I could have that kind of discipline.

Bastien was quiet through the meetings we attended

every week, but this time as we helped stack up the chairs he paused to kiss my cheek. I loved the way his perpetual five o'clock shadow felt when it brushed against my smooth skin. "I think we should skip next week's meeting," he suggested. "I see how much it tears you up not to have a chip like Marianne's."

I conjured up a smile that told the world I was totally in control, but Bastien saw right through it. "One day I'll get mine."

"This isn't the same thing, and you know it. You can't live without... ketchup." It was our super-secret code word for blood. I know. We're total ninjas. "Living without alcohol is a fine thing for anyone's body. You can't survive without ketchup."

"We've been married for a year and a half now. I've been drinking ketchup for way too long. You'd think I'd get better at this. I mean, you got your one-year bronze chip months ago." My knuckles tightened on the folding chair before I stacked it with the others. "Why can't I get better at this?"

"Me being sober isn't the same thing as what you're trying to do. You're too hard on yourself. It's those night-mares that are making you so down today. You need a solid night's sleep."

"If only. Too many nights of the same creepy dream, and it still makes no sense to me." Every night when I finally fell asleep, a voice came into my mind. He never had a face or a body, just a voice that was low and deep. It was like the best kind of radio DJ, but with an Irish brogue and a penchant for skeeving me out. At first, I hadn't been able to understand him. Now, after months and months of the same nonsensical dream that always left me feeling disturbed and unsettled, through the random syllables I could make out a low command of "Come."

Nothing scary about that, right?

Bastien got me. He didn't freak out or demand we go back to Avalon to see if a healer could find us some answers, but held me patiently when I woke him with my tossing and turning. We made love half-asleep last night, and most nights that I woke him mid-slumber.

"Come here." Bastien pulled me into his embrace, kissing the square-shaped diamond he'd put on my finger. The three aquamarines on each side sparkled up at us, shining as brilliantly as they did the day we'd gotten married at the Justice of the Peace in a quiet joint affair with Lane and Reyn.

Bastien was more relaxed in my world. He smiled easier and laughed often. When he started to hum and turn us in a slow dance only we were invited to, I fell in love with him all over again. He had the smile that could transform the dismal meeting room with drab walls and uncomfortable chairs into a ballroom with merely a slight curve of his perfect lips. He hadn't been the type to dance to woo a woman, but he learned to waltz for me. Bastien had learned so many things, living in my world. We were inseparable and insatiable, and unapologetic on both those points.

"You look hungry. Let's get you home," he suggested, corralling me past the coffee and stale donuts toward the door. "These clothes look like you've been wearing them for too long."

I guffawed. "Hello, it's only one o'clock."

"I need you," he confessed, tucking me into his side as we waved goodbye to the facilitator. "That little red number of yours that we broke in last night? I think it needs a repeat."

I unlocked our car and slid into the driver's seat. "Well, it's not going to get a replay. You ripped it clear down the middle, if you recall. Such a greedy boy."

Bastien adjusted his jeans as he buckled. "You can't scold me like that. You know it makes me crazy. I'm two minutes away from throwing you down in the backseat."

"You know we can't do that; you're too loud."

"Me? I'm not the one the animals were worried about. That was all you."

I blushed at the reminder of the forty some-odd woodland creatures who pelted our farmhouse with pinecones, pebbles and sticks because I screamed so loud in the throes that they thought Bastien was attacking me. Part of my birth blessing was that I could communicate with animals and hear other unknown languages. Using my magic tired me out, which was how I got to sleep every night, since Avalon citizens usually didn't have the need for sleep.

Bastien was my *Guardien*, which meant he used loads of magic to ward our property against intruders and keep me safe. I loved sleeping next to my husband. Our simple life might seem boring to some, but we'd earned a few decades of nothing harrowing tearing us apart. People underestimate boring. Lately, it's been my codename for bliss.

Bastien's hand found its way to my thigh, which was how we always drove. He still didn't have his license, since he was a menace on the road even after all the tutorials Lane and I had given our guys. "Are we babysitting Lucas tonight?" he asked idly, staring out the window.

"Nope. Tonight's bowling. Wednesday night is bowling, Thursday is babysitting my baby brother. You think he's learned a new word yet?"

"No," Bastien replied, repeating Lucas' only word. Lane and Reyn got pregnant on their honeymoon. Perhaps before they'd even left on the plane for Barbados. Lucas had that gorgeous mixed-race light brown skin, chubby cheeks, Lane's bright smile, and Reyn's long, curly eyelashes. In short, we didn't have a prayer. Whatever Lucas asked for, we gave him.

Even though Lucas was my cousin and brother, we held the roles of Aunt Rosie and Uncle Bastien. Bastien was a mixture of protective and indulgent with Lucas. Did me in every time. "We should really be stricter with him.

Last time I fed him he only ate a few bites of dinner, and had like, three suckers."

I shrugged. "It's our right as his favorite aunt and uncle. Disciplining's for the parents. The spoiling's for us to do."

Bastien squeezed my thigh, and I could almost guess the question that flowed out from his luscious lips before it came. "You sure you want to wait three years before we have a baby?"

"I'm sure. I like our life as it is. And if you try and hide my birth control again, you'll only be shooting yourself in the foot. We've never gone a whole two days without sex, but you'll be staring down the barrel of a drought if you do that again. I'm this close to getting the shot just to nip that in the bud."

"Okay, okay. Just so you know my vote, I'd get you nice and pregnant right now. Say the word, and we can pull over and make us a baby."

I shot him a squinty eye. "Three years. I still don't have my degree yet."

"That reminds me, do we need to cut bowling short so you can study with Judah over Skype tonight? You've got those two finals next week."

"Nah. Bowling is sacred. I wouldn't dream of calling that off. I'm mostly prepared." Man, I hoped that was true. I'd been studying for these finals for weeks, staying after class with my professors and studying all the live-long day. I listened to recordings of the lectures over and over again until I felt confident enough to go out at night without feeling like failing grades were going to come toppling down on my head. Oh, the joys of being dyslexic.

"You think your freaky dreams will go away once the stress of finals is over?"

I shrugged. "Couldn't hurt. I was thinking we should go camping or something in the mountains to celebrate my last semester being over – pass or fail."

"You'll pass. You'll do great. And I'd love to go camping again."

"Want to take Lucas, and give Reyn and Lane some time together?"

"I really, really don't. Love the little guy, but I've got big plans for you. Big celebrating plans that involve things children can't be around for."

My lips drew to the side as if in thought. "Hmm. Things children can't be around for. Are we going to do our taxes? No, tax season is over. Are we going to talk politics?"

Bastien leaned over and whispered in detail several unutterable things he'd been wanting to try. He tugged my earlobe between his teeth, making me shiver as I pulled onto the main road.

A shudder rippled through my body in anticipation of all he was promising. "Well, I guess Lucas can stay home if we're going to be giving *that* a try."

2

BITE ME

Bastien's blood tasted like... It tasted like happy. In my dream that night, fresh off the bowling win, I dreamt contentedly about sucking down a whole glass of the crimson joy. He was all I wanted, and oh, how I wanted. I sipped from a wine glass, looking classy as I downed the scandal in plain sight. Bastien was swimming in the pond out back, giving me a nice view of his tightly toned body. It was such a peaceful dream that when the sky darkened and the deep voice I'd grown to loathe called out for me to "Come," I scowled.

"Come where? Could you be more specific, you faceless jackfish? I mean, seriously. This is a nice dream you're interrupting." Now Bastien was gone from the pond, the world on the periphery was fading to obscurity, and the drink in my hand was clutched too tight to reflect a relaxing day in the yard.

"Come," he beckoned again, his low, breathy voice holding a firm command to it.

I answered his directive with my middle finger high in the air and plopped back down on the lounge chair where I'd been reclining. In my other dreams, I hadn't engaged with the voice, but we were going on three months of this nonsense.

A cold wind picked up, and the Princess Leia gold bikini I suddenly realized I was wearing gave me no shelter from the quickening storm. Leaves swirled around me like dirt devils. Then branches and stones kicked up, whipping around in the miniature tornadoes. There were four dangerous whirlwinds that I saw picking up speed around me, making me nervous as they seemed to move with purpose. They closed in, corralling me towards our woods, which didn't look like ours anymore. Instead of the pine and oak trees that encased our property, the trees took on a Tim Burton type of personality. They were spindly, inter-weaving and seemed to beckon me with malicious intent. I could practically feel them breathing as my toes stopped at the edge outside the wooded area. I don't know why, but stepping inside felt like giving the voice what it wanted, and I was just plain too stubborn for that.

I turned around to face nature's wrath, gritting my teeth as the sticks, rocks and leaves swirled toward me with deafening speed. I screamed, covering my body as best I could.

Then the ground started shaking.

Then *I* started shaking.

"Come!" the voice commanded again, angry at my willful disobedience.

"Bite me!" I shouted into the wind.

Bastien's voice filtered in through the heavens, bringing me relief just in time. "Rosie! Honey, wake up!"

"Mama! Mama! You're scaring me!" Hugh Jackman said. The wolverine that slept in the bed with us licked at my face, rousing me just enough to shove my middle finger in the air one more time at the voice before I awoke.

3

——————

BEST FAMILY EVER

"**G**et out of the mud and come play with the puppets, Lucas. Mr. Wigglebrows wants to say hello." I put the puppet with obnoxious hot pink eyebrows on my hand and started talking with it in the worst British accent known to man. "Hello, I'm Mr. Wigglebrows. I wanted to know if you've been a good boy for your mummy and daddy."

"No!" Lucas said on default. He reached forward with chubby hands and hugged the puppet, wiping slimy, open-mouthed kisses all over the felt face of his beloved Mr. Wigglebrows.

"You heard it here first," I said, looking up at Lane with a scolding shake of my head. "This is the problem I have with my nephew. He's too cute. Trouble in the making." Yes, Lucas was my brother. Yes, Lucas was my cousin. But I lived for being the overindulgent aunt who always had toys, snuggles and treats for him.

Lane flipped her cocoa-colored hair over her shoulder. "Don't I know it. At least I'm firm on the no candy rule. Reyn is such a pushover."

Reyn didn't miss a beat, even though he was tilling and planting in our massive garden with Draper and Bastien. "I heard that!"

"I said it loud!" she countered, cupping her hands around her mouth to call out to Reyn as he hoed. Then she turned to me with a relaxed smile, her early forties post-baby body only curvier and more glamorous as she stretched out in the lawn chair next to mine. I don't know how she did it. We wore matching baby blue tank tops and cut-off jean shorts, looking like sisters who didn't have a care in the world. The faint pink line that stretched diagonal across her face was a memory of a battle long set aside. "So, camping, huh? I think that'll be awesome. Great way to celebrate you getting your diploma."

"*If* I get my diploma. Everyone's so sure this is a done deal, but I could fail. Everything could still fall to crap."

"That's my little Suzy Sunshine. Judah said you were ready."

"He was just trying to end our tutoring session so he could go off with Jill."

"That's one dedicated girl. After all this time, I can't believe she stuck with him."

"I can believe it. Judah's one in a million." And I meant

that sincerely. My BFF since the fourth grade had stuck by my illiterate self no matter what. We'd survived difficult classes, bullying, getting abducted, and even went through parts of Avalon together. I'd seen his good sides and his bad ones, and I understood why he was worth waiting for. I was relieved Jill saw the same immeasurable goodness in Judah, as well. He moved to Tulsa to be with her, and though I missed him every day, it was healthy for us to finally cut the cord.

Though really, we talked on the phone or on Skype every day, and exchanged at least two dozen text messages before lunch, so I'm not sure how much separation we were actually enduring.

Lane watched her husband hoe in the garden with unconcealed lust. "Judah's a great person. Any idea when he's going to pop the question? He's been sitting on that ring for months now."

"He said he was waiting for the right time."

"And when might that be? This year?"

"Most likely. I think he wants to get his company further along before he proposes. He's got this whole speech prepared. He's practiced it on me like, ten times already."

"And did you accept?"

"Of course." I raised my nose in the air like a snooty lady. "I only say yes to the best of the best."

"I can see that." Her eyes fell to Bastien, who was working tirelessly in the field with my elk we'd named

Bambi by his side, and Hugh Jackman on his shoulder, clinging to his flannel. "You and Bastien doing alright? You seem happy. I've never seen anyone so devoted to you as he is. I'm glad you guys are so tight."

"That's the thing about husbands and wives, I hear."

"Yes, but it's more than that. It's the *lueur*, plus the love, plus your Vampire bond thing. Trying to have a conversation with him while you're in another room is nearly impossible. It's like he's counting the seconds until you get back. Not in a pining way, but in a 'she's back, so I can breathe now,' kind of way. It's intense."

"After how long it took us to get together, I don't blame him."

Lane picked up the slimed-on Mr. Wigglebrows and put him on her hand to dance the puppet around for Lucas. "I like seeing you happy, kiddo. Nothing better for a mom than to watch her daughter smile as often as you do."

"You're doing that thing," Bastien called across the field without looking up.

"What thing?"

"You're talking about me. You've got that goofball blush and grin about you."

I couldn't help the smile that beamed out from me whenever he looked my way. You try having a sexy lumberjack flirt with you and see how stoic you can be. "What do you know about it? I could be talking about Hugh Jackman."

Bastien paused his work in the garden to pet the

wolverine on his shoulder. "Nah. You only look at me like that." He snuck me a smile that made my toes curl in anticipation of the next moment we could be together. He had that way about him I couldn't resist.

Lane sniggered. "See? That's exactly what I'm talking about. You should get married."

I held up my hand to display my ring. "We already did. Remember that day we wore the matching wedding gowns and married the men of our dreams? Already happened."

Lane sighed contentedly, watching Reyn as he planted tomato plants with her son, Draper. "Feels too good to be true. Do me a favor? If I'm dreaming, don't pinch me."

Lucas wasn't walking yet, but he could crawl to his mommy faster than anything. He flopped into her arms and rolled onto his back, pulling up his shirt so she'd rub his tummy.

Draper raised his arms over his head and twisted at the waist, stretching out his back. His black hair fell away from his angular features, revealing blue eyes and wide lips that always smiled for me. "Mom, were there any plants in your car? I unloaded everything from the truck, but I think we're missing a few."

"I'm not sure."

I fished around for my shoes in the grass. "I'll go check." I loved it when Draper called Lane his mom. She'd adopted him in Avalon after they'd been reunited from a twenty-one-year separation. She'd helped raise him, but then had to leave in the dead of night to take me to

Common when I was just a year old. Draper drifted through his lowest common denominator lifestyle after Lane left, but upon her return, found himself once more. Lane just had that way about her. Draper's jaggoff father, Duke Henri, had disowned his gem of a son, which left Draper open for Lane to adopt.

Though Draper was around two years older than Lane's husband, we all shrugged off the weirdness that made our oddball family work. Draper called Lane his mom, and referred to Reyn as his dad. That had taken some getting used to, but I did the same thing, and claimed Draper as my brother even though we were technically cousins. The two of us were both disowned outcasts by our fathers, and had been joyfully adopted by our Aunt Lane. My own father, King Urien, had cast me out of the kingdom I'd helped build up when he found out I'd been infected by the dark Vampire magic. Fun times.

Reyn, who was the same age as my husband, didn't miss a beat, scooping me in his arms the second the ink dried on his wedding certificate. "You're my daughter now," Reyn had insisted. Ever since then I'd tried to remember to call him "Dad", if for no other reason than to freak Bastien out. My husband still categorically refused to call his best friend "Dad", though technically, Reyn was his father-in-law.

I feel like our family should be on a Narnia-inspired talk show. The roles were so mixed and weird, but somehow we all worked together beautifully.

I leaned over and blew a raspberry onto Lucas' round belly, giggling at the baby laugh that always lifted my spirits, no matter how high they already were. I stood and brushed off my light blue shorts, blowing Bastien a kiss that he wiped all over his sweaty face and scrubbed into his armpits before I went to the four-car garage. I peered in the bed of the truck to make sure they'd emptied it, and then opened up the trunk of Lane's SUV to double-check for extra plants. Sure enough, there was a flat of little planters that had been left behind.

When I leaned over to grab the long tray of twenty-four bell pepper seedlings, I hadn't expected the voice I'd know anywhere to come up from behind me. "Now tha's a pert little arse. Tell me Bastien's tapping it nightly."

4

THE MISSING LINK

I whirled around, my heart jumping and catching in my throat. The sight that filled my vision would make most women shrink away, I'm sure. Broad shoulders, messy dark-blond hair, scars littering his tall, muscular body, and tattoos of zippers snaking up and out of his green t-shirt. The neck tattoo matched mine, along with the one on our wrists. "Link?! Are you seriously here?" I didn't wait for an answer, but crashed into his outstretched arms. My arms wrapped around his neck as he engulfed me in the tight hug I'd been missing, squeezing me as he lifted my feet off the ground. I kissed his face all over, breathing in the woodsy scent of my old friend. "How? You said not for five years! I'm so glad you're here. Oh, Link! I missed you so much. Tell me you're staying for a while. Tell me my world gets to keep you as long as we like." I squeezed his thick neck through his chuckle.

He squinched his eyes shut, making it seem like someone hugging him was emotionally painful. He gripped me for all he was worth, as if that might make breathing easier. "Grand ye are, wee Rose. I thought I was making up how much I loved ye, but here ye are, stealing all the smiles and keeping them for yourself."

"Well, you've got a smile worth stealing, that's for sure." I paused to study his face up close, my brows pushing together in concern. "What happened to it? The smile that could light up a football field with a single flirt. Where is it?"

He mustered up a good enough representation to let me know that life had given him a beating, but that he was still in there somewhere. "I saved a sliver of it for ye. I traveled long, trekking across worlds to bring ye a piece of all tha's left of your old Link."

"Then I'll be gentle with such a fragile treasure." I placed a light kiss to his lips, like old times. "We'll make it better, Link. You're safe here with us."

"Aye. I hoped ye'd be as beautiful as I remembered. You're lovelier still, if tha's possible. My Common girl, just as perfect as ever."

"Oh, you."

"And your skin looks normal again, not all glowingly peachy like it did after Kerdik enhanced ye."

"Ah, you can thank spray-on tans for that little miracle.

Does Bastien know you decided to come stay here? He didn't say a thing."

"He doesn't know. I was hoping ye might have tha extra room ye promised I could stay in if I ever came to visit ye."

"We have like, five extra rooms, and you can pick your favorite." I squeezed him with my whole being, my heart singing against his.

A horn honked from the road, but I couldn't see the street from our garage. Bastien had insisted on a super tall privacy fence. Link slid me down until my feet tapped on the concrete floor. "The driver doesn't take our money. Can ye help me out?"

"Of course. Hold on. I'll grab my wallet." I scampered into the house through the joined garage door and snatched up my wallet, smiling gleefully at our friend returning to us. Link gave me a piggyback ride down to the cab, laughing the whole way. The sound of Link's laugh was marvelous, bathing me in its beauty I'd been living without for far too long. I slid off him to ask the driver how much we owed for the ride.

My head tilted to the side when I noticed a woman in an Amish-type dress sitting with her head down in the backseat. She was sitting next to a man who wore black fingerless gloves, dirty jeans and a black long-sleeved t-shirt. It was an olive-skinned, overbulked thug next to a straight up Mennonite woman. Not something you see every day. The woman's bonnet hid her face, so I glanced up at Link with a raised eyebrow.

Link shot me a tight shake of his head, letting me know that he'd fill me in on everything later. I shoved a fistful of cash at the driver and opened the backdoor for the woman. She didn't look up at me, nor did she move to exit the car.

Link leaned his head down to talk quietly to her. "Come on out, Quinn. It's alright. This is Rosie. She won't harm ye."

I held up my hands. "Oh, jeez. Of course not. If you're a friend of Link's you're welcome to stay here."

Quinn had nervous, thin fingers that twisted the fabric of her beige apron, which was draped over her gray ankle-length dress. The bodice was more fitted than your average Amish, showing off her narrow waist and tight shoulders. She kept her head down as she reached for Link's hand with a tremble to her hand.

I kept my gasp to myself when I saw the burns on her wrist. They looked painful, and I began to understand why Link, who was usually a bull in a China shop, was extra careful with her as she slid out of the car and stood before him. I wanted to hug her, to let her know she was welcome here, but girlfriend looked about ten seconds from ducking and running. "It's nice to meet you, Quinn. I'm Rosie, an old friend of Link's. Let's get you into the house."

"Aye, your majesty."

"Oh, right." I always forgot about my royalty status. My title back in Faîte was the Avalon Rose, or Queen Rosie the Gentle. Morgan le Fae and King Urien had been my parents, so I was co-ruler of Province 1 after my mother died. Duke Lot ruled Province 1 for me, but my title didn't go away.

My gaze shifted to the hulking dude who slid out of the car and towered over me. He was easily a few inches over six feet tall and was built like Link and Bastien – broad shoulders, beefy chest, bulked-out biceps, and a neck tattoo that marked him as an Untouchable. While Bastien, Mad and Link were in their young thirties, this dude looked to be pushing his mid-forties. I hadn't met two members of the Brotherhood, so I tried to stand straighter as I extended my hand to him. "Hey, man. I'm Rosie. Nice to meet you." It was either Nicholai or Antonio, but I didn't know which.

Dude eyed my hand with a skeptical expression, which I didn't think I'd earned just yet. "What do ye want?"

I shifted my gaze to Link, who sighed. I quirked my eyebrow at the new guy. "One hundred million dollars, of course."

A muscle tightened in his jaw, but he didn't drop his cold stare. "Figures. I'll get on it. Not sure how long tha'll take, but I'll take care of it."

"A handshake," I amended my demand. "I was kidding about the money, dude. All I want is to shake your hand and say hello. That cool?"

He studied my hand, as if there was a written contract taped inside my palm that might rope him in to actually wrangling me one hundred million dollars or something.

When he finally shook my hand, he said, "Tha's not all ye want. It never is with you females."

I clasped my hands under my chin and faked a swoon. "Aw, my very own sexist jackhole. Can I keep him, Link?"

Link gripped my shoulder in a half-hug. "Ye can dress him up in bows and ruffles, if ye like. When ye married Bastien, ye married into the Brotherhood. Think of us as two more strapping husbands who've come to see ye after a long one."

Yes, the Brotherhood was slightly strange in the way they viewed their women, but there was no undoing it. "Done. You got a name to go with that charming scowl, sailor?"

"Antonio."

I decided on being helpful to avoid further contact with Prince Charming. "Cool. You guys got any bags in the back?" I walked around the car, where the cabbie shot me furtive looks as he opened the trunk, warning me of the weirdos I was taking in.

I gave the driver a cheerful smile, as if to communicate there was nothing abnormal about a scarred, Irish body-builder who never shut up, a surly, tattooed sexist brat, and an Amish burn victim who still hadn't uttered more than a sentence. "Have a nice day, man. Thanks for giving them a lift." Dude couldn't handle the weirdness I'd accumulated (and was super proud of).

"No," Antonio said with an edge to his command. He

took the bags from my hands, as if me carrying his stuff was offensive.

The cab drove off, and I couldn't help the grin that beamed at having Link back. "Bastien's going to freak. I want to get it on film." I stuck my hand out to the woman, who was looking down at her shoes. "Hi. Quinn, is it? I want you to meet Bastien. He's out back."

Quinn shook my hand, but then quickly retracted it. "Yes, your majesty," she mumbled quietly, her Éirish accent just as thick as Link's.

Link waved off my inquiring eyebrow, asking him why girlfriend was so timid. "Quinn's a little shy, but she's alright." His arms went around her, and I saw her rigid body language melt a little at his touch. She was lean and tall, only a few inches shorter than Link. She leaned her head on his sturdy shoulder and brought her hand up to rest on his chest. "S'okay, Quinn. I told ye Rosie would like ye. No one's gonna hurt ye here."

My hand went over my mouth to cover the squeal of glee at Link actually showing manners and sweetness to a woman – and a modest one, at that. Link was an Untouchable, which was the biggest kind of warrior-like celebrity in Faîte. It meant he could walk into any room and women would fawn all over themselves trying to go home with him. Untouchables were literally above the law, and did as they wished. Quinn seemed like the exact opposite of his type, which was probably a very good thing.

I led the way up the slight incline leading up to the

house, and let Antonio stash their packs inside my front door. We strolled to the side of the house, just hidden from view of the others, who were gardening in our backyard. "Okay, I'll wait here with Quinn, and you sneak up on Bastien. I want to get a video of his face when he sees you for the first time. He'll be like," I dropped my mouth open and bugged my eyes, grabbed my heart and stumbled backwards.

"He'll do all tha, will he? Let's see, then. Quinn, stay right here, aye? Antonio will keep ye safe."

"Aye," she answered meekly, head still down. At this rate, I doubted I'd ever get to see the girl's face. She might have four eyeballs, and I'd never know. *That would be so cool.*

I readied my camera, corralling Quinn with my arm gently around her frail shoulders so we could hide behind the bushes on the side of the house, but still see the cuteness. Antonio stood a few feet behind us, looking over his shoulder at absolutely nothing. It had taken Bastien a few months to relax out here, too. Untouchables had paranoia engrained deep down, and it took time to undo the soldier mentality that kept them always on-guard.

Link bounded through the grass, booming out in his beautiful brogue, "Honey, I'm home!"

Bastien dropped his hoe, his mouth falling open and eyes wide as saucers. He didn't have the sense to brace himself as Link crashed into him with all the unstoppable strength of a freight train, bowling him clean over. Hugh

Jackman hissed and swiped at Link, but when Bastien let out an elated laugh, Hugh reassessed the threat level with an irritable huff.

"What are you doing here?" Bastien laughed, hugging his friend until the sweetness devolved into a wrestling match that flattened the area Draper had just tilled.

"What am I doing here? I've come to see how soft you've gotten. Living in a posh house, gardening with your family in the middle of the day? What's become of Bastien the Bold?"

"He's about to kick your ass! I'll show you soft." The two rolled around, dueling for dominance and laughs, letting out loud roars and dramatic cries of pain when the other "got one in on them." They were totally precious. They'd missed each other – needed each other, in a sense. There was a deep vein of brotherhood that ran to a permanent place in their hearts. It was difficult for anyone else to understand all they'd been through to earn their Untouchable status.

When they stopped to catch their breaths, Link's smile couldn't be contained. "Ye look happy, brother. Well-fed, too." He slapped Bastien's toned stomach, earning a punch to the shoulder.

Quinn stiffened at the punch, reminding me that she was totally out of her element and couldn't assess how much of a threat everything was at the moment. I squeezed her shoulder. "It's alright. Did Link tell you much about Bastien?"

Quinn shook her head, but didn't open her mouth.

"They're in the Brotherhood together. You know how they are. Big, formidable warriors to everyone else, but utter goofball cutie pies around each other." I kept my arm around her shoulders and rubbed her bicep gently to soothe her nerves. Or maybe that was making her more uneasy; it was hard to tell.

Antonio scoffed at my sum-up. "Ye know nothing about the Brotherhood. Ye wear our mark, so ye think ye know us."

I turned to meet his eyes over my shoulder. There was a moment when I debated taking the high road, but I quickly veered off into no man's land. "Oh, but I do know you. That's what I said, right? I know everything from your shoe size to what color dresses you like to wear on a Friday night. Green, to match your eyes. Bitch of a corset, though."

Antonio squinted at me, as if trying to figure out how pissed he was going to get at me for dishing out instead of rolling over and quaking in my boots. "Link is young," he said to explain away my comment about them being cutie pies.

"Good. See that he stays that way. I'd end it all right now if Link ever started looking as surly as you do."

When Antonio's comments simmered to a cool grumbling, Quinn spoke quietly to me. "Tha's the most I've ever seen Link smile."

"Bastien loves Link. Are you two..." I didn't know the

Amish way to ask if they were hooking up. "Are you and Link together?"

"Link is a good man," she replied, answering nothing.

"That's very true. Come on. I want you to meet everyone." I walked slowly with her, when I really wanted to bound up to Link and hug-tackle him. She had several false starts, but eventually she moved through the grass toward the others. "Hey, everyone. This is Link's friend, Quinn."

Lane stood, picked up Lucas and wrapped Quinn in a hug I knew she didn't understand. It was as if she was expecting to get jumped or something. "It's so nice to meet you. Please tell me you're staying for a while. We'd love to have you for as long as you'd like to visit."

"Aye, Ma'am. I think Link means to stay for a few days."

Draper introduced himself, but she flinched when he extended his hand to her. My big brother was a sweetheart, his blue eyes falling with pity when it became more and more clear that Quinn had been abused. He retracted his hand and bowed. "Pleased to meet you, Miss Quinn. I'm Duchess Elaine of Avalon's son, Draper." He motioned to Lane, who smiled with empathy in her eyes.

Quinn's intake of breath told me Link hadn't clued her into anything. She got down on her knees and bowed her head. "Forgive me, your majesty. I didn't know."

Lane didn't wave off her apology, but placed her hand on Quinn's bonnet. "I'm glad to meet you, my dear. This is my son, Draper, and my daughter, Rosie, and my baby,

Lucas." She motioned toward the garden with a smile. "And that's my husband, Duke Reyn."

I sniggered at the title. I couldn't help it. It was too cute. *Duke* Reyn. If only Avalon could see him humming a song and doing *The Macarena* while he gargled every morning. That's right, Lane and I set out to educate our men on the more important aspects of life in Common.

Lane met Antonio's stormy eyes, her shoulders rolling back to make her look like pure royalty. "I'm Duchess Elaine of the Tenth District of Avalon."

"Antonio the Horrible of Éireland."

Lane dipped her chin to acknowledge with respect the pain his life had held. To earn your status, you had to fight your way out of the army, which was basically being jumped and beaten down by all of your compatriots. If you escaped with your life, no one could lay a hand on you again. There were only five Untouchables in all of Faîte, if that tells you how nearly impossible the whole thing is. Lane was kind to acknowledge the pain a man carried with him if he was lucky enough to survive the brutality. "Untouchables are always welcome in our home."

Antonio looked on Lane as if she was smaller than him. I guess technically he was right, but I didn't like the way he sneered, as if trying to make her feel less. "I should say so. We're welcome anywhere we hang our hat. It's our right."

Lane didn't forfeit a centimeter of her cool. "That may be true, but being welcomed and taking rudely are two very different things. I'm happy to have any friends of my son-in-law in my home – whether they're entitled or not."

Antonio grumbled, as if Lane being awesome was something to be frustrated about.

I helped Quinn to stand from her humble bowing, wrapping my arms around her because she seemed to need the reminder that no one was going to off-with-your-head her. She was stiff in my arms until we crossed the ten seconds mark. Then she seemed to believe I wasn't going to hurt her. Her shoulders loosened and I felt her exhale.

Lane and I exchanged a look of concern, wondering what Quinn had been through that made her brace herself like that.

5

DINNER GUESTS

I heaped another serving of mashed potatoes onto Link's plate, knowing he ate as much as Bastien, which was always enough for two people. "You're a fine wife, Rosie – keeping your men fed and happy. This is quite the grand life you've got here."

"Then you should stay as long as you like." I handed Link his plate, smiling as he kissed my cheek. I'd been avoiding Antonio's gaze, which seemed to study me for signs of falsity. Though I couldn't imagine why. I couldn't possibly have done anything to piss him off this early in the game. "So, how'd you two meet?" I asked of Quinn, who kept her head down through her meal.

Quinn covered her mouth through a yawn, and I knew she was using that as a diversion so that Link would answer. "Ye look tired, Quinn. Rosie, do ye have a room with a bed for her?"

"Of course. Let me get some fresh sheets on the mattress." I'd finished half my plate of flavorless food, and didn't look forward to eating the rest. I wasn't trying to lose weight or be super into eating like a bird. I couldn't taste the food, due to my Vampire enhancements. The only thing that had a pleasurable flavor to it was Bastien's blood, and sometimes my own.

Bastien shot me a look that told me he wasn't going to scold me in public for not finishing my food, but that he noticed. "I'll save your plate for you to finish when you get back." The words were kind enough, but the threat behind them was real. The downside of being connected as we were was that he hovered a little too much for my liking.

"Somebody's in trouble," Draper sang under his breath.

"Thanks," I replied flatly, and motioned for Quinn to join me upstairs. I led her to one of the bedrooms down the hall from ours, opening the door like a tour guide. "Is this room okay for you two?"

She nodded, and then felt compelled to blurt out a nervous, "Link is not my husband."

"Oh. What about Antonio?"

Quinn blanched. "I don't know him well, and I think tha suits both of us just fine."

I tried to hide my smile. "Would you like the guys to set up in a different bedroom?"

She seemed torn between what was kosher and what she wanted. She fiddled with the hem of her apron, her head down. "I would not want to make requests of the Avalon Rose. It wouldn't be proper."

I tugged down a spare set of sheets and started making the bed. "You don't have to worry about that kind of stuff here. We're normal people in this world. No one knows about my title in Common. We've got plenty of bedrooms for Link and Antonio to crash in."

"Yes, your majesty. Thanks."

"How long have you guys been traveling?"

"It took us nearly a month to get here. We ran into some trouble leaving Éireland."

"Then why don't you borrow some of my pajamas, and I'll wash your clothes for you. You can take a shower, if you like. You'll feel like a whole new woman."

Her chin moved slowly from side to side in horror. "I couldn't let ye wash my clothes. You're not a servant."

I chuckled at her cuteness. "The machines wash our clothes here. Easy-peasy. The machines are our servants, and we are the overlords." I knew she wouldn't get my humor, but somewhere in Tulsa, I hoped Judah was chuckling at my lame joke.

I trotted to my bedroom and pulled out my least form-fitting flannel pajama pants and a gray thermal shirt. She was several inches taller than me and had a slender shape with more subdued curves. She didn't seem like the shorts and tank top type, judging by the Amish gown she wore like armor.

I gathered up a clean towel and washcloth, and

motioned for her to follow me to the bathroom. Explaining the faucets and whatnot to her took a few minutes, but eventually she understood it all. "When you get undressed, you can just leave your dress and bonnet on the floor outside the bathroom door, and I'll wash them for you."

"Yes, your majesty. Tha's so gracious of ye. I'm sure if ye taught me how to work the machine, I could do it so ye don't have to be bothered."

"It's no trouble. It sounds like you've had a long journey, and I can't wait to hear all about it. Wash up and come on down. I'll make you whatever you like for dessert, and we can commiserate on the ups and downs of traveling with Link." I grinned at her, but she still kept her head down. At this rate, I wondered if I'd ever get to see the poor girl's face.

When I made my way down the steps with an armload of laundry, Bastien took the stack and motioned me back to the table with a jerk of his head. "Dinner, babe."

I sighed, but didn't argue. "Oh, fine. Did you get out of Link what he's doing here, or who the girl is?"

"Not yet. I think he's waiting until it's just us."

"That's cool. FYI, your buddy Antonio's a grade-A jackwagon."

"Aw, he's not so bad. Surlier than I remember, but that's to be expected. He was travelling with Nicholai, last I heard. Nicholai's wife Katya is a real pill. Demands everything from everyone because Nicholai was stupid enough to mark her. The finest clothes, jewels, you name it. It would max anyone out on the female population, living with that."

"I knew it had to be a woman's fault," I said with a touch of sarcasm.

Bastien kissed me lightly, barely tasting my tongue before he pulled back to make sure we weren't putting on a show for the others, who were still in the kitchen. "I guess we'll have to be quiet tonight in bed."

"You're not so good at quiet."

Bastien snorted. "You're the loud one. You might want to mime screaming my name tonight. I don't have a problem controlling my volume."

"Oh, you won't have any trouble with that tonight, because you'll be wearing a gag. I don't want Link hearing your sex noises. He'll get jealous and want you all for himself."

Bastien dropped the clothes and backed me to the nearest wall, lacing his fingers through mine so he could pin my arms to the wall above my head. "You're going to gag me, huh?" He kissed me harder this time, trying to dominate, when we both knew he loved it when I was in charge.

I started whispering all the filthy things I wanted to do to him – things that should really only ever be shared in hushed tones.

Bastien's groan was needy as he pressed his body to

mine. "Let's pop into the bedroom real quick. No one will miss us."

"I wonder if they're over here," came Draper's warning for us to keep our clothes on. He waited a whole five seconds for us to break apart before rounding the corner with a narrowed eye. "Well, would you look at that. I followed the feral animal grunts and found them. Works every time."

"Tonight," Bastien whispered in my ear before he pulled away, giving me the shivers. He scooped up the laundry and placed a chaste kiss to my lips before he left down to the basement, where the laundry room was.

I glowered at Draper. "Next time you bring a woman home to your bachelor pad, I'm coming in with two cymbals and a whole friggin' marching band, you cock-blocker."

Draper sniggered at my sass. "Forgive me for stopping you from getting it on in the hallway when you have company staying here. Note to self: don't invite house-guests if you intend to do your Animal Planet reenactments all over your home."

"Did you have a purpose for interrupting?"

"You know, you'd think I would." He looked up at the ceiling in thought. "Lane and Reyn were taking off. Not taking off as much as you and Bastien were about to, granted, but they wanted to say goodnight. Also, Judah's on the phone. I caught him up as much as I could." He shoved my cell phone at me.

"Your jokes? Hilarious." I frowned at my big brother.

I put Judah on speaker so the two of us could talk to him. "This is so cool! I didn't know you'd be having more fantasy fiction adventures without me. Should I hop on a plane and come on out?"

I snorted. "No! You have a job and a life and a girlfriend. I'll tell Link you said hi, but that's all you'll get."

"I've got more than enough in my savings to afford a plane ticket. I've got so many questions for the Amish girl!"

I leaned against the wall, Draper rested his right shoulder on the wall opposite me. I held the phone between us as I spoke. "Speaking of questions, weren't you going to pop the question tonight? Didn't you have the big dinner with Jill planned?"

Judah's tone turned evasive. "Not the right time for it. Houseguests from out of this world qualifies as enough of an occasion to postpone dinner plans. Jill has to go in early to work tomorrow anyways."

I extended my arm to Draper to escort him as if I was the gentleman and he was the fair lady. He fluffed his imaginary long curls and hefted up his imaginary boobs before taking my arm. Yes, we were meant to be in the same family. "You know," I commented to Judah, wanting to say only enough so he'd stop being such a flake about the whole thing, "Jill will say yes. I don't get why you're stalling so much."

"Stop it with the pressure cooker, already. I'll ask her when it's the right time. Link showing up with the Amish is a good reason to cancel dinner plans. She doesn't know I'm postponing the proposal. She doesn't even know I have a ring."

I led Draper into the kitchen, where Reyn was doing the dishes. "You're a giant chicken, but I love you just the same."

"Love you, too, Ro. If I'm not coming out tonight, then soon. I'm starting to turn normal without you and Lane."

I smirked at his cuteness. "I can't imagine anything more tragic."

6

THE TRUTH ABOUT QUINN

I moved to the plate Reyn had left out for me, and inched it closer to the dirty dishes pile. I hoped he wouldn't notice, and would wash it so I didn't have to finish the potatoes, carrots and beans that tasted like ash to me.

Reyn didn't even look up from drying the dish he was working on as he scooted it back away from the to-be-washed pile that he was plowing through. "Here you go, sweetie. I thought you might still be hungry."

Reyn blessed me with all of the endearing names Urien had called me before my grand disowning. It was precious that he was trying to give me something that resembled a father. Because he made such a generous effort with me all the time, I obeyed Reyn implicitly. It was easier to pretend I was the ideal daughter with Reyn as my dad. Each time I did the simple things he asked, I felt slightly mollified, reminding myself that I'd done nothing to earn getting kicked out of Urien's kingdom. "Okay, Dad." That earned me another point, and made him smirk. Both of us loved each time I claimed my husband's bestie as my father.

I know it's weird, but it works.

I sat down at the counter on the tall stool and chewed my way through the rest of my plate, my cheek leaning on my hand in boredom. I could hear Link playing with Lucas in the living room, and guessed that Lucas was being launched into the air over and over. I made sure Reyn saw my cleaned plate before I tipped it into the sudsy water, proving that I was a good daughter.

Draper drained a glass of water and set it on the counter. "Hey Ro, do you want Antonio, Link and Quinn to stay with me?"

"Nah, it's fine. I haven't seen Link in so long; I want to spend some time with him. I know Bastien won't feel right sending him to stay anywhere else, even if it's just a few yards away at your place."

Draper bumped his hip to mine. "Do they have earplugs?" he hinted with a devious smirk.

I blushed, and then stuck my hand in the warm water just to flick a few suds in his face. "We are not that loud."

Reyn and Draper both guffawed. Reyn finished off the last dish, and then dried his hands on the towel that hung over the oven door. "Make sure they know they can stay with us tomorrow night, after they have to disinfect their ears."

I mimed laughing as I dipped a clean cup into the water that was still draining in the sink. I flung half a cup's worth of dishwater at Draper, who retaliated by turning on the sink and spraying me with the hose in the face. "Okay! Okay! I give!"

Lane trotted into the kitchen to see what shenanigans we'd gotten up to without her supervision. "Children, we have distinguished company with us tonight. Link is too refined for your antics." She grinned at Link, who bounded into the kitchen behind her.

Link scooped up Lucas and trotted over to Draper, dangling the baby by his armpits and swinging the tyke's legs to make it look like Lucas was kicking Draper. "Get him! He attacked the fair Queen of Avalon! Get him, wee baby! Defend the throne!"

Draper made dramatic noises of pain, throwing his body back with each kick from Lucas' chubby legs. Lucas' giggle was the best, and always made me smile. He was just about the cutest baby I'd ever seen in my life, and watching him was the high point of any evening. Even dripping wet as I was, I couldn't pry myself away to go change if it meant missing out on Lucas and Link in action.

"I think it's time for the mighty warrior to sleep, now," Reyn ruled, taking Lucas from Link just as he started to fuss. Fae babies slept until their magic could sustain itself – usually between three and five years old.

"You'll be here in the morning?" Lane inquired, pausing before heading out with her husband and son.

"Aye. Tell Lucas to rest up. Antonio and I will need some solid backup if we're going to take the wicked Queen on tomorrow." He pounded his fist into his hand and shot me a menacing look.

I put my dukes up, not caring that I was still soaked. "I'll be ready for all three of you. Untouchables are such babies."

Link's mouth fell open, and his hand went to his heart to cover over the stab of my words. "Tha was harsh. I think I might cry and need a nappy change."

Antonio moved in from the living room as if rolling in with the shadows. He stood in the entryway with a glower that seemed pretty permanent. Though our kitchen had cheery pumpkin-colored walls, gleaming countertops and white-frosted ceiling fixtures, Antonio's presence seemed to add a note of drab duty to the atmosphere. He said nothing, but his mere presence made me want to vacate the scene all the same.

Bastien came up to entertain Link with Draper, while I ducked upstairs to change. I caught Quinn coming out of the bathroom on my way back down, and stopped short at the sight of her uncovered face. "Oh!" I stepped back before I could censor myself. Girlfriend had a glossy burn mark running two inches from her left ear to her jaw. Finally, the reason for her bonnet became clear.

Quinn met my eyes with a jolt of fear at being exposed,

freezing like an animal on the verge of bolting. "I... Excuse me, your grace."

I caught her arm before she could dart into the bedroom. "Hey, hold up. We were going to all hang out downstairs. Could you come on down for a little while so we can get to know you better?" My nose crinkled, realizing something way later than I should've. "Wait. Link said you were tired. Why do you sleep? I thought in Faîte, you only slept if you used too much magic on a regular basis. Bastien and I sleep, but I burn through a lot of mojo because of my birth blessings, and he sleeps because he's my *Guardien*. What's your story?" It wasn't an accusation, but it was a direct question. If I was housing people, I needed to know what I was getting myself into. I kept my tone light, hoping I didn't spook her.

Quinn's eyes had a hard time meeting mine, but when they finally did, they seemed to say more things than her mouth was willing to voice. "Link should tell ye."

I realized that my shoulders were tensed, and I probably looked like I was cornering her or something. "Sorry. I haven't been in Faîte in a long time. Come on down for a little bit. You need to get to know us, if for no other reason than so that you can see we're no threat to you. You look a little uncertain of us." I knew I would feel uneasy until everything was out in the open.

"As ye wish it," she replied quietly, her eyes on her bare feet.

I led the way down the stairs. Bastien was building a

fire in the hearth with Antonio, and Draper brought in a huge bowl of popcorn. He threw a piece at me to remind me that I was still fifty calories shy of 2000 for the day. Let me tell you the joy it is to have an older brother who hovers like a father. I plopped down on the beige couch, jostling when he sat next to me and put the bowl on my lap. "Extra butter, just how you like it."

I actually didn't mind eating popcorn, since half the taste was in the smell. I could inhale the buttery fumes, and pretend the taste matched. I ate mostly for texture, and popcorn had a fun crunch it took me a full bowl to tire of. "Thanks, Drape. You going to work soon?"

"I feel like I should call off. It's not like anything there will be as interesting as all this."

Part of integrating the newbies into society meant that they got jobs. Though we didn't need the money, they needed the social norms and interactions from Commoners. Draper worked part-time doing security for a gated community not too far from us. He basically sat in the booth and read, but when he had to buzz people into the subdivision, he smiled and had little exchanges with the residents. Baby steps.

"You'll miss the bus if you don't get going, big brother."

"Fine, fine. I'll go grab my uniform." Draper kissed my cheek. "Night, baby Rosie." Then he stood and hugged Link, like two men who had seen each other through a falling country. "I'm glad you're here, Link. I'll be back in the morning."

Quinn stood on the outskirts of the living room, afraid to disobey my request for her to join us, but equally fearful of being near us for some reason. Since Link made no effort to integrate her into the group, I motioned to the spot on the floor in front of me. "Come and sit, Quinn. Let me brush your hair." Again, it was a nice offer, but I left no room for misinterpretation. I was giving her a directive. So help me, she would like us. I didn't want anyone feeling afraid in my home. The more she was around us, the less on edge she could let herself be. That was my theory, anyway.

I darted to the bathroom and grabbed a brush and a few rubber bands, and then set to work on her long snarls while Bastien filled Antonio and Link in on all we'd been up to since we'd left Faîte. "Reyn and I work outside doing construction, but only three days a week. Rosie and Lane made us all get jobs so we'd understand Common better."

"Tha sounds nice. Think ye might be able to get me a job there?"

I paused brushing, absorbing the hint that Link wanted to stay with us for longer than a little visit.

Bastien caught it, too. "Of course. So, you're staying for a while, then?"

Link took a long swig of his beer. "Aye, if tha's alright." We didn't keep alcohol in the house, since Bastien was clean now, but Draper kept a stash at his place we'd pilfered for our guest of honor.

"Stay forever," I insisted. "We want you here super way

bad."

The corner of Link's mouth twitched. "Well, if ye want me super way bad, I don't think I can say no."

Antonio's tone was firm. "We'll stay until the worst of it blows over."

No one spoke for a few beats. I brushed Quinn's long dark hair, taking my time untangling weeks of wear and tear. The straight, thick locks hung all the way down to the middle of her back, giving me plenty to work with. I started twisting her hair into two French braids that ran down the sides of her head. "How did you two meet?"

Antonio looked into the fire, turning his back on me and any attempts at being drawn into the conversation. He was swell.

"Quinn's a Vampire," Link blurted out, finally cutting to the chase.

Quinn buried her face in her hands. "No, Link! Now they won't let us stay!"

My hands froze in her hair, absorbing the new detail that painted the picture in a whole different light. "Don't be silly. Of course we'll let you stay. Which kind of Vampire are you? Are you the *Attelage* kind, like me?" I chided myself for sounding like a dummy. Of course she was *Attelage*. The *Farouche* Vampires were rabid and had no language. Quinn was perfectly composed.

She lowered her chin in shame. "Yes, your grace. I'm an abomination. I don't deserve to be in your home. Ye shouldn't be braiding my hair, like I'm a person."

I bit my lower lip so I didn't correct her too harshly. "I'm a Vampire, and I'm still a person. You don't have to worry about us kicking you out."

"You've already bonded with someone, then?" Bastien took in her controlled mannerisms with calculating eyes, and then turned to Link when the truth dawned on him. "She bonded with you, didn't she."

Link drank more of his beer, unable to look at us. "Aye. It was an accident, but tha seems to be how these things work now. It's bad, Bastien. Éireland's changed, and not in a way the Brotherhood can fix. There's all sorts of danger tha there didn't used to be – Were-creatures, Vamps and surly Dullahan."

Bastien didn't waste a moment, but cleared the gap between himself and Link so he could grip his buddy tight. Then he moved to Antonio's side and gripped him in a hug that was so strange, I couldn't look away, though I felt like I should. Antonio didn't appear to be the cuddly type, but he softened for Bastien, letting the Brotherhood traipse past the barbed wire that was set up to keep the rest of the world out.

"I'm sorry," Bastien said quietly. "Éireland deserves better than that." Only the crackling fire dared compete with him for the floor. Shadows bounced off Antonio's face, highlighting the grief that went beyond a simple woe for the plight of the Fae. This was his homeland, and it was in the throes of a war with magic itself.

"The Dullahan are the headless horsemen, right?" I

asked for clarification.

Antonio's tone turned sharp. "Tha's enough about it for the night. We just escaped a world of them; we need one whole day without mentioning their cursed names."

I could tell Bastien had questions aplenty, but he backed down. "Okay, then tell me how this one here got infected," he said, pointing to Quinn, who shrank at the attention.

"The lost magic went straight for Éireland after flooding through Avalon," Antonio explained. "It was trying to get back from where it came, I guess. Lots of *Farouche* Vampires sprouting up overnight, feeding and killing at random. Not too many of the *Attelage* kind. The population took a hit. Teams were formed. Mad, Link and I were called in, and we were told to kill on sight. See a Vampire, kill it."

I pursed my lips in consternation. When I'd served as a brief ruler of Province I in Avalon, I'd ordered the *Farouche* Vampires be locked in a dungeon, not beheaded. Though no one else hoped for a cure, I still did. I'd instructed Duke Lot to feed them animal blood from the butchers, and hoped they'd stuck to my instructions.

Link rubbed the nape of his neck. "Only there was a faction who thought they could try and purge the magic from the Vampires. They thought their methods might give us back our people, so we didn't have to kill so many. It seemed like a good idea, until I saw what they were doing to them." He leaned against the fireplace, looking into the flames as if they held the answers, so he didn't have to look for them anymore. "They were torturing the Vamps. Stabbing with silver stakes, wooden stakes, burning them, casting painful spells just for sport near the end. I saw what they were up to, so Mad and I went in to clean house. The prisoners were all the *Farouche* kind, except for this one." He jerked his thumb to Quinn, who was now weeping quietly into her hand. "Ye can tell the difference because the *Farouche* Vamps don't know who they are. They don't have language. They can't reason. They're wild animals, basically, and need to be put down."

"Oh, Link," I said, not in judgement, but sadness. I couldn't imagine having to kill so many people, all because they'd stopped being people.

"I was about to off this one, but she begged me to stop. She had words, so I knew she could survive the higher magic, like ye had, Rosie. I wasn't thinking. I let her out of the cage."

I got down on my knees next to Quinn and wrapped my arms around her. "They put you in a cage?!" I shrieked, trying to keep my fury ebbing toward compassion rather than a tirade.

"Aye. Like animals to be poked at." Link gripped the mantle with his free hand. "I didn't know she hadn't bonded with someone. I let her out, and she couldn't help her urges. She fed on me, so now we'll never be apart."

Quinn's cry of anguish left no doubt that she regretted her life, and the unbreakable tie she was now stuck with.

7

TEA TIME FOR THE ABOMINATIONS

You could've heard a pin drop; the tension was so high. The crackle of the fire filled in the gaps where conversation might be useful. None of us had words for the steaming pile Link had stepped into. It was truly the only way him being with an Amish cutie could be feasible. "So, you're together now?" Bastien inquired, trying as I was to picture a universe where Link settling down with a woman was possible.

Quinn shook her head adamantly. "No! I'm married to Bram." Her shoulders fell like a dying kite – all the air gone from her optimism. "Or, I was, anyways. He put me out when I changed, but eventually he'll understand that I'm still me. He'll want me back."

I heard the lie that even she no doubt had a hard time choking down. It was a lie of kindness that helped her through the loss of her former life, so we all let her keep the fib so she could hold it tight in her heart. "Of course he will."

"Don't lie to her," Antonio cut in. "Bram's not coming back, and any woman should be thanking their lucky stars tha they don't have to be saddled to such a weak, selfish fool." He met Quinn's eyes and nodded, as if his words should make her buck up somehow.

I chose to ignore Antonio. It was either that or sock him across the face. "How about your family? Are they cool with Link and everything?"

Quinn's chin quivered, and I knew I'd asked the wrong thing. I dabbed at her cascading tears with my sleeve and held her tight. "They disowned me. Called me an abomination. Maybe that's what I am now, but it still hurts."

My own pain rose up in me with a fierceness I couldn't put on hold. I held Quinn's face as if I knew her, and had permission to manhandle her cheeks without a second thought. I looked into her green eyes and spoke quietly so my fury didn't give way to a shout. "You listen to me, Quinn. You are not an abomination. We did nothing wrong. Mutated genetics doesn't mean we aren't still people with ideas and plans. Does Link let you feed from him?"

Quinn nodded once, the shame palpable.

"Then you're not a monster who goes around attacking at random. You're a person – a lady, for sure." I tried to think of what Lane might do in this situation, what I could give her that might restore some normalcy to her suddenly disrupted and now nomadic life. "What would you and your mom be doing on a night like this? If you were upset, what would she do?"

Quinn's chin trembled, and in my periphery, I could see Link's jaw clenching. It was like he wanted to go to her to ease her pain, but couldn't let himself admit that he cared. The stakes were too high. They were already too bonded. If he comforted her, things might get complicated, and I knew that Link didn't do complicated.

Her voice was quiet, and laced with palpable pain. "She would sit with me while we sewed and drank tea. Somehow by the time we finished the last of the pot, everything would be a little better."

Though I barely knew her, I kissed her temple. "I think we can manage that. Bastien, would you mind running to Lane's and grabbing her sewing kit? I'll put on a pot of tea."

"Not a problem. Hang in there, kiddo." Then he paused to make eye contact with her. "If you're bonded to Link, then you're family to me. The Brotherhood looks after our own. You're safe here, Quinn." Bastien cupped her shoulder on his way out, and I loved him a little bit more for the gentleness he exuded for her.

I shot Link a look that told him to get his butt over here, but he shook his head in warning. I held Quinn while she wept on my shoulder, her hiccups so dainty and ladylike. Even when she fell apart, there was a gracefulness about her. "Hey, you don't have to worry about getting kicked out ever again. You live here now, okay? You and I are going to have a blast, once you get used to Common. We'll go clubbing, take classes together, go on hikes. It'll be great." I squeezed her again before I stood to start the kettle. "Link, could you sit with her until the tea is ready?" I addressed him with a syrupy smile, knowing that he wouldn't refuse me if put on the spot.

Link mouthed a few disparaging words at me, but ultimately obeyed. He sat on the couch next to where Quinn was on the floor. He reached down with an awkward hand and patted her atop the head, like a Neanderthal. It was like watching a monkey try to mimic human behavior he'd seen from afar. "There, there." He met my eyes and shrugged, as if to ask me what I expected.

I mouthed for him to try harder, but Link had no clue what to do with women who weren't interested in sleeping with him. He was good with me, but that had taken time. I spun on my heel, unable to watch the painful act of Link learning to be a gentleman. The water warmed while I fished through the tea bags.

"Ye can just boil water for her. She can't taste anything," Antonio said, making me jump.

"Jeez, for such a big fella, you don't make a sound when you walk. Impressive."

Antonio posted himself near the entrance, keeping a wide gap between us. "Ye were nice to her back there."

"Would you prefer I yelled?"

"No. I just thought you'd be like Katya."

"Funny. I didn't think you'd be judgmental, but I guess we were both wrong." I pulled out a peppermint tea box. "Does she like mint?"

"I thought ye were also a Vampire. Ye know Vamps can't taste anything but their mate's blood."

"I know, but smells are the only thing that make the ritual of eating or drinking enjoyable. Makes me feel like I'm still a person, instead of the abomination that I apparently am. Her parents really talked to her like that?"

"They've got their beliefs. Link told me King Urien held the same views. I can't believe you're at all surprised by it. Ye went through the same thing."

I pursed my lips, trying not to let that slice sting too badly. "My dad never said any of that to my face. I was just kicked out. I like to pretend he did it because he was just making a blanket rule to keep the kingdom safe. I can get behind that, to some extent."

"Ye don't mean tha."

"Maybe not, but I want to be the kind of person who does. Someone who can think globally, instead of just about how I hurt. Urien is not my greatest adventure, and that's okay." I cleared my throat and selected Earl Gray. I didn't care for it, but Quinn seemed like a legit lady, with tastes for things like grown woman tea. "I think that's enough talk about me for a good, long time. Tell me about you."

There was a long pause before Antonio replied with a tart, "No." Then he turned on his heel and left the kitchen.

Slam dunk. I made a mental note that if I wanted some space from Mr. Personality, I only had to ask him a personal question, and he'd run scared.

8

———————

KERDIK'S LIE

hen Bastien came back, the kettle was singing, and Link was clear on the other end of the couch. He'd extended his foot to brush against Quinn's arm, as if that was what you were supposed to do when someone had lost everything, and needed a little kindness.

Feet. Link offered feet.

I'd seen him hug her when they first got out of the cab, but that seemed to be a special occasion, reserved for when no one was supposed to be looking.

Bastien led Quinn gently to the kitchen table, making eye contact with me as he took out the needle from Lane's sewing kit and poked the heel of his battle-worn hand. A few drops of his blood dribbled into my tea cup, and I loved him for the sweetness. I knew what he was doing; he was making a show of a few nonsexual ways we handled my bloodthirst, so Link and Quinn didn't have to feel so taboo about the whole thing.

Link watched the display and motioned for the needle, so he could do the same for Quinn. It was only the best tea of my life, as it was every time Bastien did that for me. Quinn's lashes fluttered with relief, and I could see her shoulders relaxing a little as she let herself breathe after the indulgence.

Bastien and Link sat at the table while I opened the sewing kit and basket of material. I didn't totally know what I was doing, but Quinn's fingers seemed relieved to be put to the familiar use. She selected two squares of fabric, and threaded her needle to start stitching two of the ends together. Since I'd never done much sewing, other than the occasional patch that had to be affixed to my jerseys, I mirrored Quinn's delicate movements with two squares of my own.

"Talk," Bastien said abruptly. "We've been away with no contact for a year and a half. It doesn't sound like Éireland's doing so hot."

This seemed to be aimed at Link, since Antonio stood in the doorway. He hovered in the background like a gargoyle, not wanting to be part of the conversation. Link took a drink of his beer and leaned back in his chair. "Aye. The lost magic took its time getting home, but once it did, everything changed. We've got both kinds of Vampires, though not a whole lot of *Attelages*. We've got banshees, who are mostly left alone, though I've seen a fair few captured and tossed in a cage to be 'tended to.'" He spoke with emphasis, and I got the feeling that even banshees were being tortured, though all they did was announce impending deaths with a call as loud as a siren. "The Dullahan are back, and they were thirty strong before I left. There was some fighting between them, and I get the feeling they're going to split off into two groups, which seems like it'll present a whole new set of problems."

"Sort of like gang wars?" I inquired.

Link touched his nose to let me know I'd guessed his prediction. "Aye. The headless horsemen ride around on their mounts, seeking out the beheaded to recruit them into their ranks. Off their horses, they're no trouble to Éireland, but once they get on their horses it's a whole other story. Whenever a Dullahan stops riding, someone in Faîte dies."

I grimaced. "Oh, jeez. Every time?"

Link nodded. "The thing is, a group of the Dullahan got angry when they saw the way some of those affected by the higher magic were being killed off. Most of the Vamps are tortured, dismembered, ye name it. The other half of the Dullahan want to continue on with their quest to recruit the dead who've lingered behind. They refuse to ride on horses, so they don't accidentally add to the death toll once they dismount."

"That's considerate."

"Aye. But the other half have a vigilante mind about them. Sometimes I see their point, and other times I wish they'd shut their headless gobs. Antonio, Nicholai, Mad and I are trying to contain the damage as much as possible, but the Dullahan vigilantes are the kill first, verify never sort of lads. Some of the bodies they've racked up are innocents. But they're the Dullahan, so there's no one to keep them in check, but for the Brotherhood. It's a mess."

I watched Quinn select a third square of fabric, so I did the same, sipping my tea. The steamy cup tasted like Bastien and smelled like perfume. "Who's your ruler over there now?"

"Queen Shavon inherited the throne when her mammy was murdered by the Brothers of Destruction decades ago. She's alright, but not a ruler alive could handle the mess tha's been dumped on her. She's been trying to summon Cailleach or Brìghde, but they've abandoned Éireland. She's got an advisory board she consults, but at the end of the day, no one's got a plan."

"What about..." I stopped short of mentioning the name of my green friend whom we never spoke of anymore. I cleared my throat. "What about Urien and Duke Lot? Are they lending any support?"

Link batted his hand at my suggestion. "Nah. They've got their hands full with their own troubles. Urien, as ye know, thinks it's best to purge his region of any darkness. Duke Lot's not a bad bloke. He's taking in all the nonviolents, and the violent ones are being gathered up, captured and contained instead of killed."

I exhaled, grateful I'd chosen Lot to take over Province

1 for me. It was one thing for me to tell him what my stipulations were, but another thing entirely whether or not he decided to follow the rules I'd laid out.

Link took another drink before continuing. "In Éireland they're mostly killing off the *Farouche* Vampires, but Duke Lot has hope they'll find a cure somehow, so he's keeping them locked up. That way they can't hurt themselves or the civilians." Link shrugged, as if he didn't know which way was right anymore. "Lot even let the Dullahan stay if they agreed to only collect the heads of the dead and stay off of horses – though there's not as big of a clan in Avalon as there is in Éireland. We got the brunt of the higher magic, for certain."

"Dude, I cannot picture headless horsemen walking around Avalon. I like to think I'm pretty spook-proof by this point, but that would freak me out. What happens to their heads?"

Antonio jerked his thumb to his back. "They carry them in a pack, usually. The heads still work, as far as talking and seeing and smelling and whatnot. They sometimes even try to refasten their heads on so they can fit into normal life. Their heads are grayish, though. Black, fiery eyes, too."

"Totally bonkers." I kept my eyes on my sewing, noticing my stitches were super uneven. Quinn's were tight and uniform, nearly as perfect as a machine's. "Dude, how are you doing that? I'm still working on my first two, and you're on your fourth square? I suck at this."

Quinn shot me a flicker of a smile so small, I doubt anyone else caught it. "It takes practice, is all. You're doing quite well."

I shot her a withering look that told her I knew she was patronizing me. This earned me another flash of a smile before she ducked her head to keep her eyes on her project. Despite the burn, it was nice seeing her face. She had a slender nose, big doe eyes and a pretty smile, once she let it out to play.

Link finished off his beer, so Bastien got up and handed him another. "How's Mad?"

"He sends his love. He's determined to teach tha little pipsqueak of his to capture the *Farouche* Vampires."

I grinned at the memory of Mad training the little girl who'd quite literally fallen into his path. He'd tried to shake her, but she'd had no one else. The cutie pie clung to him until he softened enough to let her stay under his wing of protection. I couldn't blame the girl; Mad had saved my life on occasion, too. Stoic and borderline Asperger's as he was, I understood Madigan. "That sounds like him. How's Annabelle doing in Éireland?"

"She's a trooper, tha's for sure. Mad wants to mark her," he said, motioning to his neck tattoo, "but he's waiting until she turns sixteen. Said the mark might make her soft, instead of relying on the skills he's teaching her."

"I'm glad it's working out. I'm surprised they didn't come with you, though. You two always seemed to come as a set."

"Aye. Mad's not keen on bringing Annabelle to Common. Too much work to be done in Faîte."

I grimaced when I accidentally stabbed my thumb with the needle. "So I know about the bad magic that got loose. What sort of good mojo did you all get?"

"Nothing," Link replied, a glib look on his face.

"That sucks. I thought invisibility and the ability to fly would be in full effect."

"If only Faîte were tha kind."

"That sounds ominous."

Antonio ran his hand down his face. "There are rumors tha Brìghde and Cailleach abandoned us. People are saying the immortal sisters took all the higher magic for themselves, leaving us with the dark stuff."

"Kerdik wouldn't allow that. What does he have to say about it all? I mean, he's a Rétif, and he hasn't left Avalon to ruin." Bastien kept his eyes on Antonio, avoiding my wide eyes. "Has he?" Being Rétif came with trickster implications, making people assume you were always up to something (which, let's face it, Kerdik usually was).

It was the first time Bastien had said his name since Kerdik surprised us by turning our field from grass into thousands of yellow roses, given Lane a potion to allow her to get pregnant, and left me with a vase of never-dying yellow roses to keep me safe. That was the day Bastien and I got married, and though Kerdik hadn't shown his face, I knew he'd been there that day, watching me in my married life. I could feel him watching, standing in the shadows so he could observe me in the life I was putting him on hold to live. He hadn't shown up since, so Bastien and I reached an unspoken agreement where neither of us mentioned his name. Kerdik had granted me a double-long lifespan when he'd saved me by infusing me with his blood. During Bastien's lifespan I was married to him, but when my husband passed, we all knew I would start my second life with Kerdik. That was another thing we never talked about.

Link shook his head, his eyes darting to me. "Kerdik doesn't live in Avalon, but he visits and helps Duke Lot when he can. No one knows where he goes when he disappears. Maybe he's with Brighde and Cailleach. Not exactly a chatty lad, tha one. I'm surprised he hasn't shown up here. Ye were so close."

I kept my eyes on the fabric as I stitched. "Nope. Showed up once on our wedding day, but he only left gifts and split. Never saw his face."

Antonio shot me a look of genuine surprise. "I thought those were just rumors. Ye know Master Kerdik?"

Bastien glowered at me. "I take it you haven't seen the fountain in Province 1 that he built. Carved out a statue of Rosie half-naked in the very center of it."

I kept my focus on my needle and thread, moving them clumsily along as I swallowed. "Yeah. He was my BFF in Avalon. Good guy."

Antonio scoffed. "Then ye truly don't know him at all.

Master Kerdik's not a good guy. He's heartless in his plotting."

Link held up his hand to interject. "Now, now. Tha's not as true as it used to be, and ye know it. Kerdik's been in and out of Éireland and Avalon, rounding up the excess bad magic and helping out Duke Lot when he can. He doesn't owe Éireland a thing, but he's stepped in a few times to help us in the past year and a half." He shrugged. "It's more than Brìghde and Cailleach have done."

Antonio grumbled his partial concession. "Too little, too late. He's the one who lost his hold on the higher magic. He's only partially cleaning up the mess tha he spilled all over Faîte. I haven't seen Master Kerdik in the trenches with us."

Link shook his head, looking anywhere but at Bastien and me. "I already told ye, tha's because he's also working in Avalon. He doesn't have to help Éireland at all; Éireland's not his. Brìghde and Cailleach should be helping us, and Kerdik's stepped in where he can. At least he's trying."

"Brìghde and Cailleach didn't set the higher magic loose," Antonio countered.

My eyebrows furrowed. "Um, neither did Kerdik. I'm the one who set it all loose."

Antonio stiffened, nostrils flaring. "What?"

Link sighed, his shoulders slumping. "The story's changed, Rosie. Kerdik pulled aside a few of us who knew the truth, and made us swear up and down tha the story had nothing to do with ye. The story everyone knows is tha

Kerdik was the one who lost his hold on the higher magic when Morgan le Fae was beating him."

I set down my sewing as dread washed over me. "But that's nothing like the truth!" I stood and moved closer to Antonio, my mouth dry and my eyes wide when the lie was presented to me. "Kerdik trapped the lost magic inside of a ring that he gave me." I displayed the white gold band on my right hand. The large square-shaped aquamarine had lost none of its appeal, nor had the three diamonds on each side forfeited their luster since I'd left Avalon. "Morgan le Fae put a spell on herself that if anyone tried to kill her, their magic would spill out. She would gather up her attackers' mojo and grow stronger. So I stabbed her, and the magic that was locked inside my ring spilled out. I didn't know it would do that, obviously, but it was me who set it all in motion, not Kerdik."

Bastien stood, sensing the angst that rose up in my chest when the other thing we never talked about began to flow out of me. "Daisy, you don't have to dredge it all up. You did what you had to do."

"I know, but I won't let Kerdik hang for it all." I shot Bastien a look to let him know this was a landmine topic. It had been a year and a half since Kerdik's name had come up, and apparently, it was still too soon for him, judging by the tightness in his jaw.

Antonio waved his hand at my explanation. "Everyone knows ye killed your mammy. But the bit about the ring is new. Why would Master Kerdik lie about that? People have been blaming him, furious tha we're stuck in this mess because of something he did. It's really not true?"

I hung my head, willing my rapid heartbeats to calm. I could feel the pressure building up behind my eyes, and did my best not to cry. "People really hate him because of something I did?"

Link's arms were crossed over his chest as he stared at the table. "Aye. No matter how hard he tries to help both lands, he's still the villain."

"Why would he do that? I'm not in Avalon anymore. He should tell them the truth and let the blame rest with me! Link, when you go back, you have to tell the people it was my fault!"

"And risk Master Kerdik's wrath? No, thanks. Ye really don't know why a man would take the blame for a fair maiden?"

Guilt and shame crashed over my head, dripping down my body to weight me with the realization that Kerdik's love for me was eternal, and it was hurting him. "It's not right," I said in a whisper, my chin lowered. "It's my fault Faîte's in such trouble. It's my fault you're a Vampire, Quinn. I'm the reason you lost your husband and your family."

Quinn didn't curse me or spit at me. She kept her eyes on her sewing and cleared her throat. "I wasn't mad at Master Kerdik, nor shall I be mad at ye. Even when I believed Master Kerdik was the one who let it all loose, I knew it was because he was imprisoned and tortured. He wasn't trying to hurt Éireland – and I know ye weren't neither." She shook her head with an air of finality. "Faîte does what it wants, because Faîte is what it is. I can't control fate no more than ye can."

Antonio was livid, his fists clenched and nostrils flared. He seemed impossibly taller as he stepped in from the doorway to tower over my chair. "Ye should've stayed in Faîte to clean up the mess! Where do ye get off, thinking ye can break the world and just leave it for everyone else to burn in?"

Bastien's arm tightened around me. "It's not as simple as all that. You don't know all we've been through. And you're forgetting that Urien's cast out the Vamps from his province."

Antonio was resolute. "Duke Lot hasn't. She could've stayed and helped there."

Bastien stood, his chest puffed. His voice suddenly rose to a shout that made Quinn jump. "We've bled enough for Avalon! This is our life now, and no amount of misplaced guilt can make me take her back there."

"So you're done sacrificing for the Brotherhood?"

Bastien balked at Antonio, who clearly didn't have a clue what we'd all been through, and only narrowly escaped. "You want to talk about sacrifice? Kerdik's in love with Rosie. If I take her back there, she's as good as his."

I tugged on his flannel sleeve. "Bastien, stop! We don't have to talk about this."

Antonio stared at me in astonishment. "The rumors are true, then?"

Link kept his voice level to bring about some peace to the tension. "Ye want to know why he'd take the blame on himself? Because he gave Rosie an extra bit of life. When Bastien's old and dead, she's to go to Kerdik. She'll live the rest of the life he gave her with him." Link's gaze shifted to mine. "He's cleaning up Avalon so tha your world is safe when ye return to him. I see the blaze in his eyes; he's determined to make sure tha when ye go back to him, he can give ye a good life."

I knew if we kept talking about this, I would burst into tears of regret, stress and loss. "This isn't something we need to talk about. Antonio, it's my fault there's darkness in Faîte, but there's nothing I can do about that. I tried to fix Avalon when I murd..." I choked on the word that was still too close to the gut. "I tried to right all the wrongs when I murdered my own mother, but I only made it all worse."

Link looked as if my agony pained him. "Don't say it like tha."

"How would you like me to say it?"

"Ye did what no one else but Lane could, and she was down for the count. Ye did a kindness to Avalon. The bit about the ring wasn't your fault, neither. No one saw tha coming. And Bastien's right; you've both bled enough for Avalon."

Antonio was livid. "That's quite the attitude to have. Convenient." Then his tone turned from dismissive to borderline pleading. "Can ye imagine what it would do to have a Daughter of Avalon who'd been turned by the dark magic? Ye could be a beacon the lost ones could turn to. It's a nation peppered with castoffs now. Ye could bring them dignity so they could try to have a normal life again. Rebuild."

Bastien shook his head in time with Link. "No. She's been a beacon before, and it nearly killed her too many times to count. Urien threw out the beacon of the people. All it's done is cause division – not the unity you're promising. You'll not auction off my wife to duty, Antonio. Being in the Brotherhood means Rosie's your wife, too. You should care more about her than this."

Link nodded. "Tha's part of why Kerdik took the blame on himself. If they knew the Avalon Rose was responsible for letting out the higher magic? It would break something they need so they can hold their heads up. They revere her. Half of Province 10 left Urien when they found out he banished his own daughter."

I fiddled with the hem of my shirt, anxious and wishing there was a simple solution I could cling to. "I didn't want that! I didn't make a big stink about any of it."

Link shrugged. "Ye didn't have to. Antonio's right about ye being a beacon. They followed ye from their homes when they found out your mammy had ye stripped and thrown down into tha well. Why would ye think they wouldn't follow ye back to Province 1 when ye were cast out?"

"What's this about being thrown down a well?" Antonio said, his eyebrow raised.

I ignored Antonio and rubbed my temples. "Lot's probably overwhelmed with tons of people wanting back in."

"He's handling it," Link assured me. "T'was a wise choice, entrusting your land to him."

Antonio spoke louder, demanding an answer. "Who threw an Untouchable's lady down a well?"

I quirked my eyebrow at him. "Morgan le Fae. Fun times. Nothing like starving to near death in darkness with nothing but the severed head of your boyfriend to keep you company for weeks." I felt confident in calling Demi my boyfriend after seeing the sketches he'd drawn of me. I didn't look as lovely as he'd imagined me. The softness of my features could only be captured by someone who'd truly loved me. Though I had his journal filled with who knows what, I was too protective of Demi's heart to ask Judah to read it to me. Though I couldn't save him, I could at least guard his private thoughts. Demi had truly cared about me, and I carried that treasure of truth in my heart when I started to doubt what was real and what had been fabricated by my mother.

Link brought us back to the original subject. "Kerdik's got his hands full in Faîte. Been right helpful in Éireland, of all places. He doesn't stay in Avalon all tha often anymore." His eyes flicked to me. "I think it makes him sad."

Bastien ran his tongue along his top row of teeth,

making a clicking noise to show his irritation. "Good. I hope he's pining and drowning in depression. I got the girl, and he'll accept it."

Antonio was resolute that the topic be pinned straight to me. "Ye should go back. Avalon needs ye, sure, but Éireland's tearing apart at the seams."

A dull hopelessness in Link's eyes muted the spark I'd always adored. "Screw Éireland. She was a grand beauty, but there's not much left of her youth anymore. She's tired, and I don't see much point in bleeding for her anymore."

Quinn's fingers slipped on the stitching. "Link," she admonished him quietly.

Link paused, blinking at her, stunned that she'd spoken at all. "What? It's madness back home. We barely got out alive."

Quinn set her sewing down, her fingers trembling. "I should retire. I must be tired. I'm so sorry," she said quietly to Link.

"Sleeping's nothing to apologize for, Quinn. I told ye tha before."

"Not for tha. I corrected ye in front of your mates. I shouldn'ta done tha."

My nose scrunched as I tried to recall when she'd said anything to Link. "You said his name, Quinn. That's okay."

"But I said it in a shaming way. It's unacceptable. I'll go to the bedroom now."

She stood, and Link didn't stop her, other than waving off her apology. I tugged on Quinn's sleeve, looking up at her in confusion. "You can tell Link when he's out of line, you know. He doesn't mind. Of course, it doesn't do much good, since he doesn't care when he's out of line, but you don't have to be afraid of him."

Her lower lip quivered with humiliation. "It's not proper, and I know better. Goodnight, everyone. I'm sorry to've spoiled the night. Thank ye for the tea, your majesty." She bowed her head to me, and then to Link. "And thank ye for the food."

9

FAIRE SÉPARER

*L*ink tipped his head to Quinn before she left, his eyes fixed on the wood of the table that Bastien, Draper and Reyn had built together. There was a matching dining table in all three of our houses, uniting us on yet another level.

I waited for Quinn's steps to disappear up the stairs before I leveled my finger in Link's face across the table. "Explain yourself, young man. Why the crap is she afraid of you? Did you do something to her?" Even as I said the words, they didn't ring true. Link didn't value relationships, but he'd always been sweet to Lane and me.

Link held up his hands. "She came to me like tha. It's the clan she was raised in. They're tight-knit and keep to themselves. It's a different culture with the Faire Séparer, which is the clan she's from. They have a different view on women than most of Éireland."

"And what view is that?" I asked, afraid to hear the answer.

Link didn't look at me as he spoke. "Breeders, mostly. Ye know the men outnumber the women in Faîte four to one. When a woman's born in the Faire Séparer community, she's betrothed from birth. When she's given in marriage, it's expected she'll pop out as many babies as she can until she can't no more. She doesn't get a choice. The women are expected to only birth babies, and do nothing more. Their husbands speak for them. The women can't even decide when they get pregnant." He met my eyes with a weight in his stare that made my stomach turn. "Quinn couldn't give her husband a baby. When she got cursed with Vampire magic, it was the perfect excuse for Bram to put her out."

I made a noise of disgust. "I hate this Bram guy!"

Link nodded in agreement. "They don't take kindly to their women speaking in town meetings. On the seventh day of the week, none of the women are allowed to talk at all."

"Not a word?"

"To teach them tha their husband owns their voice, and they should use it only to please him. Worst part about it all? She begged Bram to take her back. He slapped her across the face right in front of me – in front of the whole clan."

I shivered, understanding that Quinn's greatest ambition in life had been to be married to a man she hadn't chosen, and to carry as many children as her body could, all while being silent, and not having a say in her life. She'd wanted this, and then the Vampire madness had gotten her kicked out of a life of servitude. I couldn't decide if her Vampirism had been a blessing or a curse. "How's she even upright after leaving such a strict life? I mean, it doesn't sound like she understands how the world works outside of her clan."

"She doesn't, but she's a strong one. Not many would survive the torture they did to her. Ye saw the burn on her face?"

Bastien nodded. "Regular citizens in Éireland did that to her? Non-military?"

Antonio took over story time. "They call themselves the Master's Vigilantes. Queen Shavon disbanded her army a year ago – said they were doing more harm than good. Factions started re-forming, taking it on themselves to round up and kill off the Vampires. They did lots of cruel things to the prisoners. For some of them, it was a kindness to let them die."

Link stared at his empty beer. "Quinn's afraid of her own voice most days, but when she talks back to me like she did tonight? I almost believe she has a chance – tha she can make it."

"You care about her."

Link narrowed his eyes at me for calling him out on having a heart. "I care about her as much as I do all the Fae I saved in those cages. I don't save things, not caring if they survive the next day." Link played with the lip of his empty bottle. "This isn't bad. Got anymore?"

Bastien checked the fridge. "It's craft beer. Lane and Judah are pretty picky about the brands. Judah keeps his stash at Draper's for when he visits. There's another case over there. I don't touch the stuff anymore, though. Been clean for a year and a half."

Link's eyes widened in appreciation. "Well done, brother."

"Thanks. I'll be right back." Before he left, Bastien kissed my hand, making the butterflies in my belly dance at the gentlemanly gesture. "I like it when you talk, just so you know. I couldn't stand living in a place where you had to shut up one day every week."

"I love you." I gazed up into the caramel eyes that enraptured me. "Thanks for not being a tool who hates women."

"Thanks for being worth listening to." He motioned for Antonio to follow him. "Come on. You can pick whatever kind you like. Give our bride some breathing room."

THE LAST GOOD WOMAN IN ÉIRELAND

I watched Bastien leave with a sigh of rapture. I couldn't help but fall in love with my husband on a daily basis.

"Now tha's what I like to see. Watching ye be hung up on both your blokes was hard to stomach. Ye seem happy here."

"I am." I pointed to the frown that had taken over Link's features far too many times in one night. "You seem sad everywhere. Talk to me."

Now that Bastien and Antonio were gone, it was just us. I knew Link would open up to me if given the invitation. He ran his hand over his face. "Quinn's so quiet, and she cries all the time. I don't know what to do when she does tha. I mean, she's not loud about it. Sometimes I don't even know she's been weepy until I see her wet face. She wasn't allowed to be alone with any man – not even Bram until they were married, and he didn't ask for what he wanted, if ye know what I mean. I'm afraid I'll spook her if I get too close."

"Oh, yikes. That does make things complicated."

"She wouldn't sleep in my house because it wasn't proper for her to be alone with a man who wasn't her husband. Annabelle and Mad had to move in for a while to keep her from sleeping in my backyard."

"You're not serious."

Link nodded. "I thought I understood their culture, but it was an outsider's view. It's intense up close. How could she be so sad to leave all tha?"

I shrugged. "It's hard to gauge the level of dysfunction you're steeped in when you've been raised in it. Plus, she lost all her friends and family in one go. I don't think anyone handles that without a few tears."

Link pointed to my face. "Ye lost your Da the same way. The same week ye lost your mammy, too. I don't see ye crying all day and night about it."

I scratched the back of my neck, lowering my voice. "Urien didn't raise me, so it's not the same. And I murdered my mother, so there's not much love lost there." I crossed my arms over my chest. "And just because I don't cry about it all doesn't mean it doesn't tear me up. I can't cry about it."

"Oh, because your tears are blood? Tha's one thing I didn't miss about ye. Terrifying, tha was." He shuddered at the memory.

"Not just that. I know that if I give Urien one tear, I'll never stop sobbing. That's why Quinn can't stop. She gave them that first tear." I sipped my tea, pretending to be a lady. "Rookie mistake."

Link was quiet a few beats to respect the shifting mood between us. "Quinn still doesn't speak on the seventh day. She keeps to most of the clan's rituals, too. I think she's hoping they'll take her back, but they won't. It's been over a year we've been bonded, and they never once came looking for her. One of them even posted a sign on my property: Quinn of the Green Hills Faire Séparer Clan is Forever Cast Out." He shook his head. "I took the sign right to their property and set it on fire, but she still cries about it all."

"How are you holding up?" I asked, realizing I hadn't asked how the eternal bachelor felt about moving a conservative woman into his home.

"It's hard. I feel guilty if I look at another woman, even though we're not together. I want to help her, but I don't know what to do with a woman I can't sleep with."

"Hello, you've always been great to me."

His light blue eyes softened. "I missed ye, Rosie. Éireland's not what she used to be. When it was Mad, me, Bastien and ye, the obstacles didn't matter much; I knew we'd find a way. Without ye both, it all feels like, what's the point? Nab one *Farouche* Vamp, and three more pop up."

I got up and moved to the chair next to him, wrapping my arms around his waist so I could lean into his warm side. "You sound like you could use a break. I'm glad you decided to chill with us."

"I didn't have much of a choice. No matter how much I've explained tha *Attelage* Vamps aren't dangerous, Quinn's life's been threatened too many times to keep on living in Éireland."

"You had a choice. You could've left her to die."

Link swallowed. "If ye knew her like I did, you'd know tha was never an option. She's a good person. Sometimes I think she might be the only good thing left in Éireland. I feel like if she dies, Éireland doesn't have a prayer." He tapped his chest with a pained expression. "My homeland, Rosie."

"I hope you've told her you think that about her. It's the sweetest thing I've heard you say about any woman ever."

"She writes her family, ye know. After all this time, she's never said an ill word about them. She keeps a clean house for us, cooks, and saved my life a few times when we were out on hunts."

"She hunts *Farouche* Vampires with you?"

"Aye. It was too dangerous to leave her at home alone. Too many break-ins to try and get at her." He ran his fingers back and forth across my arm that was banded around his tummy, like he was strumming a guitar. "She makes clothes for the children who've lost their parents to the higher magic. I bring home material, and she's got it made into blankets, pants and shirts the next day. She's a sweet lass. Didn't deserve what she got."

"You're a good man, Link."

"Aye. Don't remind me. I could be buried deep in some barmaid right now, but instead I'm cuddling my mate's wife and bemoaning how I wish I could get the girl who won't look me in the eye to stop crying."

"I just love you. Every bit of you – the sweetheart parts and the boneheaded caveman parts. I'm sorry this is so hard."

Link kissed the top of my head, sighing contentedly. "I love ye, too. Best wife the Brotherhood could ask for."

My nose scrunched. "I think it's weird that I'm supposed to be your communal wife."

"Be a good lass and darn my socks for me."

I squeezed his sides, giving him a solid tickle. I loved Link's high-pitched laugh. It was infectious, and could cure the worst ailments. I'd missed the scent of Link, the sweet notes with the earthy undertones. The longer he held me, the more he seemed to unwind from everything that never had the right to keep such a free spirit so tightly coiled. "Enough about me. You've got quite the life here. How's the Vampire element working itself into the picture?"

"It's actually not too bad. I'm not being hunted, which makes things less complicated than they've been for you and Quinn. I keep trying to go for longer in between drinking from Bastien, but I've only been able to make it a few days. I'm working on it."

"I give Quinn a little every day because she's too polite and scared to ask for what she needs."

"I'm surprised you're not covered in teeth marks. Bastien's got most of his on his shoulders."

Link's eyebrows raised. "Ye bite him? Ye bite him every time ye feed?"

"A few times a week, yeah. Sometimes he does what he did tonight and pricks his finger or something."

Link shivered. "Quinn only bit me tha first time. It was too intense. I nearly lost my mind and stripped Quinn naked in the middle of all those cages. Is it like tha every time for ye and Bastien?"

I nodded. "Oh, yeah. He takes my virtue every day. Some days I take his," I said deviously.

Link chuckled, moving my arm with his trembling abdomen. "Always make those jokes with me. My life's been on eggshells for the past year. Quinn's so proper. I don't want to make her uncomfortable. I guess the addiction works well when you're married. Not so much if you're friends."

"What addiction? Blood isn't something I choose to want, Link. It's part of the Vampire genetic code or something. It's like being addicted to water."

"I wasn't talking about ye. Bastien. When the Vamp feeds on her mate, he gets addicted to her." He quirked his eyebrow at my dumbstruck expression. "Did ye really not know tha?"

I balked at him. "Does this look like the face of someone who knew she was secretly a crack dealer? How does that even work? Bastien doesn't take anything from me; I drink from him!"

Link barred his teeth to me. "It's in your fangs. When ye bite into a person, they get a rush of pleasure tha's hard to find elsewhere." He adjusted his jeans uncomfortably. "Trust me, I've tried. Quinn's singlehandedly ruined my sex life. After tha first bite, nothing's felt as good."

"Tell me you're joking. You're saying Bastien's addicted to me biting him?"

"Of course he is. How have ye not discussed tha?"

"I... I don't know. Why wouldn't he tell me?"

"Maybe he's afraid you'd take away the good stuff. If he's getting bit regularly, it's a happy life he's living, no doubt. It's no wonder he's been able to stay sober this long."

"I don't know how to feel about that."

"Feel grateful he's your husband. Be happy ye can both take what ye want from each other. Trust me, the other side isn't all tha grand." He snuggled me tighter to his side. "Sing me one of your Commoner songs. Sing the one I like. I miss this."

I grinned, reaching for his favorite tune. "'I like it when you call me Big Poppa. So raise your hands in the air, like you's a true player. 'Cause I see some ladies tonight who should be having my baby.'"

"'Baby,'" Link echoed, not missing a beat.

I'd missed Link so very much. As his body relaxed in my arms, I knew he'd missed us, too.

11

COME AND PLAY

*A*ntonio and Link guarded the house while the three of us slept. I knew Bastien rested far easier when someone was awake to watch the grounds, though we'd never had anything resembling a threat out here.

As soon as the darkness surrounded me like a black fog in my dream, I sighed dejectedly. "This stupid dream again?" I huffed, and some of the black smoke feathered out from my mouth.

"Come," the fog said in answer.

I lifted my chin heavenward. "Look, whoever you are. I'm not interested in going wherever you feel like leading. I mean it. Keep this up, and you and I are going to have more than just the one word."

"Come," the nebulous man beckoned in his deep timbre.

I gave him the finger and conjured up a basketball to

distract myself with. I wanted to shoot hoops, but I couldn't see anything to make out where a basketball net might be. The black fog was too thick to do anything fun.

"Come."

I dribbled the ball, gritting my teeth against my frustration. "Come and get it," I all but growled. "You want to be the big man with the plan? Show me your face, you coward."

When nothing happened, I shot the ball into the darkness, hoping to hear the comforting "swoosh" sound that meant I'd sunk a three-pointer. Instead I heard the voice that shook my very skin against my bones. "Come."

The ball rolled back to me, slower than if it had hit a wall and meandered back. I picked it up and launched it in the direction of the voice, which seemed more localized now. He was in front of me, maybe ten feet or so, standing where the ball had rolled to me from. "You want me to go with you? Fine! Let's go, dude. You and me." I lobbed the ball hard where I hoped his face was, but the satisfying smack never came.

My bravado began to shrink when the black fog started to mist away. The fine wetness glistened like black glitter on my skin, making me wary of whatever I'd triggered to make such a drastic change in the dream that had been haunting me for way too long.

When a man's long arm extended itself to me from the darkness, I jerked back, though the palm was open and inviting. "Come," he said, though this time the echo-y quality was gone. He was standing right in front of me, and sounded like he was finally asking gently, instead of commanding, like he thought he was some deity from above. The softness in the beckoning released my shoulders from their guarded position, and I exhaled the last of my gusto.

Warning bells blasted for me to back away, and my gut even tugged me in the opposite direction the hand wished for me to go. But I was so sick of this unending dream. I was tired of resisting the voice.

Against my better judgment, I placed my hand in his. The palm beneath mine was warm, uncalloused, and seemed to tremble with anticipation. The trepidation tingled in both of us, making me jumpy.

"Dude, why are you here, and who are you?" I asked quietly, hoping we could have a legit conversation instead of a shouting match.

The belabored pause made frustration rise up in me that he might say, "Come," again, instead of actually giving me an answer. My shoulders tightened when his reply came back a steady, "I'm here because you heard me. I've been calling out for so long."

I chewed on that, wondering if it confirmed that I was five peanuts shy of being a nut job. "Okay. Who are you?"

"My name is Dub. Do you know who I am?" His voice touched on a note of insecurity, as if it had been so long since his last conversation, he wasn't sure if that was his name at all anymore. Like he hoped *I* could tell him who he was, so he didn't have to wonder anymore.

The black glitter clinging to my skin was getting darker, changing me into a walking shadow. I knew I should run, but the cool wetness was only unusual, not painful. I rubbed my thumb along the back of his smooth hand to comfort him. "I'm sorry. I don't know who you are, but I'm a good listener. Why don't you tell me about yourself."

"I... I'm not sure that's a good idea."

"You could start by letting me see more than just your hand. Face-to-face conversations are helpful in meet-and-greet kind of situations."

The hand tightened on mine, though not in a threatening manner. It was almost as if he was bracing himself for my rejection. I knew that hesitance. I'd felt it every first day of a new school year. Walking into your class with a lazy eye and a hump didn't exactly endear people to me. Those things were gone now, but I remembered well the sting of isolation. Dub's was palpable, even as he stepped out of the black mist.

I was expecting some sort of horrible monster, but what I got was a five-foot-ten man with a long, narrow nose and high cheekbones. His leonine build was partially concealed under a black cloak, though I could see his slim waist and slightly broader shoulders peeking through the shade. Dub's face was... normal. He had black eyes and matching coal-colored hair, angular features, and a mole cluster on his left cheek that would've made him look impish, if he gave smiling a shot. The triangular design of the three small moles on his cheekbone seemed to wink out at me with all the charm of a dimple. He had one of those hard to place age ranges to him. I pegged him at around forty years old or so, but his erect spine and rigid deportment made him seem about a thousand.

"Hey, man. It's nice to meet you. See? Was that so hard? Next time you want to talk to someone, this is the way to go about it. Show your face, shake hands and, you know, be normal."

"I'm afraid I don't know much about normal."

I let go of his hand and picked up the basketball at my feet. "Well, it's not bellowing like a jackhole for me to go where you say. You've got to know no girl's going to go blindly with you like that."

Dub's eyebrows furrowed, flummoxed by this gem. "Oh. I didn't realize. It's been so long since I've conversed with a woman. I used to give commands, and they were swiftly obeyed."

I snorted and started dribbling the ball. "Aw, that's cute. We don't do that here. This is my dream, which means I give the commands."

Dub frowned, his lips taut with displeasure. "I'm not sure how I feel about that."

"I'm not sure I care." I squinted at him through dribbling the ball, doing a few flashy tricks just to pass the time. "Do you think I've enjoyed you giving the orders every single night for a year and a half? Pay the piper, dude."

He rolled his shoulders back, readying for the gavel. "Very well. What sort of payment do you require in this world?"

I quirked an eyebrow at him, tilting my head to the side to size up his sincerity. "Come," I answered in an ominous imitation of him, a sardonic smile painting my features. I tossed the ball to him, but it bounced off his stomach and lost its gusto on the way down. "You're supposed to dribble the ball. It's a game."

"A game?"

It was like talking to E.T. "Yeah. I'll show you. Watch how I do it." I made a show of dribbling, going slow so he could see how the pros do it. That's right; in my dream, I'm Michael friggin' Jordan. I started singing Montel Jordon's "This is How We Do It" in time with the bouncing ball.

Dub's erect posture married with his frown to make for a snooty disposition. "I didn't call you so we could play games and sing ludicrous songs."

"I don't care why you called me here. This is my dream, and this is what we're doing." Yes, I was being bossy, but whatever. Dude had haunted my nights for way too long for me to follow him blindly into whatever supernatural abyss he had in mind. I had to get a feel for him first. Let him know he couldn't snap his fingers and expect me to come running. I hated that even my dreams had political landmines.

"Very well. Let's get this over with. A game. How do you win?"

"You're too green to think about winning just yet, but I like the hustle." I waved my hand around in the dark, glittery air. Goosebumps broke out on my wrist from the slight chill. "Can you clear some of this fog up first? It's totally distracting. The hoop's over there, and we need to be able to see it."

Dub held my gaze for a solid three seconds, letting me know by the tightness in his stare that he was none too pleased to be taking orders (or polite requests).

I know the feeling, pal.

He sucked in his breath and then blew it out in a long gust, clearing the wet glitter out of the way so we could actually see. Beyond the darkness that had plagued me was an empty, dim room the size of a gymnasium. The concrete walls and floors gave way to a sky that was lit only by the occasional flickering star above. "Is that to your liking, mortal?"

"Actually, my name's Rosie, not mortal – not that you bothered to ask. I'm cutting you all kinds of slack, here. It's best behavior time. Roll out those company manners and put on a smile for me." I shot him a beamy grin as I dribbled. Trotting a few steps closer to the hoop, I took my shot and hit it on the first try, dark though it was. That's right. In my dreams, I'm amazing. I told you – Michael friggin' Jordan.

"Can this part be done now? I've something important to show you."

I retrieved the ball and called, "Catch!" as I tossed it to him, warning him this time.

Dub participated, catching the ball and doing his best imitation of me. He was awkward and couldn't make heads or tails of how to walk while bouncing the ball. "This is the game?"

"It's not the whole game. Would you relax? We'll get to whatever it is I'm supposed to go see with you when we're finished."

He looked like he wanted to ask how soon this could be over with, but the breeding that gave him his erect posture made him hold any petulance from his tongue. He shot the ball, but midway through the arc the ball slowed, correcting its trajectory and landing itself clean in the hoop.

"I saw you cheat, dude. You can't magic it into the hoop. Try again."

Dub exhaled through his flared nostrils as I tossed the ball back to him. He took another shot and missed horribly. His temper began to take over his shoulders, making them hunch inward with grouchiness. "Very well. I played your game, much to your amusement. Let's go."

I shook my head. "That was a very respectable shot for your first time without magic." I dribbled the ball nearer to him, lining myself up for a hooked shot I liked to show off with. "I'll tell you what. We can go do your outing once you can hit all five of these in a row without magic." I demonstrated by starting at the far left of the unmarked court – easily a three-pointer. After the net swooshed for me, I did a straight shot three-pointer, and then hit one from the far right of the court. I did a right-handed layup, and then a left. I missed the feel of the court, and reminded myself to see if I could catch a few pickup games after finals released me from their studious stranglehold.

Dub's expression kept vacillating back and forth between furious and overwhelmed. "I can't do that without magic. You know I can't."

"Then I guess you'll just have to practice. If you want something bad enough, you should work for it. Bossing me around gets you nothing; it's time you learned that."

"This is important. You need to understand the seriousness of the problem."

"If it's that serious, you'll learn how to hit those five shots in a row. Maybe you'll even have a little fun in the process." My eyes didn't hold back their compassion when I said, "You don't look like you've had a whole lot of fun in your life."

Dub's eyes steeled with a touch of sadness. "My life was so long ago; I scarcely remember the ritual of it all."

"Then I'm glad I met you, Dub."

He looked taken aback, confused at my declaration, as if no one had ever been pleased to see him before. "You can't mean that."

I dropped a bit of my swagger and trotted over to him,

chucking him on the shoulder. "I'll see you tomorrow night, alright? We can play together on the court for as long as it takes you to learn the game. It'll be fun."

"Fun?" he spoke the word as if it was a language he had yet to understand.

I extended my hand to him, ready to put the lid on the dream I'd finally made some progress in. "Goodnight, Dub."

12

BREAKING THE WORLD OVER BREAKFAST

When the morning light cascaded through the navy curtains, I all but purred against Bastien. I liked to start my day with a tiny bite, getting us both going and moaning in tandem. I climbed on top of him, waking him up "the fun way," as we'd dubbed it.

Bastien's eyes didn't open, but his hands knew the dance well enough, squeezing and caressing until we worked ourselves into a frenzy. The sheets tangled around us and became problematic when Bastien proved particularly acrobatic once he was more fully awake. It usually took us an hour to "wake up", and even though we wanted to get to our guests, that morning was no exception. Some things were too good to be rushed.

The shower was warm, and I welcomed my husband's capable hands that took their time washing his favorite parts of me. I returned the favor, teasing and stroking until the water ran cold. It was the best way to start our day.

My feet barely felt like they touched the floor as I flitted down the steps. I hummed to myself as I started making breakfast for everyone. My grin came easily when Bastien tripped down the steps, his body loose and clumsy from the morning workout. His arms went around my waist as he pressed his front to my back while I scrambled eggs in the skillet. His hand gripped my thigh and tugged upward, letting me know he wasn't finished with me yet. "The eggs will keep. Turn this off and come back upstairs."

"We have guests. They'll know what we're doing if we don't come down until noon."

Bastien's hand dipped under the hem of my blue cotton soccer jersey, climbing upward until he reached payday. I shuddered against his hard torso, dropping the spatula as my body started to sing for him. If this was the turn his addiction took, I decided not to complain. "How about I take you right here?" he growled low over my shoulder, biting on my earlobe. "I don't think Quinn's up yet, and I haven't heard the guys moving around the house."

As if on cue, the sliding glass door opened, and Link and Quinn stepped inside, stopping when they got an eyeful of our morning ritual. "Ho! I didn't think ye would still be going. We can go back out for another walk, if you'd like."

Bastien's hand slid out from my shirt, situating the

material and dipping his head to Quinn apologetically. "Sorry about that. Come on in. Rosie's making eggs. You guys want juice or coffee?"

"What's coffee?" Link asked.

Bastien cast the two a lazy smile. "It's a legal drug Commoners use to wake up."

"I don't need tha. I don't sleep. Ye want some, Quinn?"

Quinn shook her head, her eyes wide in fear. "I don't use drugs." She was wearing the jeans and t-shirt I'd set out for her. She kept adjusting the shirt, pulling out the hem to make it more shapeless on her form. She looked like a normal girl now – a skittish one, but still. She kept her chin tilted down to obscure her face, but I caught glimpses of the pretty woman that had been marked with the burn.

I cast Bastien a simpering look. "Bastien's being a dork. Coffee isn't a drug. It's just a drink everyone here has in the morning."

"Whatever ye wish, I'm grateful for," Quinn replied subserviently.

I set an empty mug down on the counter for her. "My wish is for you to choose what you want to drink. Coffee, milk, water or juice."

It was too many options for a girl who'd had her whole life decided, but I knew she was also a person who wouldn't dare disobey. I'd given her an order to choose something, and difficult as that was for her, it was a necessary start. She fiddled with the hem of the purple t-shirt, shifting her weight from one foot to the other. "Water, please."

"Coming right up." I showed her how to use the faucet, in case she wanted a refill and was too scared to ask for what she needed.

Link came around the counter and grabbed a cup of water for himself. "What's the plan for today? I don't know what the dangers are, so I've been making the rounds all night with Antonio, not knowing what to look for."

"Oh, Link! I'm sorry. I didn't know you were going to do that. There aren't any dangers here."

Link scoffed at my assessment. "Oh, to think like ye do." He pulled me into his arms and pinched my nose, as if I was five years old declaring I wanted to be a candy taste-tester when I grew up. "Tell me about the beautiful sugar-soaked world ye dream about. One where Vampires can walk around with no threat to them at all."

I squeezed his sides, loving the squirm he did that made him look like a little boy. I was the perfect height for him to lean on, so I remained in his arms, despite his patronizing tone. "Well, Vampires aren't real here, so no one's got their torches and pitchforks, screaming for our heads on a stake. That's one point for Common."

"Aye. What about people trying to steal your throne or your jewels?"

I shrugged. "I don't have a throne. Avalon doesn't exist here. No one knows about all that, and they definitely don't know about the jewels. We've got those in different safety deposit boxes. Nothing harrowing comes sniffing around here, except the occasional prowler, which the animals are good at intercepting." I leaned my cheek to his firm chest. "You can relax with us. You're home, Link."

He stiffened, but then slowly tightened his arms around me, leaning his chin atop my head. "I don't know what tha means anymore," he admitted.

"It means we take care of you for a change, instead of you trying to take care of everyone else."

Bastien scooped the food for all of us while Quinn set the plates on the dining room table. "You can keep an eye on the house while I go to work, or you can come with me. They build houses completely different here. I'm learning so much."

"Ye build houses? Tha doesn't sound too bad."

"Go with Bastien. I'll just be studying with Draper all morning until I have to go to school this afternoon."

Link frowned at me. "Ye are too old for school."

"Not here. There's school for all ages here, if you want to do it. After this week, if I pass my exams, I'll finally get my degree."

"What does tha mean?"

I grinned into his t-shirt. "It means that I can apply for a job as a healer for animals. I mean, not a full-on veterinarian, but a veterinarian's assistant, at least."

"But ye can talk to animals and treat them well enough without your degree. You've been doing tha for years."

"Yes, but no one in Common knows that. I'm just a regular girl here."

Link squeezed me tight. "I didn't trek all the way across worlds for a regular girl."

I pulled back and grinned up at him. "I know you didn't. You came here for Bastien. Well, you can't have his hot body. It's mine!"

"I think everyone in the country must know tha by now. He shouted your name enough times last night. Then again this morning." He tried to iron out his accent to impersonate Bastien. "'Oh, Daisy. Just like that. Tug on my hair! Hold on tight, baby!'"

I blushed and whirled on Bastien. "I told you that you were the loud one!"

Bastien glowered at Link. "Keep it up if you want to eat your breakfast off the floor. I can be as loud as I want in my own home." His shoulders slumped. "I was really that loud? I was trying to keep it quiet for you guys."

Link cupped his hands around his mouth to produce an echo. "'Right there. Oh, just like tha. Daisy, you're driving me crazy! Stop teasing me!'" Then he went off on a tangent of unintelligible noises that sounded like animals going at it. I'd like to think we sounded more refined than that.

Quinn turned crimson and choked on her water. Poor girl stood on the furthest reaches of the room, looking like she wanted to melt into the floor to escape the three of us. I cast her a friendly smile. "You hungry?"

"Yes, your majesty. But I shouldn't eat at your table. I can take my food outside."

I waved off the formal address. "I'm just Rosie. You can save the manners and titles for the people in Faîte. I don't need them. I'd like you to eat with us. My table's yours."

She was hesitant, but eventually bowed her head to me. "Yes, your grace."

I sighed, but kept a polite smile affixed to my face. I sat with her, leaning into Bastien when he took the chair next to me.

Link shot out question after question about our world, ranging from the mundane to the absurd. I expected nothing less than ludicrousness from my sweet Link. He paused his demolition of the eggs to stare at Bastien and me when I fed my guy a bite from my fork, smirking at his appetite. "I shoulda come to Common a long time ago. Ye look happy. Both of ye. I didn't think it possible, after everything Avalon put ye through."

"That's the thing about marrying the man of your dreams," I replied, not caring if I sounded cheesy. Bastien and I had managed to hold onto each other, which was no small feat. "One day, you'll meet the man of your dreams, and you'll never stop smiling."

Link winked at Bastien, who chuckled. "Oh, I already have."

"Speaking of dreams," Bastien inquired, changing the topic. "I didn't have to wake you from your nightmare last night. I can't remember the last time that happened. Did you actually have a normal dream for once?"

I weighed out my answer while Bastien clarified for the newcomers. Then I filled the three in on the turn my nights had finally taken. Yes, these were the harrowing events of our world. Nebulous nightmares. It was a wonderful thing to be able to complain about such innocent inconveniences.

"Wearing a black cloak, eh? Tha must be a dangerous fella. What's his name?"

"Dub." I took in the frozen body language around me and shrugged. "I know it's a weird name, but I'm so happy the nightmare shifted to basketball lessons that I don't care." I smirked at Link. "See? Aren't you glad you're in a world where that's our biggest problem? Annoying dreams are as bad as it gets here."

Link put his fork down. "Please tell me you're joking."

"What?" I glanced at the fear in Quinn's face and took in the rigid posture of the man at my side. "What'd I say?"

Link jabbed his fork in Bastien's direction. "Ye must've mentioned the Brothers before to her. Ye know about Dub, right?"

Bastien shook his head. "I've never told her about your land's history. We left Faîte behind, Link. The most we've talked about our life before was with you guys last night. We left Avalon to start over." He shifted in his seat to address me directly. "Rosie, did you hear about Dub from anyone else?" I knew he was skating around mentioning Kerdik's name.

"No. I don't think so. I only just met him in my dream. He's a real dude?"

"Not anymore." Link drummed his thick fingers on the tabletop. "Three black freckles just here?" He pointed to his left cheekbone. "Dark hair, black-eyed bloke?"

I nodded. "How'd you know?"

"Because he's one of Carman's sons – the three Brothers of Destruction."

Bastien closed his eyes. "Dub's the Brother of Darkness. That would explain why you've dreamt of nothing but the black for a year and a half now. It's Dub. He's calling to you."

I pressed my lips together, hoping this wasn't something I should be afraid of. I wanted to be done with fear. This was my home, and I hadn't invited anxiety into it. "'Brothers of Destruction' sounds ominous. I'm guessing they're not a Girl Scout troupe, or a band of Christmas carolers?"

"Aye. Ye don't want to be near them. Ye should put this Dub out of your mind at night."

I scoffed. "I don't think you understand how dreams work. I've been trying to shake this dude for a year and a half. I can't get him out of my head. I don't have a choice in it, Link."

Link met Bastien's eyes. "It's dangerous, Bastien. How's he getting into her mind? Ye can't be sleeping with her no more. What if Dub goes from her brain into yours? If he can control an Untouchable, what then?"

I held up my hands. "First off, I'm not being controlled by anyone. So let's just clear that up right now. Dub just wants to show me something. I don't know what, but it's important. He said it's serious."

"No," both Link and Bastien ruled with finality. "Whatever he wants, the answer's no."

Bastien nodded to enforce Link's edict. "Dub's a bad guy, babe. The worst."

"I feel like I might need a touch more than that. Are we talking someone who doesn't recycle, or is he full-on Voldemort?"

Bastien had read all the *Harry Potter* books to me because he's just that sexy. "The Sons of Carman are more like the spawn of Voldemort. Carman's long gone though, so at least we don't have to worry about her."

I sighed over my flavorless breakfast. "Give me the 101 on it all. I seriously have no idea how freaked out I should be right now."

Link drained his cup and helped himself to more eggs. I smiled, loving that he was already making himself at home with us. I liked Link in my house, taking up space at my table and in my life. He sat back down with us and started in on the story. "Carman was an immortal witch. One of the few true witches, actually. Not many exist anymore. It's because of her they were hunted down and driven into the ground. She worked against Brìghde, withering up the crops when the spring came around, and basically doing all she could to terrorize the Éirish. She loved chaos, and treated the Fae like puppets."

"She sounds swell."

"She had three sons, all warlocks themselves. They could touch ye and inflict their will on ye for a few minutes. Dian was the warlock for violence. A touch from Dian would make the gentlest soul turn vicious just long enough to murder the person next to them, and come out of the fog none the wiser. Dother was the middle brother, known for imparting evil."

My eyebrows furrowed together as I took in Quinn's shiver. "Just a generic evilness, or are there actual specifics to the mayhem?"

Quinn spoke up when Link paused to drink my water. "A brush from Dother, and all love drains from ye. You're capable of true ruthlessness. Ye can commit unthinkable acts with no threat of conscience. This was all before our time, though, so most of it's knowledge tha's passed down from our grandparents."

"Dother sounds swell. Bet he doesn't get invited to many tea parties."

Quinn managed a polite smile at my humor. "I admit, I cannot picture him sitting with us, stitching blankets and sipping hot tea."

Link picked up the story. "Cailleach and Brighde finally contained Carman decades ago, and Kerdik did away with the brothers. No one knew how, but it makes sense tha if Kerdik could lasso the higher magic in Faîte, he could stuff the brothers into your ring, as well." Link hung his head. "Kerdik put a ring around your finger tha had the Brothers of Destruction in it! When ye set loose the lost magic, Dian and Dother escaped back into Faîte."

I gasped in time with the color draining from Bastien's face. "Are you serious? I let out two immortal super bad guys?"

Link didn't pull any punches. "Aye. They've returned to Éireland, twisting the Fae as they did decades ago before we were born." Link shook his head. "Ye can't talk to Dub if he comes back into your dreams. Master Kerdik locked them up for a reason. We've been trying to find a way to contain Dian and Dother, but it's hopeless. They're immortals. It's a fight tha's over my head."

I leaned my elbows on the table and rubbed my temples. "Super. And Dub was the dude for darkness? He touches people, and... what? Makes them blind or something?"

"Tha's halfway right. He makes them blind, but during tha time he can control what ye see. Used to torture people with their worst fears. Make them watch their families being torn into pieces just for a laugh with his brothers. Dub was the oldest of the three, and had more control over his gift than the others." Link met my gaze with a stern seriousness. "So if Dub's in your dreams, don't touch him. Don't go near the fog he gives ye. He'll torture ye, Rosie. Make ye see things a sweet girl like yourself couldn't even dream about in your worst nightmare." He reached across the table and stroked my knuckle with the tip of his index finger. Some people assumed the Untouchables were cold brutes, but I knew better. Link didn't hold back any of the compassion in his gaze, but soaked me in his tenderness. "You've seen enough horrors."

I opened my palm so his heavy hand could rest in mine. I squeezed his fingers, letting him know that I understood how permanent our friendship had become. "Okay. I won't go with him into the darkness."

Link patted my fingers with his free hand before sitting back in his chair with a lazy smile. "Why can't ye just dream about me, like ye used to do?"

"If only," I teased.

"Dian created the Leprechauns, you know. Took a few of the Fae and twisted them so they only wanted gold. They were supposed to go out, find treasures and bring them to him. When the Leprechauns didn't comply and started keeping the gold for themselves, he slaughtered them all."

I swallowed hard, suppressing my "They're after me Lucky Charms!" jokes, that only I would appreciate.

When Draper came in through the side door, it was with my schoolbooks in hand. "Morning, all. Did you save me some breakfast?"

"Of course. Help yourself, and then we can get started." I motioned to the skillet on the stovetop.

"That's my cue." Bastien leaned in to kiss me, as he did

every morning when Draper came home from work. Draper's nightshift ended an hour before Bastien had to be at work. He rubbed his chest with a frown. "I feel like I should call in today. I don't like that Dub's in your head."

"It's just a dream. Nothing's going to happen to me while I'm awake. We're overthinking all of this. It's been going on for a year and a half. This isn't a big deal." I really hoped that was true.

Bastien nodded. "You're right. If he had any power over you, he would've made you go to him instead of asking you to come."

I smiled at the solid logic, and then took another bite of my eggs. My face fell with the weight of Faîte coming down to ruin our breakfast. "All the lost magic that came tumbling out of my ring... It's bad, right? I released two super villains. I mean, it sounds like Avalon and Éireland are on the brink."

"Aye. But tha's not for ye to worry about. There's nothing ye can do about it anyways. It's for the immortals to look after the magic when it goes amuck. Kerdik's doing all he can to try and capture Dian and Dother, he just hasn't had much luck yet."

My voice was small, but carried through the kitchen. "I'm half immortal. Maybe this is my battle. Maybe this is part of my adventure."

Nobody moved for several weighted seconds as my words hung in the air. Link stopped chewing as he exchanged a heavy look with Bastien. Draper's jaw was tight, and Quinn was a statue.

Bastien shook his head. "I'm calling off for work. No way, Ro. You're not stepping foot in Faîte. You don't have powers like the immortals do. You go toe-to-toe with this higher magic, and you'll lose. If you lose, I lose. We all lose." He moved to the door and locked it. "I know that look. You're staying in the house until that's out of your head. I won't lose you to Faîte."

I scratched the back of my neck, unable to look up at them. "Maybe Antonio was right. It's my fault the lost magic spilled out into the world. Then I just left Faîte to deal with it. I didn't help clean up my mess."

"Because it's not your mess! You're talking about going straight to Violence and Evil, and... what? Starting a fist-fight? You'll lose, Daisy. Plain and simple. Kerdik never should've given you that responsibility, especially without explaining the risks. There's a million reasons why he shouldn't have put a ring on your finger. This is on him. You didn't ask to be the one to carry evil and violence around on your finger, but that's what he did to you. His gifts always end up being curses. Never forget that."

A fierce indignation rose up in me, immediately protective of Kerdik. I swallowed down my tart retort that I knew would get us nowhere. "It sounds like Kerdik's trying, but he's drowning with it all. I know he shouldn't have given the ring to me. I mean, obviously. I broke the world. But it doesn't sound like Kerdik can fix it all on his own. Where the crap are Cailleach and Brìghde?"

Link shrugged, but Quinn offered a passive answer. "It's not for us to question the immortals. They do as they please. All we can do is hope that we might somehow please them."

Her words came out rehearsed, like a mantra she'd prayed as a child. I let her words exist for a few seconds, not wanting to contradict one of the few things she'd been bold enough to say. I patted her hand gently, and felt her body lean in toward the contact I could tell she'd been starved for. "I really wish we had immortals who loved Éireland as much as you do. Hopefully they'll see how hard you've fought, and realize it should've been them on the front lines."

13

GREEN AT GRADUATION

My heart was beating a mile a minute, and not just because I was wearing heels. Lane had convinced me this was a dress-up occasion, though I didn't see the point, since my cap and gown covered up my mid-thigh light gray pencil skirt, and the cleavage-peeking high-necked white blouse that had ruffles running down the narrow V on my chest. Lane and Reyn had bought me a white gold necklace, and I smiled when it poked through the narrow curtain of white ruffles. The circular pendant bore the inscription "Know Who You Are" in a font Judah had designed.

My gray heels clicked on the hard floor as I walked on rubbery legs toward the other graduates. I'd waited so long for this day. Though it had been postponed past my original plan, I'd managed to get back on the horse and ride that sucker to the finish line. Through much painful effort on Lane, Draper, Bastien and Judah's parts, I was graduating.

Judah offered his arm to steady me, smirking at the heels he knew I couldn't manage with grace. "Want to borrow my shoes?"

"If I said yes, would you wear my heels?"

Judah scrunched his nose and shook his head. He pushed his Buddy Holly glasses up as he grinned at me. "I feel like I might handle those things slightly less elegantly than you."

"Thanks for flying in for this. You're the best, Big Daddy."

Judah smirked at me. "Thanks, Hot Mama." He looked older now, taller somehow. The distance between our addresses gave him the space to grow up into a man who'd put aside his weekly D&D games, and donned his entrepreneur's cap. He'd told me it was facing all the crap we'd gone through in Avalon that made him step up to the plate and start swinging. I like to think that tenacity was there all along, our world waiting with bated breath for someone as wonderful as Judah to make his mark. His online business was thriving, making trips across the country for my graduation a thing he didn't blink twice at.

Bastien kissed my temple. "You got everything you need? We'll be just out in the crowd. Tenth row. I think Lane made signs. You can't miss us."

"I think I'm good. This is it." We reached the back area in the hallway behind the gymnasium where the graduates were congregated. I saw the mass of navy gowns, and it hit me afresh that I was one of them. I was one of the people who would get their diploma. I'd worked tirelessly to earn a Bachelor's Degree, and now my moment had finally come. So many emotions were poking at the edges of my composure. After Bastien kissed me, Judah made to leave with him. "Wait, Bastien? Could I have a second with Judah?"

Bastien squeezed my hand before letting go. "Sure, Daisy. I'll see you after."

When it was just me and Judah (and about four hundred graduates), I leaned forward and pressed my forehead to his. I didn't know what I wanted to say to him, but I knew I needed him there. This was just as much his journey as it had been mine. Instead of waiting for me to find the right words, he chose the perfect ones. "I'm so proud of you, Ro. I always knew you'd make it to this moment."

"You did? I lost my faith quite a few times. Judah?"

"Yeah?"

I let out a long breath to make sure I didn't cry. "Just so you know, none of this would've happened if it weren't for you. I wouldn't have graduated high school, and I definitely wouldn't have had the guts to even try college. You... And I... And you should know that... I super way love you, man."

Judah chuckled, his lashes sparkling with tears as he pulled me in for a hug. We gripped each other as two friends who had gone through a war could. He'd stayed with me through it all – helping me study for classes he wasn't even taking, negotiating with professors so I could have more time to get through a paper, and making up rap songs at all hours of the night so I could remember the more complicated details and reproduce them on a test.

Judah held me tight, speaking low into my ear as his voice cracked with emotion. "I'm so, so proud of you, Ro. There was never a doubt in my mind that you could do anything you set your mind to. I wouldn't have survived the bullies in junior high without you, much less the rest of my life. You're my best friend, and I'll never stop needing you."

"I'll never stop needing you."

There were no more words, only repeats of the sentiments that were too big for sonnets. Shakespeare himself couldn't encapsulate all that Judah meant to me, how much he'd saved me, and made my life better.

Instead of a speech, Judah sang quietly to me. "'I thought I knew what getting older would feel like.'"

I smiled through the effort of trying to trap my tears inside. "I love you so much!" Lost and Forgotten was our favorite band in the universe. When there were no words, Judah reached for lyrics that we'd sang over and over as we'd planned out our lives together.

"'But here you are now, and I didn't have a clue.'"

"'I keep wishing for more time, but what I should've

asked for was more and more of you,'" we finished in unison.

Judah kissed my nose. "I love you, too. Wouldn't have changed a thing about us, or how we got here."

"What about the time I farted on your pillow because you hid the remote?"

"Not even that. Now, go graduate. I'll be out in the crowd. My sign says, 'Go, shorty! Get your diploma, girl!' Lane's says, 'My baby girl is a college graduate!' Reyn's says, 'My daughter's got her degree!' Bastien's says, 'Marry me.' Draper's says, 'My sister's smarter than your sister.' Link's says, 'I'm taking her home tonight!' Lucas is too young to hold a sign, and Antonio and Quinn are staking out the perimeter."

I sniggered in his arms. "You're the best dorks a girl could ask for."

Judah's dark hair was cut short now, and he looked like a true grownup. He tugged on my cap, making sure it was straight. "I think this here crown makes you Queen of the Dorks for like, a solid week, at least."

"I'll take it. Now go, before you make me cry. I've made it a year and a half with no tears. I'm not about to start bawling now."

Judah shoved his hands in his pockets, humming the hook to the Lost and Forgotten song we'd sung to each other as he walked away. There was still plenty of time before I actually had to line up, so I hung by the drinking fountain in an unlit corner to compose myself. I inhaled and exhaled, willing myself not to cry. I'd wanted this for so very long, and didn't want to miss out because I'd gone spontaneously blind from blood clouding my vision.

My back pressed to the cool concrete. I wished I could be one of those people who didn't feel things so very much. I closed my eyes to steady myself, breathing in and out with great effort.

"Now, now. You're not to cry unless you know I'm here to wash away your tears for you."

My eyelids flew open, and a small shriek escaped my lips at the voice I'd know anywhere. He'd made me melt, made me furious, made me laugh, and made me insane. "Kerdik? What are you doing here?" Before he could answer, I leaned up on my toes and threw my arms around his neck. My eyes darted around, but no one seemed to be paying us much mind. Dark as this corner was, I prayed no one would see his beautiful green skin and freak out. He wore gloves with his usual chocolate-colored pressed pants, white dress shirt and charcoal vest. There was a scarf added to his ensemble to cover his neck, and his Newsies cap that had been pulled low over his blue hair, shading his face from view.

He stepped further into the dark corner with me, and tipped his hat up to reveal a smile that was laced with scandal at making an appearance in a world where he most certainly didn't belong. "I came to see you on your big day. This is important to you, and it's not something I'll get to witness in our life together. Just because I don't get you now, doesn't mean I don't want to be there for the grand moments."

"You're really here? I'm not hallucinating? I don't understand! How did you know? How are you here? *I* didn't even know I'd be graduating until last week when I got my grades back."

"I have my ways." He pulled back, grinning at the warm welcome I'd given him. "You are a sight for sore eyes, even wearing this ridiculous hat." He drank in my face, memorizing the features he knew well. There was an ache in his eyes, like being near me shifted something he'd needed to breathe properly. "Tell me you're happy. You certainly look well cared for."

I nodded, taking in the scope of the man I tried never to think about, lest I miss him too much and break down. "I am. We've got a nice, uneventful life here."

Kerdik let out a sigh of relief, as if that was the only thing he needed to hear. "I can't tell you how glad that makes me. To see you happy? I know it's all worth it. I was afraid Avalon and I had broken your smile for good."

I shook my head. "You gave me too many smiles for me to lose them all." I sunk into his embrace, memorizing the scope of his toned back with my palms as he did the same to mine. "You really came all this way just to watch me graduate?"

He seemed like he wanted to say something else, but instead gave me a tight nod. "I did. Just to see you graduate. I'll be your husband someday, so I should be here to see your big moments."

"Oh! Hold on." I unzipped my cumbersome gown, and dug my phone out of the pocket in my skirt. "I need a picture of us. In Avalon, people have to draw portraits from memory, but I have this. It lets me get an instant portrait."

Kerdik's mouth was opened until he swallowed the lump in his throat, gaping at me instead of examining my phone. "You're beautiful. That's what you wear here?" He pointed to my bare legs with an almost pained look in his eyes. "I thought I was overselling your hold on me, but if anything, I underestimated it. Rosie, tell me you're still holding me in your heart."

I whipped off my cap and moved next to him, positioning the camera so it could capture us both. "Of course I do. Now, smile. Pretend you like me," I teased.

Kerdik's eyes flitted to the screen, perplexed for a few seconds before he remembered he was supposed to smile. It was the perfect shot of the two of us, grinning with our mismatched skin on my special day. We took another with my graduation cap on, so I could remember that he was there for me without being asked. It was when I pressed my cheek to his to get that second snapshot that I realized Kerdik was sweating.

"K? What's going on?" I felt his forehead, and fresh heat rolled off his skin. I swore, taking in the bags under his eyes that I hadn't noticed in all the excitement. "Talk to me."

Kerdik shook his head. "Go graduate. I'll watch from backstage and meet you at your house after. We can catch up then."

"But you don't know where I live."

"Oh, darling. Don't you know? I can always find my way home to you." He leaned in, fingering my face as my heart fluttered.

I pulled back, tempted, but firm in my resolve that I wouldn't be cheating on Bastien. "I'm married, Kerdik. I can't... We can't... Let me be good at this. Let me be a good wife. Don't rip me in two. I'll be yours when it's time. And when I'm yours someday, I don't think you'd want me kissing other dudes."

Kerdik's eyes closed. "Yes. Apologies, my love." He cleared his throat. "Apologies, Mrs. Avalon." He took my hand instead, giving it a solid shake to accompany his forced smile. "You're right. When you're with me someday, I'll expect you to be with only me. I can behave."

"Thank you."

"Get your hands off her!" came Antonio's rough and booming voice.

My head jerked to the rude intrusion that drew too many eyes. "It's fine, Antonio." I winced when Antonio neared and let out a horrified gasp at who he'd just barked at. For all his talk about Kerdik screwing things up, he was speechless before the widely-feared immortal. "Kerdik, have you met Antonio? He, Link and their friend, Quinn, have been living with us for the last few weeks. Antonio's an Untouchable." Though, I'm sure Kerdik could've verified that easily enough by the neck tattoo that matched my own.

"Your majesty," Antonio said with a curt bow. I could tell by his constipated expression that he was trying to figure out if he should leave me with Kerdik and run, wondering what good he would actually be if he stayed by my side.

"Go on back with the others. I'm safe with Kerdik."

"I should say so," Kerdik sneered, lowering his Newsies cap to cover most of his face from the few people who glanced toward our disturbance. Kerdik wrapped one arm around me and whispered in my ear, "Go on, love. Have your moment and smile for me on that stage. I'll see you tonight."

I jumped when Kerdik vanished. Putting my phone in my pocket, I zipped up my gown and jammed my cap back on my chestnut curls, which were now sufficiently messed. "See you after, man." I tried to walk away, like what just happened was no big thing, but Antonio caught my arm before I could escape.

"He's a danger, ye know."

"He's no danger to me."

"Master Kerdik is a menace to all of Faîte, make no doubt about it. Be careful. I don't want ye alone with him."

I flipped my hair over my shoulder and stomped off to join the rest of the graduates, leaving Antonio to scowl by himself.

14

____

KEEP ME

What I had hoped would be a bubbly evening filled with conversation and high-fives had quickly devolved into a staring contest. Lane was in the crosshairs for not telling anyone that she'd been in contact with Kerdik, informing him of my big life events. Antonio stood behind the couch, leaning over it every now and then to shoot menacing looks at Kerdik, who couldn't have cared less. Quinn was hiding out in Draper's house with Judah. Link was whistling, I'm pretty sure just to unnerve us all. I was stressed that no one was getting along. Bastien? Well, Bastien was just plain pissed.

Lucas was immune to all our nerves, playing with a noisy plastic wombat. The toy broke the tension with intermittent high-pitched squeaks, which he giggled at. Reyn was on the floor with his son. His shoulders were tensed, giving away that his calm smile was a farce. I knew he was on the floor partly to guard his son from Kerdik's oft-swinging temper.

"Is no one going to offer me some tea?" Kerdik finally asked, amused that his mere presence caused this much upset, no matter which world he was in.

I made to stand, but Draper put his hand on my shoulder. "No. You don't wait on people. I'll get it."

I scoffed. "Hello, your status is the same as mine."

Kerdik waved off my protest. "Your brother's right, darling." Then he pointed his finger at Antonio. "That one. He can fetch me what I wish. Tea is what I've asked for. I shudder to think what might happen if I have to request it a second time."

Antonio gripped the couch, but didn't argue. Kerdik held the ultimate trump cards, even over Untouchables. Antonio stomped off to the kitchen, muttering to himself all the way.

I glowered at Kerdik. "Do you have to be such a blowhard? You know he's an Untouchable."

"All the more reason to set the precedent early on. He'll serve me, you, and Lane if I say so, and thank his lucky stars for the opportunity. It's good for a man to know his place."

"You sound like a tool when you talk like that."

Link's whistle stopped, no doubt anxiously bracing himself for Kerdik's retaliation at my sass.

"Why are you here? You saw her graduate. Now you can leave." Bastien was in no mood, which surprised me zero.

Kerdik pursed his lips, and again I caught a glimpse of that tired look in his eyes. "I need to speak with you, Rosie and Lane."

"I don't keep secrets from my husband," Lane insisted, her lips in a tight line.

"I'm certain you do," Kerdik countered, "though I don't care if Reyn stays."

Draper didn't move to leave until Lane gave the okay. She reached over and placed her hand atop his. "Why don't you take Lucas back to our place. See if you can get him to eat something. Link?"

Link deferred to Bastien, who nodded. "It's fine, Link. Let's just get this over with."

The others left, taking Antonio with them and shutting the three of us in the house with Kerdik. "Why do you look tired?" I asked, cutting to the chase. "What's wrong?"

Kerdik's eyes met mine. "You always could see right through me. That's one of the reasons I'm here, actually. I came to see you graduate, and I was hoping to ask for a favor while I'm here."

Lane replied for all of us. "Of course. What do you need?"

Kerdik lowered his chin, looking ashamed of his admission. "I need to sleep. For just a few days. I've been burning through too much magic in Avalon, trying to set things right again."

My fingernails dug into the leather of the caramel-colored couch. "You've used up so much that you need to recharge? Kerdik, that's not safe!"

Kerdik shrugged, as if he couldn't have cared less about things like helmets and seatbelts. "Avalon's a mess, but it's nothing compared to Éireland. Dian and Dother escaped from your ring, Rosie," he announced, but then continued when he assessed our lack of shock. "They've been... I've been stepping over there when I can, but Duke Lot has his hands full. I don't like leaving him alone for too long. He needs the backup."

I noticed a wet ring surrounding Kerdik's armpit, and a slight tremor in his hand when he adjusted his collar. "Kerdik?" I gasped and made a beeline for him. "Lane, he's burning up! Here, hun. Let's get you to bed and put your feet up." I hiked him up and coiled one of his sweaty arms around my shoulders. Bastien won my heart when he took Kerdik's other side without being asked.

Bastien nodded toward the stairs. "Quinn's bedroom," he suggested. "She can stay with Link, or at Draper's."

"I can make it up there without assistance," Kerdik insisted with mild irritation. He took a single step – with our help – and let out a groan as his knee buckled.

Bastien, hero of my dreams, scooped Kerdik up in his arms. His eyebrows were drawn together as he put aside his many issues with Kerdik, so he could help the only being that might be able to save Avalon. "Up we go," he grunted as he used his hefty muscle mass to carry Kerdik up the stairs.

I scampered around them, darting into Quinn's room and pulling back the sheets. I gathered up her belongings and moved them to Link's room, my palms sweating at how bad things must be if Kerdik came here for some peace and quiet.

Bastien laid him down on the bed while I started taking off his shoes and socks. My fingers rubbed his toes, which were heated, like the rest of him. He moaned at my touch, and I guessed he didn't have many people in his life who stroked his feet. "Rosie," he murmured, his eyes closed.

"I'm here. I'm not going anywhere. You're safe with us, alright?"

His hand rose, searching the air for me until his damp fingers rested atop mine. "Home," he exhaled.

"Cold packs," I suggested. "We have to get his temperature down. I think they're in Reyn and Lane's freezer."

Bastien nodded, letting Lane into the room while he trotted down the stairs.

Lane's fingers fumbled on Kerdik's vest and shirt, unbuttoning with a "let's do this" kind of expression that told me she would rather be doing anything else. "We have to lower your temperature," she explained apologetically.

I didn't wait for instructions, but carefully unbuckled

Kerdik's brown pressed pants, swallowing hard when he shifted his hips so I could tug them all the way off.

"This isn't how I imagined this," he said quietly, and I could see a thin sheen of sweat covering his legs. "I've been good. I stayed away so you could be with him."

My cheeks heated that he was saying all of this in front of Lane, who kept her eyes averted. The more his green skin was exposed, the more she fought to hold back her grimace. "Thank you. I'm doing well, here. Bastien's good to me." I tentatively reached out and brushed my knuckles down his cheek, my heart lurching as he leaned into my touch. "We don't have to talk about any of that now. Tell me how you're burning through so much magic."

"So many Vampires. So many needing to be locked up. The magic keeps floating. If I lose my patience and kill one Vampire, the evil migrates to a new body. It's slippery. I can't grasp it."

"How'd you do it before, the first time when you trapped it into my ring?"

"The darkness flocked to the three... It doesn't matter. I can't do it the same way without endangering you."

Lane studied Kerdik's moist features. "What do you mean? Is Rosie in trouble?"

"No. I won't let anything hurt her. She's safe." He said it like a mantra that kept him warm at night. "She's safe."

Lane nodded, as if that settled it. "You came here to sleep? Let your magic restore a bit?"

Kerdik tugged me closer with his weakened grip. "I

can't trust my body will be safe in Faîte. There are too many I've angered. Too many on the prowl. I knew Rosie would keep me... keep me..." His words trailed off, and I almost thought him asleep, until his chest rumbled with a cry of, "Mother!"

Lane went from wary to maternal in a heartbeat. "I'm here, Son. You're safe here. We'll watch your body. Don't think on it another second." She clutched his other hand. "It's alright, it's alright."

I didn't have the guts to tell Lane that Kerdik might have been calling out for his own mother. No one knew that Kerdik had been born – it was a secret I didn't understand, but was important he keep tight to the vest. I let her think he was calling out for his future mother-in-law, which I hoped was the case.

I let go of his hand so I could situate the covers to the side, but the second the contact was dropped, the walls of my house started to tremble. An ominous rumble made Lane cry out at the spontaneous earthquake, but I knew the cure. I scooped up Kerdik's hand and pressed his palm to my cheek, so he could feel I was with him. "Sleep, sweetheart. Get some sleep."

Lane eyed our connection warily. "It's him. He's going to bring the house down on our heads if you leave his side."

"I know. I forgot, but he did that last time. Even though he's asleep, he's still mildly aware. I just have to stay with him, and everything will be fine."

Lane pinched the bridge of her nose. "If I haven't told you before that one man is more than enough for any woman, let me say it now. This isn't going to go over well with Bastien."

I swallowed thickly, hoping I could maintain the line I'd traipsed across too many times for Bastien to trust me.

15

WATCHING KERDIK SLEEP

I cradled Lucas from my spot in the chair Bastien had brought in for me. Hugh Jackman sat on the bed next to Kerdik, harrumphing that he was put on hold for a baby, of all things. I cooed to my giggly nephew while I sat by Kerdik's bedside. My bare feet were propped up on the mattress, my toes resting against Kerdik's so he didn't freak out in his sleep and bring the house down on our heads. "Are you the sweetest baby in the world? Yes, I think you are." I don't care what the baby books say. You try being around a baby as adorable as Lucas, and see how much your vocabulary shrinks, and how high your pitch can soar. "Are you the sweetest baby in two worlds? Yes, I think you are." I lifted him up over my head just to hear him squeal with delight. "I just love you so much! Who's your favorite aunt? Auntie Rosie. That's right. Auntie Rosie loves you with all her heart." I brought him back down and kissed his face all over.

"And you say you're not ready for children," Bastien commented quietly, tossing me half a smile. He bumped his shoulder to mine, leaning his chair back on two legs and twining his fingers together behind his head.

I zoomed Lucas over my head again, and then made him dive for Bastien, who took over the airplane festivities Lucas was so fond of. "Thanks for being so cool about all this." I motioned to Kerdik's sleeping form.

"I know you had nothing to do with it. You didn't ask him to come here. And his reason for coming is solid. He's right not to leave his body unguarded like that in Avalon. If it's as dangerous as Link and Antonio were saying, then he shouldn't risk sleeping there. Can't fault the guy for being pragmatic."

"You're pissed."

"Not pissed. Actually, I'm fine. You asked me to be with you while you sat with Kerdik, which means you're not hiding anything. Things are different with us now. I don't have one foot out the door, and you've got my ring on your finger. You're doing what you have to do for the kingdom because you're the Queen of Avalon. I get it, and I'm cool."

"The coolest? Like, popsicle, cool? Like, Kool Moe Dee, cool? Like the Abominable Snowman, cool?"

"Yes, to all the cools. I'm pleased to say I know what all of those references are. I'm as cool as they come, babe." He blew a raspberry on Lucas' cheek. "I've been doing some thinking. Talking with Lane, actually. I don't want you to live the second half of your life alone. The more I see Kerdik not being such a violent tool, the more at peace I can be with the whole thing. I want you to be happy – after your years of mourning my death, that is."

"Granted." I rested my cheek to his shoulder, grinning at Lucas and wondering how it was that we'd gotten this far in our relationship. I pondered his words, unsure how true it all sat. "I'm not sure I'm doing all I can for the kingdom. I mean, it sounds like Faîte's falling apart over a serious mistake I made." I rubbed my stomach, and Hugh Jackman climbed from Kerdik's body up my leg, so he could curl up on my abdomen. I ran my fingers through his coffee-colored fur, smiling at his contented noises. "It feels wrong to be so content over here while Avalon's falling into chaos."

Bastien sat Lucas on his lap and bounced the baby on his knee. "You're one person, Ro. You can't put an entire kingdom's wellbeing on your shoulders. Not even Kerdik can do that. That's where Avalon gets messed up. They put it all on him, and that's just not practical." His gaze fell to the man stretched out on the bed. Ice packs were on his ankles, wrists and forehead, but they had to be replaced every hour, since they turned warm so quickly. "How's his temperature?"

I leaned forward and touched Kerdik's cheek with the back of my hand. Hugh Jackman grumbled at being jostled. "He's not as molten as he was when he first got here, but he's still too warm."

"I can't believe the grocery store only had a dozen ice packs. I hope it's enough."

I yawned, and then stuck my tongue out at Lucas, who tried to grab onto it. I wondered if my own parents had played such silly games with me when I'd been small enough to zoom through the air like a plane.

Probably not. Urien's love had turned out to be a steaming pile of fool's gold, and my mother had never loved anyone.

"You went all quiet. Where'd your mind go just now?"

I stroked Lucas' brown cherubic cheek, marveling at the wonder that was my baby brother-slash-cousin-slash-nephew. "Do you think Urien misses me? Do you think he regrets kicking me out?"

It was the thing we never talked about. My father's name, like Kerdik's, was rarely mentioned in our new life. Bastien rested Lucas on his wide chest, patting his back while his free arm stretched around my shoulders. He brought me closer so he could kiss my forehead. "I can't imagine anyone not regretting every second you weren't in their life. He did what he thought he had to do for his region, not what he wanted to do."

I nodded, knowing the logic made sense. Still, the ache clawed at me in my vulnerable moments, making me question everything I thought was rock solid about life. Dads were supposed to move Heaven and earth to make sure you had a good life. Superman wouldn't have hesitated to welcome me into his home. My voice was quiet when my words finally surfaced. "When we have kids someday, promise me that no matter what stupid things they do or who they turn out to be, that you'll love them, no matter what. Promise me that your love will never look like abandonment."

"I promise, Daisy."

"I don't know how to be a mom," I admitted.

"You didn't know how to be a wife, but you're the best one I've ever had. Of all my wives, you're number one."

"Aw, you say the sweetest things. You're my favorite wife, too," I teased, and then yawned again.

"I think it's time to turn in. I'll go take Lucas down to Reyn. Get ready to be nice and cozy with the men in your life, honey."

I grimaced. "I'm really sorry this is happening. I know this is awkward. For the record, you're dealing with all of this way better than expected."

"It's almost like I was meant to be your husband. I get it, babe. I get it all. This isn't your fault."

"Still, I'm sorry this is hard."

Bastien waved off my apology and zoomed Lucas out into the hallway. Hugh Jackman practically purred as I pet him, nuzzling me and telling me how glad he was that the baby was gone. *I'm your baby,* he insisted.

"Yes, you are."

We were quiet for a few minutes, giving me a chance to

be alone with my thoughts while I studied Kerdik's even breathing. I wondered so many things, not the least of which was how Avalon could be so bad off that he required sleep, which was something he only did once every decade or so. I didn't like that he was taking the blame for letting the magic loose, even less that he was taking shots from who knows how many angles. He didn't have a support system. I was his support, and I'd left him to wander Avalon alone.

At least he had my dad to keep him company.

Since no one was there to witness the crime, I shifted Hugh Jackman onto the bed and leaned forward. Kerdik's lips were light and curvy, drawing me in, as they always had. My traitorous finger traced the slope of his top lip, breathless at the intimate contact I knew I shouldn't indulge in. I was happy with Bastien, and didn't want things to change. Still, having Kerdik spread out before me brought back a myriad of memories I'd tried to put in the past. His stern jawline that only knew how to smile for me. His leonine form that could hoist me up without a problem, yet looked positively dashing in dress clothes. His green skin and sky blue hair, which people looked on as if it was something to fear, instead of the work of art I knew he was. In rest, Kerdik had no sarcasm, no anger, and no superior lilt to his mannerisms. He was uncomplicated and beautiful, and I'd missed his companionship.

I gathered Hugh Jackman up onto my lap when I heard Bastien bounding up the stairs, and sat back, my toes touching back on Kerdik's. Bastien had changed into gym shorts to sleep in, since sleeping naked wasn't an option tonight. He handed me a tank top and shorts, watching with rapt attention as I did a sexy dance for him while I stripped and dressed for bed.

"You can't get me worked up tonight," he warned quietly. "As cool as Kerdik and I are trying to be about it all, I don't think he'll be thrilled if I throw you down on the bed next to him and pound you into the mattress." He adjusted his shorts and motioned me forward. "Get on in, you teasing vixen."

I bent over to change out Kerdik's ice packs with the fresh ones Bastien had brought back up, giving my husband a nice view of my backside. His hands made themselves at home, massaging my butt and giving it a light slap before I climbed into the queen-sized bed. I didn't want to crowd Kerdik or add to his body heat, so I tried to only hold his hand when I slid in next to him.

My heart lurched in my chest when Kerdik cried out a desperate, unintelligible sound of relief and pain that mingled together when he felt me lying next to him. His eyelids remained shut, but I could see the agony in his twisted expression. "Hey, hey. It's alright," I assured him, not totally certain that he could hear me. "Kerdik, I'm right here. You're safe."

"Forgot my phone in the bedroom. I'll be right back."

When Bastien trotted off, I pressed a kiss to Kerdik's cheek. I couldn't help it; I loved him too much to be able to stand back stoically when he was in pain. I gasped when I felt moisture on my lips, and saw that a single tear had escaped Kerdik's infinite composure. I licked my lips, savoring the flavor of something so very rare. My kiss calmed Kerdik's upset, and within a few breaths, he was at peace, breathing evenly by my side.

"What time do you want me to set the alarm for?" Bastien asked when he came back into the room.

"Whenever you have to go to work. I don't have anything in the morning. Even if I did, I'm pretty sure I'd have to cancel it. I wish we hadn't missed the soccer game tonight. I bet the guys got creamed."

"You and I do carry the team, I'll admit. Though a night without Nick staring at your rack is a good night in my books. I wonder if he actually scored a goal, since you weren't there to gawk at." Bastien did an exaggerated imitation of our horny teammate's ogling, which wasn't too far off the mark. He stretched, and then started his nightly calisthenics that we usually did together.

"Nick doesn't stare. He's..." I paused when Bastien froze mid-pushup to quirk his eyebrow at my denial. "Oh, fine. You're right. Nick's a little pervy."

"A little? Link nearly took him out back for a swift reckoning after our last match. I had to talk him down."

I smirked at how quickly Link had assimilated into our world. Quinn was still on the outer edges of normal, but Link was comfortable in his own skin no matter which world he was in. There was a certain charm about someone who could radiate that level of confidence. Then again, he had that kind of appealing smile that if he walked into the mall wearing a tinfoil hat, a hot pink halter top, and no understanding of how revolving doors work, he'd still pick up four numbers (which he'd have no idea how to use, since he still can't handle the responsibility of a phone).

Bastien did twice the pushups he usually did, letting me know that as much as he was trying to be okay with everything, he truly did not want to share a bed with Kerdik, and was putting it off until the last yawn. When the mattress shifted behind me, he turned me on my side so he was spooning my body. His hand palmed my belly so that he could tantalize the underside of my breasts beneath my cotton tank top whenever he felt like it during the night. Hugh Jackman slid between me and Kerdik, ducking his body between my arms so he could snuggle under my chin. As I dozed, my hand relaxed, and rested against Kerdik's shoulder, linking me to him as he slept.

I wasn't expecting my dream to pull me in so quickly, but soon the glittery darkness was all I could see.

16

DUB'S FAMILY

"Where have you been?" Dub thundered, his voice filling the abyss of my dream.

I dribbled the basketball I couldn't see clearly though the black, glittery fog. "Never thought I'd miss you telling me to 'come' over and over again, but I've got to say, it's a far sight better than being yelled at. Care to rephrase?"

"Where have you been, you Commoner?" Dub was in no mood for my sass, but I didn't much care. "You were supposed to come back so we could play your game, and then I could show you what I needed to."

"Well, I'm here now."

"Do you have any idea how delicate everything is? I can't control you in here, so I need you to come to me willingly."

"I super-duper don't care about the madcap plans of any man who shouts at me and demands things."

"You are an infuriating woman!" he thundered, his fists clenched.

I was about to spit out a "Back at you, Princess!" but my spine straightened when I heard the voice I'd know anywhere.

"I don't think you want to be yelling at her. You have no power here."

"Kerdik?" I turned, a giant grin taking over my features. I dropped the ball and ran to where I guessed he might be, crashing into him in the foggy darkness. "What are you doing here? For a year and a half, it's been only me and Dub. How'd you get in?" I nearly strangled him with the tightness of my hug, drawing out a contented chuckle that moved his chest.

"How I've missed being greeted by you, darling."

Dub stiffened, for a moment perplexed that Kerdik was joining our little nightly ritual of antagonizing each other. "Kerdik, after all this time. How good of you to join me in my kingdom."

I rolled my eyes and turned my chin over my shoulder to bark at Dub. "Oh my gosh, do you hear yourself? You sound like an arrogant tool when you talk like that."

Kerdik stroked the side of my face. "I believe you said something similar to me when we first met. My body's resting next to yours, but my mind is still quite sharp."

"You're really here in my dream? I'm not just imagining it?"

"Yes, and yes. Dreams are imaginings, but yes, when I wake, I'll remember this as vividly as you will."

"I missed you," I admitted. "I mean, I'm happy here, but it's been too long."

"A mere moment apart is too long." His lips puckered against my cheek.

"Spare me your lover's reunion," Dub said, clearing away a bit of the fog so he could join us. "My, my. It's been many years, Kerdik."

My head whipped from one dude to the other, unsure how this would play out. Kerdik had trapped the Brothers of Destruction decades ago. There was no telling how deep the grudge went.

Kerdik's abdomen tightened as his eyes narrowed on Dub. "I should've known you'd find a way around my snares. How long have you been in her mind?"

Dub motioned to the air around him. "Not too long after the higher magic started spilling out and my brothers escaped, I started to hear her voice." The way he spoke about his brothers made it seem like he was annoyed by them.

Kerdik glanced around, his neck tense. "Where is the rest of the lost magic? I don't want Rosie exposed to it."

Dub tapped his shoe to the concrete floor. "This place is built in layers. The rest of the higher magic that remained is trapped on various levels of this place. The floor is mine alone. I built it when everything shifted, and the higher magic started spilling out. It's quiet here, so I can listen in on Rosie's life more clearly from this vantage point."

All color drained from my face. "You can hear me in the daytime?"

Dub looked at me as if I was a dummy. "Of course."

"Why are you here with her?" Kerdik demanded, his tone sharp.

Dub straightened, staring Kerdik down with a cool intensity. "When the magic spilled out, I elected to stay behind. Let Éireland deal with Dian and Dother. I've had to listen to my infuriating brothers for decades, trapped in here with them. You wouldn't believe how restorative the quiet can be." He let out a satisfied sigh. "When I get bored, I listen in on Rosie's life. Mildly entertaining."

Kerdik quirked his eyebrow. "You elected to stay imprisoned when you could've escaped back out into Faîte?"

"Not everyone wants to frolic about Faîte and be hunted by you and the other immortals. I wanted space from my brothers, which you gave me, dear." He tipped his head in my direction, his black hair falling forward like feathers. "That was a well-timed murder on your part."

Kerdik's body was tense as a fiddle's string, and seemed likely to snap in some unreconcilable way. "You'll leave Rosie's mind, Dub. I can hunt you, no matter what plane of consciousness you're in. I'm giving you this one chance to leave her dream, out of respect to your brother."

Dub's smile turned evil with the simplest twist. "Tell

me, nephew, how is it after all he's put you through, that you would imagine either of us respects your father?"

I knew that I wasn't supposed to know Kerdik had parents. He'd murmured about it in his sleep before, but that was a secret he held tight to the vest. "You're related to Dub? Dub's your uncle?"

Kerdik pinched the bridge of his nose. "I don't suppose I could ask you to forget you ever heard that, can I?"

"In that case, I didn't hear a thing."

"Good girl," Kerdik said, and then he shifted me to stand behind him, blocking my view of Dub. "Very well, let's get to it, then. You know I had no control over the spell once it was cast. I told you I was going to do it, and you even encouraged me in that direction." Over his shoulder, he said quietly to me, "When Éireland was overrun with too much higher magic, and some was starting to migrate over to Avalon, I cast a powerful spell that wrangled the darkness into the ring."

"I know, babe. You told me that already."

He reached around behind him and held my hand, guiding it to wrap around his taut abdomen. He leveled his gaze at Dub. He was protecting me, sure, but I knew he was drawing me closer so that he could assure himself that he wasn't alone in this fight. I made Kerdik stronger, which wasn't a responsibility I took lightly. "I told you it was a possibility that the Brothers of Destruction would be swept in with the higher magic, but you agreed that it was worth the risk. You said you'd stay in the ring if it would take your brothers and the more dangerous magic from Faîte."

Dub's tone was acerbic. "Yes, well, call me an optimist, but I wasn't expecting that to actually happen. I was stuck with my insufferable brothers for decades. Forgive me for not giving you as cheery a greeting as your little tart."

"Tart?" Kerdik was livid.

I didn't give a crap. "I've been called worse. It's cool. I think you stink too, man," I said good-naturedly, tossing Dub an air high-five, which he didn't understand the mechanics of.

Kerdik's thumb moved over my knuckles. "If you're in her mind, then you're not content with your decision to stay behind when the magic escaped, contained as I have you. What are you here for? You'll not make more of your minions." He rolled his eyes and blanched. "Your Fear Gorta experiment was a disaster."

Dub finally dropped his aggression that I could tell was a family trait. He looked on Kerdik with an intensity that bespoke of things more important than a blood feud. "Dother and Dian won't be captured again."

"Yes, they will. It's just taking me longer to get my grip on them. But I bested them before and trapped them in the ring. I can do the same thing again."

Dub shook his head. "No, Kerdik. That's what I've been trying to tell your little friend for too many months now, but she won't listen to me. When Dother and Dian were stuck in the ring with me, they made it their mission to absorb as much of the higher magic as they could. They're far stronger than they were all those years ago. Far more cunning and slippery. You aren't powerful enough to best them, and you'll spend the rest of your immortal days trying."

Kerdik's face soured. "You're going to spend your time trying to convince me that I should give up? What sort of a fool do you take me for?"

"I know how to take them down," Dub insisted. "I wanted to show the plan to Rosie, but she's been resisting me."

"That's because she's smart." Kerdik's hand reached for my other wrist, and wrapped it around his hips so my palms could press across his abdomen, encircling him in my love. He was nervous, so I held him together as he argued with his uncle. "Why should I believe you'd want to help me capture your own brothers? You stayed behind in the ring to be rid of them. Why would you help me trap them with you in here again?"

Dub rolled his shoulders back, the fog surrounding him like heavenly clouds. "I don't want you to capture my brothers. I want you to kill them."

17

CANE AND RING

Neither of us had been expecting Dub to come back with an answer like that. Kerdik scoffed, but I could tell his curiosity was stronger than his disbelief. "You lie. Immortals can't be killed. It's who we are. If there was a way, I would've found it. I would have killed my father long ago, or he would have killed me. It cannot be done."

My eyes closed against the pain words like that whipped Kerdik with. To want to murder your own father, and to fear being offed by him? I squeezed my arms tighter around Kerdik's waist to let him know that I loved him.

Dub's voice thundered across the space that seemed to stretch on forever, yet still felt claustrophobic with the black clouds that pressed at us from all sides. "If we can be born, we can be killed!"

"Very well, then tell me how such a thing can be done. And why would you give up such a guarded secret, if it would end your own brothers, and I assume you, as well?"

Dub's chin shifted from side to side. "They are no brothers of mine." His gaze locked in on Kerdik's. "Dother and Dian know where Carman is hidden, and they'll stop at nothing to free her. We felt her presence the same day the higher magic spilled out. She called to us."

Kerdik squinted his eye at his uncle. "You don't know where we trapped Carman. We put her somewhere separate from the Brothers of Destruction exactly so you couldn't find her and free her."

Dub shook his head. "We felt her presence. Our prison touched hers. We know she's in Cailleach's cane."

I recalled the blue-haired old woman who had a hump and a wonky eye, otherwise known as "the hag". When I'd hugged her, only then could I see that she was actually a smoking hot woman in her prime. She'd told me she'd been cursed by Carman, I think, so that only pure souls could see her true form. It was a rough way to live.

I inhaled sharply when I remembered Cailleach's staff that had turned hot when it brushed up against my right hand. It was such a small thing back then, what with all the harrowing events surrounding my first meet-and-greet with her in my bedroom back in Province 1, but now it blared at me like a five-alarm fire. "When Cailleach bumped my ring with her staff, it turned so hot in her hand that she dropped it. She looked confused by the sudden shift, like it wasn't something that happened all the time."

Dub nodded, looking relieved that I said something that proved he was telling the truth. "That was my mother sensing us nearby. You must hide Cailleach's staff, Kerdik, otherwise Dother and Dian will go after the hag to try and free Carman."

"Cailleach is gone," Kerdik commented, shocked that the puzzle was starting to make a little sense after all this time. "I haven't been able to find her or Brìghde since the higher magic spilled out."

Dub nodded. "Then she must know that Dother and Dian are looking for Carman. The hag is smart. Always has been."

Kerdik rubbed his chest as he thought aloud. "A war between immortals would be catastrophic for the Fae. Cailleach cares about her people. Éireland wouldn't survive the magnitude of such a fight if Dother and Dian went to war with her. Maybe it's best she's stayed away."

Tired of hiding behind Kerdik, I moved out to the side, my hand on my hip. "What about you? Why didn't you fly out on the nearest broomstick and jailbreak with your brothers? Why the altruistic streak all of a sudden? Don't you want to free your mom, too?"

Dub laughed, which I'll admit, I didn't expect. "How little you know of darkness, little one. I stayed *because* my brothers escaped. Family doesn't always stick together. I like to control what people see, not guess at how much pain I can make them endure. I get no pleasure from watching Dother and Dian rape, pillage and maim. I grew tired of Carman's mind games." He touched a midnight cloud with a wistful expression. "Letting them out was the greatest gift you could've given your old uncle, Kerdik. I'm eternally grateful for the peace you've given me in here without them."

"Don't mention it," Kerdik grumbled. Though he didn't shove me behind him again, he inched his shoulder in front of me, subtly shielding me with his body as much as I would allow. I took his hand and pressed a small kiss to the back of his shoulder, earning a glimmer of a smile when he turned his chin to glance back at me. Then he turned to Dub with a stern expression. "Why have you been in Rosie's dreams? What do you need her for?"

"She holds the prison on her dainty finger," Dub answered succinctly. "Such an odd choice of vessels for you to choose to carry such a large responsibility. She's merely a child."

"I'm twenty-four, you jag," I grumbled.

"I gave it to her because she was pure of heart, and didn't abuse the power she already possessed. I knew she wouldn't try to crack open Pandora's box and let Destruction out into the world."

Dub's calculating stare lasered between Kerdik and me.

"You love her." When neither of us denied it, Dub scoffed. "Love makes men foolish."

"What do you want her for?" Kerdik spat through gritted teeth.

Dub held out his hand in invitation, and before he said the word, I knew his only response would be "Come."

18

SÍOCHÁIN

*K*erdik turned to hold me, kissing my lips before I could protest, and flooding us both with the rush of togetherness. Then he stepped back to compose himself before I could scold him (and myself). "You'll stay here. No matter what, don't leave this spot. I'll come back for you once Dub shows me what he wants from you."

"No," Dub interjected. "She needs to see. She's the vessel the Destruction rests on. This involves her, too."

Kerdik turned and glared. "You will not lay a hand on her, Uncle."

"If I wanted to harm your love, I would've done so when she first defied me." He turned and motioned for us to follow. "Now, come."

Kerdik held tight to my hand, posturing as he led us through the puffs of black that glittered on our skin with a sticky wetness. His grip was unyielding. His tension made me nervous, but I tried to keep my cool through it all, stroking solidarity on the inside of his wrist with my thumb. We walked together, following Dub for what seemed like hours. After so many months of dreaming in darkness, I didn't trust the scene that unfolded before me when the clouds began to clear.

A bright sky broke apart the clouds, chasing the midnight away with a cheery blue and gold that emanated from above and warmed my skin with its glow. We found ourselves at the edge of an ocean, which glittered with peaceful waves that lapped in the distance. I looked down and saw that I had no shoes on. My toes dug into the sand, which also looked like it was made of pure gold glitter. "What is this place?"

Dub's voice was gentler now. "You trusted me. That's good. Both of you. Trust is crucial in this. It's why I didn't force this vision on you, Rosie. I needed you to trust me enough to follow me here."

"I'm here now, so why don't you tell me what I'm looking at?"

Kerdik's voice came to me filled with wonder. "It's Síocháin. This is where immortals are born. When my mother gave birth to me, this is where she did it. Something about the water here has a property that bathes the babe in a unique flow of power. It preserves us."

Dub nodded, moving to stand on Kerdik's other side. "Not many of us still know about this place. It's gone out of use, since none of the immortals have thought about procreation since Dother and your mother did it. We all know the disastrous turn that took." He sniffed at Kerdik's green skin dismissively.

"You'll watch it with that kinda talk around me," I warned Dub with a snarl.

"I've thought about it," Kerdik admitted, his eyes not blinking as he took in the splendor of the glistening sea. When he squeezed my hand, emotion flooded through my arm and traveled into my chest, where it made my heart clench with something precious. Though he was thought by many to be a monster, Kerdik was often my something precious.

Dub turned his chin to study me behind Kerdik's back. "Yes, I can see you've been contemplating the near-impossible." He cleared his throat and returned his gaze to the ocean. "This is where you can get the power you need to capture Dother and Dian once more. Bathe in the ocean six times, and then you'll be able to overthrow them." He raised his eyebrow. "Bathe in the waters seven times, and it would give you the strength to end them once and for all."

Kerdik's gaze cut to Dub. "You're exaggerating. Immortals can't be killed."

Dub didn't waver. "Many confessions are made to the darkness. People underestimate me because I don't come out the gate with vengeance and mayhem. I hold more secrets than you could guess at in your love's entire lifetime. Immortals can be killed, and this is how. If you want to end your father and your Uncle Dian, you must first go here."

I pressed my lips together when the math aligned. If Dian was Kerdik's other uncle, then that meant Dother was Kerdik's father. I closed my eyes when I realized that Kerdik's dad was the Brother who was known for inflicting Evil on Faîte.

Kerdik got down to business, skating over the emotion he wouldn't voice in mixed company. "Do Dother and Dian know the power to kill an immortal rests in the waters of Síocháin?"

Dub chuckled, giving me the shivers. "You overestimate our brotherly bond. They dismissed me as lesser ages ago. Dother only used it for your conception. They don't think beyond their baser instincts. It's time for their reign of terror to end."

"How do I get here?" Kerdik asked, swallowing hard. When he kept speaking, it was almost as if he was talking to himself. "My mother wasn't a true immortal. She was like Rosie – a mortal my father gave an extra life to. I have no one to show me the way. I doubt Brìghde and Cailleach even know where Síocháin is. They've never bathed in these waters before."

"Carman wore a pendant. Do you recall it?"

"Onyx," Kerdik confirmed. "Heart-shaped, long as a finger, and heavy. I remember. You know I remember. You saw her beat me over the head with it when I didn't remember a detail of my lessons."

My hand stayed tucked tight in Kerdik's grip. Thinking of him as a child was perplexing enough. To think of him being abused tightened a sailor's knot in my chest that I knew would never come undone.

"Find Cailleach and summon Carman from inside her staff. If you can convince your grandmother to lend you her onyx, that would transport you to Síocháin. There you can find the power to overthrow Dother, Dian and even Carman herself if you bathe in the waters seven times."

Kerdik was still for several minutes as he studied the vision of the place he was born. Then his eyes steeled, and I knew what he was going to say before the words tumbled out. "No. I won't risk letting Carman loose for this. I'll find another way."

Dub's tone flashed from instructive to irate. "There is no other way! You have to end them, Kerdik. Don't tell me you have some sort of attachment to your father. After all he did to you, don't tell me you wish Dother spared."

Kerdik's scowl tightened. "I wish him dead more than anyone. I remember your kindness to me, Uncle. I remember being beaten for months on end by him, and you would come by to distract him, giving me visions of a better life, if only I could escape him. I know you convinced him to let me go and build my own nation, and I appreciate all you did for me. But I won't risk letting Carman loose on your word alone. It would be the end of Éireland if she got out. And after Éireland? They would take their wars to Avalon. Avalon wouldn't be able to stand against the likes of Carman, Uncle Dub." His temper climbed as he clutched my hand. "Rosie and I are going to live together in Avalon someday. I won't have it destroyed before I get to start my life with her."

My free hand moved to Kerdik's chest, rubbing his sternum to soothe him. "Hey, it's okay. We'll figure this out, alright?"

Kerdik's eyes turned mournful as his gaze fell on me. "Bastien did as he promised; he gave you a good life in Common. I need to be able to keep you safe, darling. I can't start our life together in the middle of a war that has no end."

I leaned up on my toes, and lightly as I could, I brushed a gentle kiss to his lips. "If you say it's too risky to try and get the onyx from Carman, I believe you. We'll find another way."

Kerdik let out a gust of nerves, his sweet breath washing over my face. "Thank you. Thank you for trusting me in this."

I was about to reply, but shrieked when Dub moved behind me and jerked me out of Kerdik's grip. "Let me go, you jackhole!" I shouted, stomping on Dub's instep and thrusting my elbow back into his abdomen.

Black ties that had a slight fog around them wound around me, securing my arms at my sides. I didn't much care for being dominated, and thrashed around as best I could.

"Not another step," Dub warned Kerdik, who made a

grab for me. Dub dragged me backwards, unperturbed by my cussing and kicking. I even tried to knock him out by bucking my head backward in hopes I could break his nose or something, but he was prepared for my antics. "You'll do as I say, Kerdik. You'll find Carman, take her onyx and go to Síocháin. You'll bathe seven times in the lake there. Then you'll end their reign in Faîte. You think you're the only one who cares about the kingdoms? Do you think I don't bleed for Éireland, as well?"

"You did your fair share of inciting fear and chaos, Uncle Dub. Don't pretend you were the saint in all of it. Let Rosie go right now!"

"I've had decades in here to ponder my ways. I was impetuous back then, but I kept myself locked inside the ring to pay for my many crimes. Dother and Dian have no conscience to call them back here! I'll not stand back and allow Faîte to crumble at the hands of my brothers! You know I'm the only one with a sense of what's best for Faîte. When my Fear Gortas grew out of hand, I slaughtered my own creations for the good of the world. I didn't hesitate to do what needed to be done, nor will I hold back now!"

"Give me Rosie, and we'll talk," Kerdik demanded.

Dub's voice calmed as his arm banded across my chest. His chin looped over my shoulder so he could speak quietly in my ear, knowing Kerdik could still hear every word. "I'm sorry, my dear. Take one last look on your love's face. You'll not see it again until my brothers are dead." Then to Kerdik, he shouted, "You want your future wife to look at you and know your smile? Then you'll do as I say, or she dies in darkness." He jerked me harder when I struggled with renewed vigor. "And you know, I don't think she needs your little Compass gift, either. You've cut her too many breaks. It's time you were properly motivated, Nephew."

Ignoring my struggle, Dub blew a loud gust of air on the back of my neck. Then he used the arm that was banded around my torso to tear something that felt attached to my spine out through my belly button.

"No!" Kerdik lunged for me, but Dub's hand covered my eyes before Kerdik could rip me away from Dub's clutches. I saw nothing but the inside of his palm, and then even that faded from my vision.

I saw black. Even as Dub's hand pulled away from my face, I saw nothing but unending darkness as Dub vanished from behind me, severing my bindings so I could stumble forward into Kerdik's panicked arms.

19

ONE WEEK

I hadn't cried in a year and a half. Not a single tear. Not at the birth of my brother-slash-cousin-slash-nephew, which I'd held Lane's hand through, not my own college graduation, and not any number of amazing things that living with Bastien and the crew had brought me. I'd been pushed to the brink of brimming emotion, but had pulled myself back each time before the tears spilled.

Now it was like I couldn't turn it off. Resisting for so long had built up a flood of tears I couldn't escape. The carefully constructed dam burst, and terrified, hysterical sobs broke out across the bedroom when I awoke to the same blackness Dub had sequestered me to.

"Honey, you have to calm down. Explain it again, Kerdik. Why can't she see?" Lane's voice was pinched, but I could hear the forced decorum she was trying to portray to lessen my anxiety.

"I've explained this a dozen times already! Dub's been in her dreams. I visited Rosie while we were both asleep, and Dub told me I had to go to Cailleach, try to summon Carman from Cailleach's staff, and steal her onyx necklace. The necklace is the key to getting to Síocháin. When I get there, I have to bathe in the river six times if I want enough power to capture Dother and Dian, and seven times if I want to kill them. When I said that it was too dangerous to summon Carman, Dub blinded Rosie. It'll last until I get myself to Síocháin, so I can end Dother, Dian and Carman." Kerdik's voice went from irritable to gentle in the next breath. "Darling, I'll fix this. I can get you back your sight without involving Carman."

Lane's hands slapped on something – I'm guessing her thighs. "But you can't kill an immortal. It makes no sense!"

Hands that I should've trusted wrapped around me when the darkness grew dizzying. I shrieked and flung my body off the bed, accidentally bashing my head to the wall and falling to my knees. "Ow!"

"Rosie, it's just me!" Bastien exclaimed over the mayhem.

"No one can touch me! I don't know whose hands are on me, and I'm freaking out enough!"

"Okay, alright. I won't touch you without letting you know it's coming. You banged your head pretty good there. Are you alright?"

I heard too many things – rustling of heavy fabric, footsteps coming from too many directions, coos of sympathy, and then more hands on my arms and shoulders. "No! Don't anybody touch me!" I felt around until I was stable on my hands and knees, my chest heaving and my breath coming in syncopated pants, like a beast.

"Why are her eyes bleeding like tha?" Antonio shouted. "It's demented! Make it stop!"

It was when Lucas' sweet voice mutated to a wail of empathetic fear that I started to really lose my shiz.

Lane's voice rose above the din. "Okay, everyone out! Bastien, Kerdik, you can stay, but everyone else, go downstairs. It's too much when we're all confused like this. Everyone needs to take a break." When her edict was met with hesitance instead of a swift shuffling of feet, Lane started doling out tasks. "Reyn, take Lucas outside, please. He doesn't need to see his aunt like this. Link and Antonio? I need you to do a round of the property. Look for anything suspicious. Anything at all. If Dub can control her body from inside her ring, I want to know how he's doing it. Quinn? Honey, if you could put on some tea and gather up cleaning supplies so we can get the blood off the walls and floor, that would be great." When footsteps started padding on the hardwood away from me, I started to draw in full breaths again. "Draper, honey, go downstairs and start picking up anything Rosie might trip over."

"I'm not leaving when she can't even see. She's my sister, and I'm not going anywhere."

Lane's voice came out through clenched teeth over my pathetic whimpering. "Draper, so help me, you'll do as I say. When Judah gets back from the grocery store, you can explain it all to him. Now, go."

Draper moved closer instead of turning and leaving. I heard the creak of him kneeling down on the floor and felt his unsteady breath on my blood-streaked nose. "Rosie?"

"I can't see you!" I was heartbroken and scared. My tears ran into my mouth, leaving the rusty taste of blood on my tongue and lips. "I can't see your handsome face! I can't see your eyes. I don't know what you're saying with your eyes!"

My brother's quiet calm couldn't be faked. That was just who Draper was. "My eyes are saying that this is probably very scary for you, but I'm not worried."

"How can you not be afraid? I'm b-blind!" I tapped my stomach. "Dub stole my Compass! I can't feel where things are anymore! I can't sense it."

"I know Kerdik will do everything he can to get your sight back. This is temporary. Can you hang on for a week? Take a break from my ugly mug for just seven days?"

"No!" I replied, but then started to factor that into the equation. "Seven days?"

"Just seven measly days." Draper's voice was steady, while mine was crackly and broken. "I've seen you play soccer with a rolled ankle. I've seen you take Bastien to the mat in your Ninja Warrior classes. You can do anything." His voice was soothing, reminding me there was gentleness in the world when it felt like there was only the crash of darkness. "I'm going to wipe your face, now, okay?"

I was hesitant, jerking away twice before he even touched me. My hands flailed around until they finally landed on Draper. I had to see if his features were as confident as his voice sounded. My brother remained still as a statue while I ran my bloody fingers over his cheekbones, his closed eyes, his gentle smile and his unclenched jaw. Finally, my shoulders loosened by a necessary degree. "Okay. Seven days. I can do anything for seven days."

Kerdik sounded unsure. "Um, about that..."

Draper cut him off without apology. "Come here, pumpkin. I'm here for you. By the time your week's up, you'll be so sick of me, you'll beg for your blindness back just so you don't have to look at my face."

I don't know how I managed a nervous chuckle, but one spilled from my lips anyway. I stayed still while Draper ran a wet washcloth over my face, throat, and hands. "Please don't leave me," I whispered, my voice tight with pain.

Draper's composure gave way to emotion that pinched his voice. "Never." Then he pulled me slowly onto his lap, leaning his back to the wall so I was hemmed in by his lean, but strong arms. My fingers feathered over his t-shirt, and then gripped the material over his heart. He moved my cheek to his shoulder, shifting my legs to the side so he could hold me close. He kissed my forehead and ran his fingers through my hair. Then he whistled loudly through the house, summoning Hugh Jackman to come and curl up on my lap.

It was just what I needed – besides, you know, sight.

"What's going on? Why can't you see? Did the new one do this to you? Should I claw his face?"

"No. It's complicated. Just tell me everything's going to be alright."

Hugh Jackman, Lane, Draper and Bastien all said, "Everything's going to be alright."

Kerdik said nothing, and I believed him.

20

WITHOUT MY SAY-SO

For the first time in a year and a half, I couldn't wait to fall asleep. I kept Hugh Jackman with me all evening, and invited every single bird in our woods to come and sing me songs. They each did their freak-out over my predicament, but I welcomed the words because they drained my magic, which allowed me to sleep through the night.

Instead of darkness, the first filters of faded light trickled through my muted vision when I finally fell asleep. I leapt at what I'd once considered darkness. The concrete floor and dark mist felt like the bright sun in comparison with the black I'd been engulfed in. "Dub!" I cried out. "Dub, get your selfish, conniving butt in here so I can kick it right good!"

For the first time, I was alone in my dream, and I didn't like it. I'd counted on him being here, telling me to "come" or whatever. Though, I'd already seen what he'd wanted me to witness with Kerdik, so perhaps he wouldn't be back. I looked down at my hands, marveling at the small freckles that dotted two of my knuckles. Though it had only been a day, I missed the sight of them, and sought to memorize every inch that had been kept from me.

"Good!" I shouted to the midnight fog, my hands clenching to fists. "You should be too scared to show your face. You should run from me! You know what I'm going to do once I get my hands on you? It'll be the first time an immortal bites the dust without your stupid Síocháin. Try me, you jackwagon!"

"My, your fury is tiring. I'm not surprised Kerdik put a world of space between the two of you."

My head whipped around, but I couldn't tell which direction his voice was coming from. It seemed to boom from all around me. "Where are you? Get over here, Dub. You blinded me, you bastard!"

The fog before me started to roll away just enough to let me know movement was coming, but it didn't clear completely. The dewy wetness clung to my skin like slick glitter, making me not just pissed, but now irritable on top of it. I squinted, grateful I could see in here, however muted the landscape might be. Dub's angular chin and high cheekbones looked as if they'd never cracked a smile in all of his many lifetimes. "See how frustrating it is when you tell someone to come, and they dally? Imagine a year and a half of that, and you'll grasp my frustration."

I didn't bother with a blithe response, but came out swinging. My fist flung out with precision and victory, nailing him square across his sharp jaw. My right fist was jealous of the action, so I caught his gut with a right hook that held all the fury of Mike Tyson on a match day. "Give me back my sight!" I swung again, angry that he'd taken something precious and treated it as if it wasn't a requirement for everyday functionality.

For all my violence that I unleashed on Dub, the jag didn't even flinch. He simply stared at me, barely blinking as I punched him over and over again. When I paused for a breath, he sighed. "Are you quite finished?"

I punched him once more, smack in the nose with a money shot that would've broken the bones if he'd been susceptible to my strength. "Give it back," I seethed, my aching fists clenched at my sides.

"You'll see again once Kerdik does as he should. If he values your sight, he'll make quick work of ending Dother, Dian and Carman. If he stays focused on the task instead of bothering himself with the lesser lost magic, you'll be looking at his face again, I would guess in a week or so." He scratched his chin, which didn't even look pink with my assault, the superior jackhole. "Or is it your husband you'd rather be looking at?" His chest rippled up and down with mirth. "Ho, you are a beauty when you're enraged. The blush in your cheeks is stunning."

I pointed my finger in his face. "You don't get to comment on my life, dude who's hiding from the world inside a ring. Your whole universe sits on my fist. Never forget that."

"I'm curious, was it Bastien first, or my nephew? How did it work? I didn't start to be able to hear it all until the magic spilled out. Now I can hear your life quite clearly when I wish for a little variety."

"How clear are we talking?"

"So clear that I can tell you how many times a day you brush your teeth, every conversation you have, and the responses of anyone near your ring. I know how you prefer your eggs." He smirked at me, the bastard. "I even know how many times you make love to your audibly grateful husband. I must say, your aggression in the bedroom is quite spectacular. The women weren't like that in my day."

His smug smirk earned another punch. My indignant scowl couldn't be helped. "Well, don't listen!"

"I can't believe your husband can move about the next morning, what with how acrobatic your trysts sound."

"Dude, you're out of thin ice to skate on with me. Please, tell me more reasons why I should hate you."

He waved his hand to dismiss my rage. "I care nothing for your temper. I care that everything Faîte's been built to be isn't destroyed by my family."

"Then care less about getting on my last nerve. You've blinded me. You took my Compass. I would think poking me about my sex life, which you certainly were not invited to listen in on, would be clearly off-limits."

He waved his hand to the fog. "I could've blinded you

here as well, or left you on your own in the darkness, but I gave you a little light in your dreams, along with some company."

I shot him a withering look. "I'll pass on the company. I used to have decent dreams before you came along, you controlling jackfish. You're about the last person I want to use my limited vision to see. And forgive me, but you call this light?"

"Ah, but a little light is better than none at all. Look at your hands. Aren't they exquisite? I saw you admiring them before. People take the simple things for granted until I take them away completely. They thought I was wicked for casting my blindness." He shrugged, picking up my hands to examine my palms. "Sometimes I was, but other times I simply wanted people to finally open their eyes. Some need blindness to truly see what's important."

I ripped my hand back and slapped him across the face with it. "Spare me your philosophy on what a philanthropist you are for taking away people's ability to see."

For some reason, my fists had only amused him, or maybe even bored him, but the slap was a disrespect that made his nostrils flare. His hands reached out and coiled around my wrists, tightening as I thrashed through his punishing grip. He was determined that I would understand his patience had a limit, and I was in danger of crossing it. "You will behave yourself, or things could get far worse."

"How could they possibly? Look what you've done to me!"

Of all things, Dub chuckled. "Oh, little firefly, people always think things can't get worse after I take their sight, but you know? I've never found that to be true. I'm limited in your mind, but I'm not without power. I could make our time together a walking horror show." He exhaled in my face, and I got a strong waft of licorice that stung my nose. I winced and blinked, and when my eyes fluttered open, I gasped at the terror that was splattered everywhere.

The fog had lifted completely, but it was still dim in the football field-sized concrete room we were in. As far as I could see, there were bodies splayed out all around us in varying stages of torture and dismemberment. Severed heads, missing legs, gangrened arms, warty fingers, scaly faces and decaying mouths were everywhere, groaning and moaning at me.

I let out a bleat of fear, but there was nowhere to run when they picked themselves up and started ambling toward the center where we stood. One of the leprous hands reached out and snatched at me, jerking me away from Dub with surprising strength. I shrieked when another hand squeezed my hip, raking his nails across my tender flesh and shredding it like taffy. The strange thing was that I couldn't tell if it actually hurt or not, but the image was so real that my brain manufactured enough memories of pain to go with the illusion.

My scream was fresh from a slasher flic, but I didn't

run. I started punching the zombie-like faces as tears fell down my face. In my dream, my tears were normal, which was the only mercy I knew when more of the zombies pulled at my body.

Dub simply watched, studying my fear in the way a doctor might take vitals.

It was when one of the zombies grabbed at my breast that I lost my shiz, my breath coming out in hyper-spasmic spurts. Flashes of the heartless soldiers who'd taken Lane against her will and molested me in Avalon lit my insides with panic. I felt their filthy fingers and knew afresh the hopelessness of my screams. "No more hands! Get the hands off me! No one touches me ever again! It's my body! Mine!" I punched without aim, my terror making my jabs erratic. "Kerdik!" I screamed in desperation.

Dub whistled as if he was wrangling a heard of dogs, and just like that, every single body on the field vanished, leaving only Dub and me. I fell to my knees, trembling as I wrapped my arms around my torn and bloody midsection.

Dub took four steps to stand in front of me, and then placed his hand atop my head. "So you see, there are things far worse than blindness. I don't want to scare you, so if you can calm yourself down during our visits, I can show you beautiful things instead of more of that. But if you continue to test me, I will retaliate." He paused for my response, but I was too beside myself to deal with him. He slowly lowered himself down on one knee to examine my side. "Let me heal it. It's not a real injury, you know. This is all just pretend. If you could let your mind understand that, you'd realize it's not even truly painful. It's a vision I can cast. But it'll stay like that, bleeding and uncomfortable until you wake if you don't let me help you."

Tears dotted the grass as I batted his hand from my hip the moment he made contact. I covered my breasts with my arms, my gaze darting around to make sure no one was coming for me anymore. "No one touches me without my say-so! Go away! You're a bastard for doing that!"

Dub's voice turned softer. "Little Firefly, I won't do that again if you can behave."

"Go away! I don't want to see, if it means I have to look at someone as horrible as you! Leave me in the darkness, if this is all I get. I don't want to look at you another second." My nose ran as true anguish set in. "You have no idea all I've been through! It takes all the denial in my arsenal just to get out of bed some days, and there you go, throwing everything I'll never be able to erase in my face."

Dub sounded actually ashamed when he started with, "Rosie, I..."

"Go away!" I bellowed, my voice cracking. I could feel the hands on me still. It wasn't just the zombies, who grabbed without purpose or intent. It was flashes of the soldiers who'd done as they pleased with Lane, and then started to move onto me. It was the soldier in Morgan's castle who'd grabbed me and threatened ungentlemanly horrors that still haunted me with their depravity. It was the men who'd wrestled my clothes from me before I'd been lowered down the well in only my underwear. It was all of them, piling up into a big ball of lechery and filth. Their hands felt stuck to my skin like painful burs that ripped as they fell away, leaving scars that hadn't healed, and might never fade.

Dub's voice was gentle when he finally spoke from his place next to me. "Perhaps that was too much. It's been a long time since I've been around a woman, or people other than my ruthless brothers. I... Rosie, I'm sorry."

"No one touches me," I chanted like a promise to myself, shivering as I rocked back and forth like a true basketcase. "I have a good life now. No one puts their hands on my body unless I say so." Tears dribbled down my cheeks still, and I felt freedom in the normalcy of that simple act. It was normal to weep over being molested. It was normal to cry tears of salty saline instead of fat drops of blood. It was normal to be distraught over something distressing.

I was normal, and I welcomed the weaknesses and warts that came with such things.

Dub's hand on my back made my spine stiffen, so he retracted it. "Tomorrow night I'll not bother you. No matter what you must think, I don't want you to fear me. You're the only person I've been able to talk to other than my brothers in so very long."

"Then you probably shouldn't have blinded me, if you wanted to make a friend. You've been cryptic and irritable, and you want to hang out still? You attacked me! I can't see my husband because of you!"

"That, I'll not apologize for. Your pain in it, I regret very much. I don't wish harm on you. For a year and a half, I've asked you to come with me on your own, when I could've just forced the vision on you." His hand found its way to my back again when I cupped my mouth and wept into my palm. "Dother and Dian will destroy Faîte. Your discomfort was the only way to motivate Kerdik. I've seen it in his eyes; he would move Heaven and earth to save you. That's the equivalent of what I need him to do now."

"Go away," I whispered, not wanting to hear his altruistic reasons for mentally attacking me and taking away one of the only five senses a person had, plus my secret sixth sense. "Just go away."

The hand on my back disappeared, and so did Dub, finally leaving me to weep in the dark.

21

STUPID BLEEPING BALL

"Listen for the ball," Bastien instructed with all the patience of a saint.

Really? Really? No kidding! I kept my grumbling internal, knowing Bastien was doing the best he could with the situation we'd been handed. I'd missed two matches, and was determined that by hook or by crook, somehow I would get back on the field. I bent my knees and tried to keep my ear tuned to the fancy ball Judah had bought online and shipped to me. It was a soccer ball that beeped, so blind people could hear the ball they couldn't see.

We. The ball *we* couldn't see. I was having trouble blocking out the millions of other sounds that hadn't been a huge issue until recently. I could hear crickets, the flutter of bird wings, and Draper and Lane chatting near Lane's house on the deck. Lucas and Reyn were making adorable noises at each other. The animals were cheering me on from the sidelines. They had taken to following me around after Hugh Jackman had reported my total breakdown to the other woodland creatures, the snitch. With all the little noises and pockets of conversation, it was hard to tell where the ball was, and how fast it was rolling toward me.

"You're terrible at this," Antonio commented, being his usual cheerful self. The ball was somehow now behind me, chirping away that I'd missed yet another goal. "You're supposed to listen for the beep. Bastien, this is a waste of time. She's never going to figure this out. You're bending over backwards so she can relearn a game." He said the last word as if it pained him. "A *game*, Bastien."

I pursed my lips to rein in my temper. "I think I'm done for tonight." The ball continued to beep behind me, letting me know that I sucked at blind soccer. I couldn't even run with any real confidence. I usually played striker, or right middy. Now I was stuck trying to figure out how to tell if the ball was inching near the goal. My soccer coach when I was in Little Kickers ruled that I had too much aggression to play goalie. He was not wrong.

I heard the slam of a book, and knew what Draper would say before he opened his mouth. "You want to try reading again?"

"No, thanks. It was a sweet effort, and I tried, but I'm just as dyslexic at Braille as I am at regular reading."

"You're still just learning the letters, Ro. You're not giving it an honest try. Give it some time before we throw in the towel."

Once again, I pursed my lips together, willing my mouth not to belt out anything unkind. "It's decoding, Drape. Whether it's visual or tactile, decoding letters is where I hit a wall."

I moved slowly over to the right side of the goal, feeling around until I located my cane. Bastien and I were resolute that I would learn to do as many things as I could without assistance. Though I could hear his heavy tread as he ran to stand a few feet from me, he did not pick up my stupid, terrible, I-want-to-shatter-it-into-a-million-pieces cane. He let me feel around, trying to remember the exact spot where I'd put it. I was twenty-four, and used a cane to get around. Give me back my hump and wonky eye, turn my hair blue, and I'd be Cailleach, in the flesh. Minus Kerdik's evil grandmother living in my cane, of course, but close enough.

Bastien walked beside me, gently taking my free hand and wrapping it in the crook of his elbow. "You hungry?"

It was cooler out, so I guessed the sun was on its way down. "Not really. I can make you something, though. How about some eggs?" I joked. I'd tried to make him breakfast two mornings ago without anyone hovering. In the short time Bastien was in the shower, I'd managed to light a potholder on fire, douse the stovetop with water (extinguishing the pilot lights), and cut myself with the stupid steak knife when I was trying to slice up some bell peppers to go in the scrambled, wet mess. All that aside, I'd managed what I hoped was a nice representation of breakfast. I made it halfway up the steps before I tripped on the stairs, and did a faceplant in the warm, goopy eggs (which was how I learned that there were a few jagged shells in the mix).

Bastien kissed my temple, his breath a comfort to me when my senses were so very overwhelmed. Sweetheart that he was, Bastien had helped clean me, the kitchen and the stairs, and then insisted he finish every salvageable bite – shells and all. It's a good man, the one who makes a meal out of your mess. "I was thinking of taking you out, actually."

I frowned. "Out? No, no. I can't go out."

"You got another hot date?"

"Hello, look at me. I can't go out like this. I wouldn't be able to see the menu, I can't drive, and I couldn't leave my stupid cane at home. People would stare."

"People always stare at sexy women. I should think you'd be used to that by now."

"Bastien, you know I can't."

"Why? Is there something wrong with a blind person going to a restaurant? If you owned a Chinese food place, would you kick a blind girl out?"

I shook my head. "Kerdik might come back tonight. I

don't want to be out if he comes home with a cure or something."

Bastien's sigh was loud. "Babe, it's been a month. Before he left, he told us that Draper's promise of seven days wasn't something he could hold himself to. He's trying to find a cure without accidentally unleashing Carman from Cailleach's cane."

My voice came out flat. "You don't think he'll find a cure."

Bastien squeezed my wrist closer to his ribs, securing my hip to his side so we walked in-step. "I think you need to be patient. You're doing a great job at acclimating to all the changes. Hold out a little while longer. Quinn and Link want to go with us – make it a double date."

I didn't respond, only practiced breathing in through my nose and out through my mouth. Quinn and I had been doing yoga together every morning. Well, Link too, but his version of yoga consisted of breathing like an ape while trying the simplest positions, falling over, and then leaving the room after cussing a few times. It was the best part of the ritual, for sure. Link being terrible at yoga meant that when I couldn't find my center of gravity because the darkness was still so disorienting, I still wasn't the biggest klutz in the room. Something about having my Compass gone messed with my balance a little. "Double date? I don't think so."

Bastien stopped walking and turned to face me before we reached Lane and Reyn's deck. With his free hand, he ran his finger along my jawline, angling my face up so he could look at me as if I could see his features. Oh, how I missed the look of Bastien. "How many things have I asked you for, Daisy?"

My shoulders sank. "Nothing. This whole time, you've asked for nothing. You've bent over backwards to help me, and you haven't wanted a thing for yourself."

"I want to go out with my wife for a couple hours. I want to eat a meal and show you a good time. I want to feel normal again, even if it's an altered version of normal. I want to try."

I wanted to plead with him that this would be the furthest thing from a good time, but I chewed on my lower lip to keep from crushing his simple request. "If this is what you really want, then okay. We can go out."

I didn't have to feel his smile to know it was there, but my fingers climbed up to touch his lips all the same. Bastien never grew impatient or annoyed when I needed to touch his face so I could gauge his expression. I leaned up on my toes, and that was all I needed for him to come the rest of the way. His lips were my anchor when I felt so very turned around in the daily storm I couldn't seem to shake. Supple and soft, and always ready for mine, Bastien's lips told limitless stories with a simple kiss. His five o'clock shadow prickled against my palm, zoning me in to only him and cancelling out all other distractions. Only my husband could sweep me away from the dismal mood I often found myself sinking in these days. Bastien always knew how to sweep me.

Bastien and I made love quickly up in our bedroom, since he didn't want to miss the reservations he'd already made in anticipation of me caving. After we finished, it took him all of three minutes to get ready, but I was still at a loss. I only wore my jeans, t-shirts, soccer clothes and pajamas, though I knew Lane had bought me a few other things here and there that she held hope I might try on one of these days.

I sucked in a deep lungful of air and stood from the bed in Bastien's long t-shirt. "Okay, out you go. I need to get dressed."

Bastien's hand on my elbow was firm, but gentle. "I can help you. What do you want to wear?"

"Now, how am I supposed to surprise you with how much of a bombshell I can be if you see the whole assembling process? Lane's at her playgroup with Reyn and Lucas, right?"

"Till seven."

"Could you ask Quinn to help me out?"

"Sure, babe." He sat me back down, knowing I was pretty much a menace in tight spaces. Even though our bedroom was fairly large, I could trip over a flat surface these days, and hit every single piece of furniture on the way down. I'd gone from athlete to klutz overnight.

Quinn's knock was light and gentle, just like her. "Rosie? Did ye want some help?"

I was so proud of her for finally dropping the "your majesty" nonsense. It had taken a solid month of reminding her my title didn't matter up here. We were finally starting to become girlfriends – sewing together, drinking tea, her reading to me, me telling her all about life in Common outside of our little commune. I genuinely liked the little dormouse. She'd even started speaking on the seventh day of the week, which was a great departure from her upbringing in the oppressive Faire Séparer. "That'd be great. Come on in, Quinn."

Her footsteps were light, but I could hear them well enough to know she was standing in front of me. "What would ye like to wear tonight?"

I shrugged. "Whatever." Then, upon consideration, I pursed my lips. "Actually, a skirt. Something I would never wear in public. Let them gawk; I can't see them anyway. If I can't see myself, at least Bastien should be able to enjoy the view." I described the miniskirt Lane bought me that had vertical peach and cream stripes, gesturing towards the unused back portion of my closet. The skirt still had the tags on, and I could hear the hesitation in Quinn's voice when she helped me slide it on.

"It's nice, but are ye sure there isn't more to it? Like, another piece tha attaches to make it longer?"

I shook my head. "Nope. Bastien wants to go on a date? I'm giving him date attire." My goal was to get him so worked up that he would cut the date short, so we could head home and make good use of our bedroom. I fell down less when I was laying in the bed. I didn't want to be in public a minute longer than we had to.

I described a light gray blouse to Quinn, knowing that I could leave the top two buttons undone to give him a discreet peek down my top from his superior height. I paired it with a black lacy bra, knowing the dark cups would be just visible enough through the light gray blouse to tease Bastien with the ever-present reminder that I was packing Double D's. "You can pick something from my closet to wear, if you like."

Quinn's reply came back uneasy. "Um, I don't think I could wear something like tha."

"There's the gray pencil skirt I wore for graduation. That's knee-length. Pick whatever you like; Link will go bonkers."

"I'm sure I don't know what you mean. I'm bound to Link, which isn't the same thing as marriage. Link doesn't fancy me." Quinn's nervous denial made me smirk. It was obvious to everyone and their mother that the two were into each other. They were both just too scared to rock the boat with something that was already so complicated.

"You're in Common now. The limitations of the Faire Séparer Clan and the rules of Faîte don't apply here. If you want to wear jeans, you can. If you want to look like we're girlfriends who hang out on the regular, then you're welcome to mix it up a little and wear some of my clothes. You've got a life with choices now, Q. It's time you made good use of them." When Quinn took a tentative step toward my closet with new purpose geared toward what would look nice on her, I laid back on the bed and blinked up at the ceiling. "Link won't know what hit him."

My fingers knew how to French braid without my eyes needing to get involved, though I had Quinn check herself in the mirror for final approval. Quinn banded my hair in a ponytail atop my head, and then braided my thick mane. She wrapped the braid around the ponytail, making my bun seem more sophisticated and intricate than the sloppy mess I usually threw together.

I straightened the collar of my blouse for the sixth time, just in case the ends had turned upward without my knowledge. "I'm not sure if I've said it before, but I like having you around. I didn't have a ton of girlfriends growing up."

"I can't imagine tha's true. You're kind, generous and friendly."

"What about you? Did you have lots of friends in the Faire Séparer?"

This was usually the point where Quinn clammed up, cutting out all conversation about her previous life by excusing herself from the room. Maybe it was the borrowed gray pencil skirt that made her bare her soul, along with her calves. "My mammy was my best friend. I had two girlfriends: Sheila and Kelby. They were the only ones near my age. Sheila was thirteen, and Kelby was thirty. I didn't have much in common with them, but they were okay."

"I know you're trying to be polite, and keep from saying they're jerks. You can tell me the truth. I won't snitch on you."

Quinn guffawed with a grin in her tone. "I wasn't gonna say no such thing."

"Whatever, Q. I know you."

The words settled between us for a few seconds before Quinn continued. "Sheila used to leave all the darning for me. There were always excuses why she couldn't help out, but eventually I stopped needing to hear them. Kelby had seven children, so everything she did was superior to me, and she never let me forget it. Whenever she got pregnant, I had to rub her feet every night." She cleared her throat. "I don't mind, of course. I was happy to serve the Faire Séparer. It just would've been nice to be asked, instead of ordered."

I gaped at her. "Yikes. Well, if I'm doing something that's crummy, let me know. Man, that sucks, babe."

"I like us because we help each other. I get to help dress ye, and ye help me figure out Common. Plus, ye put a roof over my head. I'm so grateful for ye, Rosie."

I stood and felt around, accidentally grazing her boob, and finally was able to wrap my arms around her. "If there's anything I can do to help you out, let me know."

Quinn's hesitance was telling. I was getting good at reading non-visual cues. I held on tighter so she couldn't escape and brush her feelings aside for the sake of decorum. "I... There's something you can do tha I wish I knew how."

"What is it?"

Her voice dropped to barely a whisper. "How do ye talk to Link like ye do? It's so natural." When my grin took over my face, she started to splutter through her nerves. "I mean, it's your right. He calls ye his wife. I was already married, so I know I can't be his... I don't know what I'm saying! Never mind."

I giggled at her cuteness. "You know how the Untouchables work. You marry one, you're marrying them all. Sure, Link calls me his wife, but he also calls me his sister." I grinned in her direction. "I don't think it matters what you say to Link at this point. I think he's just hoping you'll look his way at all."

I could practically see Quinn's blush rising in her cheeks. "Ye don't know what you're saying!"

"Oh, I think I do. Just be yourself with him."

"Ye make him laugh all the time. I've never been able to do tha. He's always so serious toward me, or he avoids me."

My smile couldn't be helped. "Well, Link and I don't crush on each other, so there's nothing at stake for me. You're both so careful around each other – afraid you might rock the boat. Maybe you could stop running away whenever he comes near. That's a start. Link's a goofball. He's a good guy. You can be yourself around him. You don't have to be so perfect. You also don't have to be invisible." Then I paused, steeling myself to speak aloud the thing I knew she felt, but was afraid to put into words. "If you piss him off, he's not going to throw you out."

Quinn froze, and then exhaled. "Thanks. I think I needed to hear tha. You're a good sister, Rosie."

I beamed at the compliment *I* needed to hear. "Let's go see what sort of trouble we can get into."

22

BLIND DATING

The clinking of heavy silverware was like background music for the fancy restaurant. I could hear no less than four dozen people talking politely over their meals. I was hit with the smell of beef, mushrooms, and some kind of air freshener that reminded me of floral peaches. Or maybe they were serving peaches with flowers on the side, or something crazy fancy. There was violin music, but it didn't sound like it was coming from overhead.

Bastien moved slowly to accommodate my unease, which was only made worse by the gray high heels Lane had bought me that I insisted on wearing. They made a clicking sound when I walked, and silly as it seems, it gave me a degree of peace to know at least which sounds came from me. Though, it only took five minutes for me to realize that heels took practice, and being blind didn't lend itself to being super helpful in learning curve types of situations.

My hand was tucked into the crook of Bastien's elbow while I tapped the hard floor before me with the end of my cane. I both loved and loathed the sound that my cane made on the floor. On the one hand, it allowed me to have a better chance at not tripping and falling on my face. On the other hand, it was a sound that drew attention to the blind girl walking through the restaurant in heels she hadn't fully mastered yet.

Bastien's voice was low and methodical as he described the room we walked through. "There's a wall of tall windows on our right, facing out onto the main road. The kitchen's a little ways in front of us, and there are two swinging doors on either end. The tables are square, and they've got white tablecloths on them."

I smiled, despite my nerves that people were no doubt staring at the blind chick. "That sounds pretty. I've always wanted to go on a date to a place with white linens."

"Why didn't you tell me that?" I could practically hear the frown in Bastien's voice that I'd held back a desire from him.

I shrugged. "Can you really picture me in a place with white linens?"

"The visual's pretty stunning, actually. You should always tell me what you want, Daisy."

"Are there candles?"

"Yes. How did you guess?"

I grinned. "Judah read me a description of the restaurant before we left. Googled pictures, and talked me through it all. Did I freak you out with my Spidey senses?"

"A little. And after my fiftieth superhero movie with you, I'm happy to say that I totally get that reference."

"I'm so proud of you, you handsome Commoner."

"The tables have white cloth napkins, and there's a silver chandelier we're walking under right now. It's got dozens of crystal teardrops hanging from the ends. There's a musician in a long, black dress in the corner, and she's playing the violin with her eyes closed. There's an older couple – probably late sixties – dancing cheek-to-cheek to the music. She's got a smile, and he's whispering in her ear, just like us."

"Tell me more." I could listen to Bastien describe things for hours. Maybe that makes me weird, but it was like having a sexy narrator in your ear, making everyday non-events seem like something exciting, and borderline sensual.

"There's a couple talking through their teeth across their table. It looks like they're arguing, but they're in public, so they've both got these demented fake smiles on." He paused for my snigger. "We're going to walk around a table here," he said as he steered us to the left. "Link keeps wiping his palms on his pants. Quinn's got him all nervous, dressed in your clothes like that. I'm guessing you had something to do with that?"

"A lady never tells."

Murmurs of, "Oh, that poor girl," and "She can't even see how pretty she looks," reached my ears, making my jaw clench. I debated between shrinking into Bastien's side, and holding my head up in defiance of the whispers that seemed to multiply the further we moved into the dining area.

When we reached the table, Quinn took my cane for me. Bastien moved to stand behind me, just as the specialist for the blind had taught us in our rehab sessions. His movements were fluid, his arms wrapping on either side of my body so he could affix one of my hands on the back of the chair, and the other on the lip of the table. This way I could sit with some amount of confidence. He waited until my knees were touching the side of the seat, and then gave my butt a discreet bump with his pelvis, letting me know he wanted me, and also that it was safe to sit. I glided into the chair with what I hoped was a cool ease. I'd never worried about decorum before, but now that I couldn't see myself, I was hyper aware of looking like a bumbling ape.

Bastien moved behind me to push my chair in, making me feel like I was in a movie – a proper lady on a date being escorted by a dashing gentleman. Bastien was often brutish, but it was nice to know he could polish his manners and bring them out to dine just for me. He leaned down and gave my neck a little nibble, as if I was the treat that tempted him. "I know what you're doing with this skirt."

"And what, exactly, would that be?"

"You're thinking I'll get so turned on that I'll end the date early, just so I can see what this scrap of material looks like in a pile on the floor."

"I don't know what you're talking about," I said, feeling the heat rising in my cheeks. "But if you want to go home and make love all night, that's fine by me. Maybe this skirt is too short. Maybe you should just take it clean off of me."

"Nice try. You've got no idea how many men I'm this close to taking a switch to. Everyone is staring at your legs."

I swallowed hard, relishing being gawked at for the muscular calves I had worked hard for, rather than for my cane, which I definitely hadn't earned. "They're probably just staring at my neck tattoo," I said in an attempt to dismiss the compliment.

"Good. Let them all see that I marked you." Bastien reached down and laced his fingers through mine. He made sure to keep his words just between us with a gravelly, "When we get home, I want you in nothing but this skirt. I think I might tie you to the headboard again, and take my time reminding you how dangerous it is to tempt me in public."

"Now, now," Link interrupted without apology. "Don't go whispering all the best sweet nothings in Rosie's ear. Save some of the good stuff for me, sweet-ums."

I heard Bastien blow Link a kiss.

The waiter came to the table just as Bastien took his seat between me and Quinn. "Good evening. I'm Nathan, and I'll be your server this evening. Can I get you all something to drink?"

"Water for now," Bastien replied.

"Sir, what would your partner prefer?"

I frowned, wondering if I somehow looked like I was also deaf.

Bastien's reply was wary, but he tucked enough of the irritation away to appear polite. "I don't know. Maybe you should ask her."

The awkward tension kept building the longer Nathan couldn't muster the words. "Um, how do I…"

"Ye just talk to her," Link scoffed. "She can hear ye just fine."

After a long pause, the waiter leaned down and shouted in my ear, "Um, miss?"

I jumped, my hands flailing out and knocking one of my utensils to the ground. I kept my chin down, clenching my jaw, so it didn't start quivering on me in public. "Just water," I mumbled, mortified that people were probably staring for all the wrong reasons. I wanted to be gawked at for my scandalous skirt and my wicked neck tattoo, not because I came off as mentally challenged – which apparently, this waiter assumed I was. I moved to pick up my utensil – I couldn't even guess which one it was I'd bumbled – and ended up whacking my forehead on the edge of the table. I let out a bleat that announced my public shame, but I kept my tears locked tight inside.

The violin music stopped. The pockets of conversation

stopped. I didn't need sight to know that I was the focus of everyone's meal at that moment.

"I've got you, Daisy." Bastien picked the silverware up off the floor and set it on the table. Then he set about lecturing the waiter, who couldn't stop apologizing.

23

BLOOD AND SPAGHETTI

Link got up to help settle me in my seat once more. His strong hands steadied my trembling arms, not wavering when I gripped his thick forearms as I tried not to panic. "Link?" I whispered, ashamed at how blatant my fear made itself known when I spoke. "I can't do this!"

"I'm so sorry, miss!" the waiter said, fumbling with my place setting, I assume to correct the damage I'd done.

"Missus," Link corrected him. "Can't ye see she's married? I'll take ye out back and set ye straight if ye disrespect our wife again. I'll have a pint of your best stuff. Quinn?"

Quinn was appalled. I could hear it in her silence, and the slow way she placed her drink order. She waited until the bumbling waiter left, and then leaned forward across the table. "Rosie, honey, would ye like me to read the menu?"

I shook my head, unable to entertain the idea of stomaching a single bite now. When Link leaned in, I thought he would offer a steadying embrace. "Have a dance with me," he requested quietly.

"What?"

"Have a dance with me."

His suggestion was just out of nowhere enough to divert my chagrin to confusion. "But there's no music. I made the music stop! I can't. I'm too clumsy now."

Link picked up my hand and brought it to rest on his lips. "Dance with me," he said, and this time I felt his plump lips move. It was the details I missed. It's not like I could go up to my husband's bestie and ask to put my hands all over his face so I could remember the nuances that made him charming.

"Link, I'm scared." I'd climbed up a seemingly bottomless shaft to get at the Jewels of Good Fortune without a safety net. I'd faced trained soldiers, and stared down the barrel of too many obstacles that were life or death, but dancing in a restaurant was the thing that felt like one push too many.

Slowly, so that I could pull away if I wanted to, Link drew me up from the chair and led me a few paces out from the table. My legs were rubbery, but I managed not to trip and fall. He put his large hand at the small of my back and raised his voice. "If only there was a bit of fiddle music in this place, then I could dance with my lovely wife."

The violinist took the not-so-subtle hint and started playing a melodious tune that spun emotion out of thin air. Violins had that natural magic about them. "Link, how much space do we have? Am I going to bump into any tables? Is my butt in anyone's face?" I didn't want to sound like I was fretting, but there was so much more to think about, now that I couldn't see where I was going. I took a breath and tried not to freak out. I'd taken so many things for granted, but I promised myself that I wouldn't let this moment go unappreciated. Link was trying to give me back my dignity, and treat me like a woman when I felt like a fool.

"You've got a solid three feet on all sides, love. We're just going to turn in a circle for now. Nothing fancy." He leaned in to speak quietly to me, adding a slight tease to his tone. "Always keep your firm breasts pushed to my chest. Then you'll never lose your footing. No doubt our lad's counting down the seconds until he gets ye into bed."

I snickered at his caddish behavior, which most people would probably find offensive. "Your boobs are so much prettier than mine." My hand migrated to honk his left pectoral under the guise of feeling my way through life.

"Aye. Some things can't be helped." His sentence started off light, but ended on a minor key, making me ponder once again just how long I might be stuck in the dark. I hadn't seen or heard from Dub since he'd blinded me, though I knew he had to be there. My days, and even my nights, were now shrouded in darkness.

I felt constantly lost without my Compass, and without the whole chunks of my independence I'd forfeited to blindness, I feared I was also losing myself. I didn't have the confidence to do a simple thing like slow dance with my friend without questioning every move. "Lie to me, Link," I whispered. "I think I need a lie right now." The truth of my reality felt far too grim.

He was gentle with my fragile psyche. Instead of a lie, his voice deepened to sing the song his mother had blessed him with when he'd been a boy. "'In the dark of night, my eyes can find ye. My eyes can find your heart wherever it roams. There's nothing in all of Faîte that could separate us. 'Cause wherever ye lay your head, I'll find my new home.'"

I sighed with a wave of contentment. "I love when you sing to me." Link slowly turned us, our hips fused together so I swayed in time with his agile pelvis. "Link? Do you think..." I didn't want to voice my fears that this might be permanent, but the question was there, hanging between us like a gavel of doom.

"I think a great many things, and all of them point to your life being grand." Link moved my hand to his lips once again, only this time, it was so that I could feel them moving closer to mine. "Just grand, Rosie." I heard several coos of "aw" and "how sweet" when Link's full lips touched on mine. The Untouchables treated me as if I belonged to all of them, with the understanding that Bastien got top benefits. I know it was strange to dance with my husband's BFF and kiss him in public, all while my man watched with what I hoped was the same contented expression he always wore when the Untouchables doted on me.

The violin sang to us, muting out a lot of the other noises that overloaded my already frustrated brain. There was a sweet note in the sadness, and as I turned with Link, I willed myself not to tear up.

"I'm sorry, I've never done this before," Quinn said, her voice coming from my left. She had gotten up from the table, and was now probably an arm's length from us.

Bastien was patient. "That's alright. Here, let me pull you closer, and then we hold hands out to the side."

I smirked at Quinn's flabbergast. I could hear how flus-tered she was getting at the close contact from a member of the opposite sex. "Bastien, people are going to think I'm your wife, but I'm not!"

"You're in Common now, Quinn. It's time you started acting like it."

Through our pressed-together cheeks, I felt Link's mouth curl up at the corners in time with mine. It was cute to listen to her verbally worry over the scandal. My spine relaxed when I felt Bastien's hand on my shoulder. "Can I cut in? Quinn might need a dance partner with more experience."

So fast, I could barely understand the choreography of it all, Bastien shoved Link at Quinn, and slid around to take the place of my partner. He held me close to his body, chuckling at Link and Quinn, who couldn't stop apologizing to each other.

"Oh! Tha was your wee foot. Sorry, Quinn."

"It's alright. Ow! I didn't mean to bang your head like tha. I'm sorry, Master Link."

Link sounded put out, finally voicing the thing we'd all been thinking for months. "You've known me for too long to still be calling me your master."

"But you're above me. It wouldn't be right to speak disrespectfully."

"Call him a wanker!" I whispered, earning a pinch to my side from Link.

"I'm a man, Quinn. I just want to feel like a beautiful woman like yourself would want to be seen dancing with a lug like me. When ye act like you're beneath me, it reminds me tha we're adults. I don't want to be an adult tonight."

Quinn's voice came back with a hint of a smile to it. "Well, what do ye want to be, then?"

My breathing hitched as I waited for Link to please, please, please say the right thing. He paused for so long, I wasn't sure he was going to answer her until he finally said, "I want to be the man who's lucky enough to be standing here. Right here. With you. Let me be tha man."

I swooned on Quinn's behalf. "Link," she said like a prayer. "We shouldn't say such things. It's not proper."

"*I'm* not proper," he pointed out the obvious. "I don't need ye to be perfect. I need ye to be the woman who makes me wonder."

"What do ye wonder?"

I had to lean in to hear him whisper, "All sorts of things, Quinny. I wonder all sorts of things about ye."

When the song ended, Bastien led me back to the table, requested a different waiter, and read me the non-meat dishes (one salad, and spaghetti. Here's an angry shout-out to all the vegetarians who get stuck with a garden salad being their only other option for the main course). For a non-native, Bastien had taken to my world with surprising grace, learning how to make himself at home and appear totally normal as he leaned back in his chair, with his ankle looped around mine under the table.

My stomach was in knots, because though I couldn't see the eyes on me, I could feel them staring, watching me smile along with the conversation, while my chin pointed in the wrong direction. Lately, it felt like I was always going in the wrong direction. I ordered with some sort of competency, and the waitress was even kind enough to narrate where she was putting things on the table in front of me when the meal came.

Let me tell you a little thing about eating spaghetti. It's not one of those dishes you can eat gracefully, even if you can see what you're doing. Add being blind to that, and you've got a recipe for disaster. I felt noodle after noodle smack the front of my blouse before I tried my hand at cutting my pasta. I thought I remembered where the knife was, but I misjudged the distance and bumped my spoon against my glass of water. If you ever want to feel like a graceful dove, I recommend not spilling your water all over the table. I heard ice cubes crackle out of my goblet, sliding across the table as Quinn and Bastien tried to hurriedly right my glass and dab at the mess I'd made by simply showing up.

"I'm sorry! I'm so sorry, guys. I don't know what's wrong with me!" I added my napkin to the mix, even though I'm sure my outfit would benefit from dabbing something clean on my no doubt stained gray blouse. I wanted to help, but only managed to knock my righted goblet over again. Now I *knew* people were staring.

"It's alright, Daisy. You're okay. It's just a little water." Bastien was gracious, but I already had myself guilty as charged for being the biggest klutz in the universe.

Quinn reached over the table and held my hand. "It wasn't your fault; it was me. *I* spilled the water. I knocked it just a second before ye did."

Hearing Quinn take the blame for something that was so obviously my fault made my eyes shut tight, though that action was purely engrained habit that accompanied wanting to melt into the floor. I used to be made of tougher stuff, but apparently I was such a wuss now that my chin wobbled over a little spilled water.

Despite their many attempts to draw me into conversation, I knew that if I spoke too much, I might burst into tears. At least the blood stains would be camouflaged by the spaghetti splatters on my blouse.

This didn't use to be my life. It didn't use to be me.

But now it was.

24

I CAN DO IT MYSELF

*I*f only I could run to my bedroom and lock the door, so I could cry in private. After I banged myself on the doorframe three times on my way through the house I used to know like the back of my hand, I fell up the steps (easier to do than it sounds), banging my shin and my chin, all in one go.

When Bastien's hands reached down to pick me up, something explosive shot out of me without filter. "Do not help me! I can do this by myself!"

"You need your cane, Daisy. You can't go whipping around the house like this."

"Yes, I can! Normal people do it all the time. I don't need a cane! I'm twenty-four!"

Bastien was frustrated, but kept his cool, standing near me as I knelt on the step to reassemble my bearings. "I didn't mean it like that. It's all temporary, remember?"

"Everyone keeps saying that, but it's not true. If there was a way around getting the onyx out of Cailleach's cane to kill Carman, Dother and Dian, Kerdik would've found it by now."

"You're not giving him enough time. He'll figure this out." Bastien's voice came back pained. "He wants you to see more than anything."

"You don't get it. There is no other way!"

"Then he'll get the stone from Carman, and it'll be solved the way Dub said it should be!"

"That's suicide! I won't let Kerdik flush a whole world down the toilet just so I can see again. One person's discomfort isn't worth letting an evil witch out to torment a nation. He captured the three brothers before without using the mojo from Síocháin; he can do it again."

"Kerdik won't let you suffer like this."

"He won't know, then. I'll get myself together eventually. I just need some time to adjust, is all." I couldn't see Bastien's face, so I didn't know if he was pissed, or just chewing on his response. Either way, I was done being the girl with two left feet. "Look, it was a nice try, but I'm not ready for being so exposed like that. I need..." I shook out my hands as I leaned my hip to the railing. "I just need a little space right now. That was hard for me. I know you don't want going out to eat to be something that's rough, but it was."

Bastien didn't tell me he was going to grab me and kiss me in a sweeping series of motions that startled me and made me lose my balance. I flailed, letting out a bleat of panic into his mouth that I know hurt his pride. "I'm sorry," he said, righting me like a gentleman. "I didn't mean to scare you."

I touched my forehead, cursing myself and my rotten luck in all of this. "It's not you. Obviously. I'm the mess. Go hang with Link and Quinn. They're more fun than I'll be tonight."

"Let me at least help you to the bedroom."

"I need to learn to do this by myself. Everything's fine, Bastien. I just need to lie down, okay?" I mustered a smile that was probably the worst fake happiness of my life. "Really, I'm fine. I just want some space."

I could feel him watching me as I felt my way along the wall, counting the doorknobs I passed until I reached the third one on the left at the end of the hallway. I stumbled into my bedroom and locked the door behind me, unable to hold on for a single second before a sob rolled out of my mouth and landed in my hand.

25

___

SO MUCH DIRTIER

My shirt was ruined from the spaghetti I'd dropped on myself with all the grace of a rhino using chopsticks. I sniffed and sobbed as I unbuttoned what used to be pretty gray silk, and used the ruined fabric to mop the tears of blood from my cheeks. Though truly, I was probably just smearing them all over my face. My black, lacy bra was sexy, but itchy, so I unhooked that and tossed it to the floor, angry at everything that caused me the slightest bit of frustration. My silver heels came off next, allowing me to feel the hardwood floor with my bare toes. The tears still fell as I replayed the night's events in my mind. I was worse than Jerry Lewis in a fine restaurant. Bastien had done his best to romance me, but I'd ruined it just by showing up.

"Stupid!" I chided myself, throwing my gut-punch

word in my own face. I was stupid to think I could go on a date with my husband and pretend nothing had changed.

"Ugly!" I berated myself, painting my naked body with hatred I'd fought so hard to overcome. I'd wanted to feel sexy and beautiful, but neither of those words seemed to suit me. I was clumsy and messy, no matter how I dressed myself up.

I didn't understand why Bastien was with me, other than the Vampire bond thing. I was so moody lately. I wasn't trying to be difficult, I was just scared. Everything that I'd once understood was foreign now. The life I'd fought so hard to free myself from Avalon to get my hands on, now made little sense to me. I unzipped my miniskirt and kicked it to the corner with my other things, knowing I had to be careful where I laid stuff, lest I trip over it.

I'd worn sheer black lace panties in anticipation of the date going well. Now the sexy material mocked me. I couldn't even see if they looked good on my frame. It was difficult to feel confident when I couldn't get through a door without banging myself on both sides of the entryway.

I sunk to the floor in just my underwear, and held myself with one arm while I dabbed at my face with the other. I did my best to muffle my sobs in the destroyed shirt, hoping my lower mood swings didn't reach Bastien's ears.

"I feel as if I've passed the point where I could've

announced my presence gracefully," came a voice that shouldn't have been here.

I startled, my head darting around the room to place the direction the voice came from. "Kerdik? What are you doing here?"

"I honestly can't remember. So many things seem to have flown out of my head at the moment. You... Those..." His footsteps neared, and I heard the slick of fabric stretching as he knelt before me. "Allow me."

Though I should've stiffened at the intrusion, my shoulders relaxed as his hands molded to my face, washing my tears away with careful fingers. "I'm sorry you're seeing me like this. It's been a long night." The act of someone washing me so tenderly brought a flood of emotion to my tear ducts, no doubt making more of a mess of things. "I'm sorry! I'm trying to stop."

"Shh. It's alright, love. I'm here now. Now, tell me clearly, who do I need to murder? Who's made you cry this much?"

"Only me. I'm... This whole being blind thing is a little more of a challenge than I anticipated." I didn't have the wherewithal to pull back and care about my nakedness. I cared that he was here, which might mean that he had good news. "Tell me you've found a way around Dub. Tell me there's some Harry Potter potion or Narnia root that can undo this."

He leaned in and kissed both my closed eyelids, making me jump at the unexpected contact. "I need a bit more time, darling. I'll find a way. I'll give you back your sight."

I bit down on my lower lip and nodded, my heart dropping so far down, it felt like a palpable plummet. "Okay. I know you're trying your best."

"I want to do whatever it takes to give you your sight, but I can't risk letting Carman out. You cannot imagine the damage my grandmother could do. I would get you your sight back, only to have you close your eyes from the horrors she would inflict on Éireland."

I nodded, having come to the same logic on my own. "I understand. Why did you come back, then, if you don't have good news?"

Kerdik's response was measured. I knew him well enough to realize I'd offended him. "I'm not allowed to come and visit you unless I can cure all your problems?"

Instead of denying it, I drew in a deep breath. "I don't want you to see me like this."

He leaned in and whispered in my ear, "Darling, I want to see you in *only* this."

"You know what I mean. Crying into my stained shirt. Stumbling through my own house like a dummy."

"Rosie," he lightly scolded me. "I love you."

"I'm pathetic!"

He brushed his hands over my face again, sweeping away the wetness. "Sweetheart, you have to stop crying. I can't dry your tears fast enough."

I sniffled a few more times, willing my nerves to steady. "Kerdik, this is hard."

"I know, love. I know. I'll fix it all; I just need more time. Do you trust me?"

I nodded, though my hesitation was obvious.

His fingers fluttered over my face, and then swept down my throat. My chin tilted back automatically so he could wash the blood off my body. I gasped when I felt his lips in the crook of my neck, his arm coiling behind me. My back arched in his half-embrace, my mouth falling open as his lips trailed lower and lower down my exposed skin. Goosebumps broke out over my flesh, and every touch was heightened from the sensory overload that combined with the forbidden nature of indulging with Kerdik too soon. My body felt like it was on fire with the sudden flair of lust overload. His nimble fingers tweaked and fondled, making me his willing prisoner as I writhed under his ministrations. I didn't feel ugly under his capable touch, my awkward parts felt beautiful finally. "Yes. Just like that," he whispered, breathless and eager.

"We can't!" My protest finally tumbled out in a frantic bleat of confusion. "I'm married, Kerdik!"

Kerdik paused, but slowly acquiesced. His lips traveled north, placing a delicate kiss on my mouth. Then he fisted my braided bun and jerked my head so he could speak low in my ear. "Tell me you want me. Tell me you're Bastien's princess, but one day you'll be my queen. For now, that'll be enough to get me through. Tell me that if you weren't married, this scrap of fabric would be gone, and I would be buried deep inside of you right now."

I blushed at his filthy words, and then nodded guiltily. "But I'm married, so we can't. Please, K. I have to get this right. I want to be a good wife. I love him."

"Alright, then. I'll behave." He did me a solid and grabbed my bra for me, giving me one last nip before helping me hook it on. "Putting clothes on you is counter-intuitive." He kissed my naked shoulder, setting my skin tingling afresh. Then he stood, and I heard the shifting of my dresser drawers as he rummaged through to find me something less damning to wear.

When the familiar flannel folded around my arms, I snuggled into the warmth. "That's Bastien's."

"I know. But if you smell like him, perhaps I'll remember I'm not to suck on your pink nipples anymore."

"Oh, it sounds so much dirtier when you say they're pink." I buried my face in my palms, regret streaking the serene expression I'd been going for. "You can't be in here. You know we can't handle it."

Kerdik helped me to stand, and then let me use him for balance as he slid a pair of cotton shorts up my thighs. He cupped my butt once my clothes were in place, making me squeak at the flirtation I was trying hard not to indulge in. "Tell me to port downstairs, as if I just got here."

"Port downstairs, Kerdik."

Kerdik helped me with the last of the buttons, and then planted a kiss directly behind my earlobe. "I'll see you soon."

26

URIEN'S CONDOLENCES

I tried to act surprised when Quinn came upstairs with my cane. "Rosie, Master Kerdik's in the living room! Maybe he has good news for ye. May I come in?"

"Sure." I felt around on the dresser for my lip gloss, but accidentally knocked the tube off onto the floor. When I bent over to retrieve it, I whacked my forehead on the edge of the dresser, wincing at the audible bang. "Oh! Stupid!" I cursed myself angrily.

"Honey, let me get those. Oh, Rosie. Sit down right here."

I was dazed as she led me to the edge of the bed, sitting me down to examine what was sure to be a mark by morning. My shoulders slumped when she kissed my forehead, adding a note of maternal sweetness to our dynamic. On any given day, it was a tossup as to who mommed who, between the two of us. It was actually a helpful synergy with us, not letting either one be the charity case for too long. We took turns being broken, and then being strong. "I'm alright. Why wouldn't that have happened? Maybe I should get myself a helmet to go with this fetching cane."

Quinn's arms went around me, encircling me in her affection. "It will get easier. It's supposed to feel like this for a while until ye get the hang of it. Remember those studies Judah looked up? It takes people months to learn to rely on their cane. Maybe ye should call him. Would tha help? He can find ye the study and read it to ye again."

I missed Judah terribly, but part of me was glad he was in Tulsa, and spared from witnessing me being such a failure at this. I didn't have words to voice my despair, so I kept them locked tight inside. "Kerdik's here, you said?"

"Downstairs. Link's nervous. He keeps cracking his neck and his knuckles. He always does tha when he's scared."

I blinked at the insight I hadn't picked up on. I'd known Link a lot longer, and that quirk had slipped by me. "Huh. Interesting."

"Come, now. Did ye want to change?"

It was painfully obvious she didn't want me receiving guests in my husband's oversized, frumpy shirt and thin pajama shorts. "Nah. Kerdik doesn't care what I wear."

"Here's your cane, then, and I've got your other arm."

We walked slowly down the hall, and Quinn made sure

I didn't tumble to my death down the steps. My cane tapped the floor, announcing that the walking klutz was nearing the living room.

Bastien took Quinn's place, his arm around my hips and his hand on my elbow. "Hey, Daisy. Kerdik stopped by and wanted a word. Reyn's sitting in the chair next to the fireplace, and Link's going to make room for Quinn, so they can sit on the love seat." I smirked at his subtle match-making that prodded the two awkward bodies closer together. "Antonio's standing in the walkway between the living room and kitchen. Did you want to sit on the couch with Kerdik and me?"

"Sure. Where are Lane and Draper?"

"Lane's putting down Lucas for the night in their house, and Draper's at work."

"Oh." Then more quietly, I muttered, "Hey, sorry I lost it earlier. I didn't mean to ruin our date. It was nice that you planned something."

"You didn't ruin anything. I think we did well for our first time out." Bastien positioned me so my calves were backed up to the couch, and then he slowly lowered me down. When he sat next to me, his considerable bulk dipped me to lean into his side, anchoring me when there wasn't anything to hold on to so I could steady myself. "That's much better." I could feel his chest moving more evenly, now that we were connected. Mine was finding that same, relieved rhythm.

Kerdik cleared his throat and delved into the news I

already knew. There was no cure he was finding, and no, neither he nor I were willing to go to Carman, and risk unleashing her on Éireland.

"So, you're just going to leave my daughter like this?" Reyn questioned with a note of indignation tightening his tone.

"He doesn't have a choice," I answered. "I'm one person. Me being uncomfortable doesn't matter in the long run. Hundreds of thousands of people being tormented by Carman isn't something that's worth the trade."

"He's right," Antonio chimed in. "Éireland would collapse if Carman got loose."

Bastien's arm tightened around me, but he said nothing. I knew his heart was sinking every bit as much as mine, but he couldn't argue that Kerdik was right.

Link wasn't taking the news quite as diplomatically. "For how long? Dub's holding her hostage, ye know. This isn't something he'll let go. Don't ye think tha if he can control her sight, there's more he can do?"

Kerdik's dismissive reply came out unruffled. "Oh, Link. How small your mind is. Dub's power is locked inside Rosie's ring. His most notable ability is darkness, so yes, that weapon has surfaced, but only in her mind. Rosie's physical eyes haven't been harmed; it's her mind he's darkening."

Link didn't hold back his flabbergast. "Tha sounds even worse! What else can he do to her brains?"

Kerdik hesitated, making my spine stiffen. "Nothing. If Dub could inflict more punishment on me through her, he would have already done so. Right now, my focus needs to return to restoring Avalon. In my quest to find a cure for Rosie, I've been putting Avalon's needs aside. The Dullahan are beginning to form sides, as Éireland's headless horsemen did. The one side is somewhat peaceful – helpful, even. The Phare Dullahan, they're called. They're rounding up as many *Farouche* Vampires as they can, and avoiding riding on horseback. But the other clan of Dullahan are vengeful – the Sombre Dullahan. They come out at night and terrorize the people. Anyone who's walking about after the sun falls is a target. As soon as I kill one, it seems another pops up. Difficult to murder – the undead. They're bent on recruiting as many as they can to add to their numbers. There's been talk of a takeover in the works. I've had to reinforce Duke Lot's security."

Link shifted his considerable bulk on the couch. "Tha was the same problem we were having in Éireland, only they didn't seem organized enough to want to take over. They only wanted chaos, to terrorize."

"Yes, well, Avalon's always been a bit more civilized than Éireland. That doesn't surprise me."

I rubbed my forehead at Kerdik's superiority complex that didn't lend itself to tact or making friends. "How's Éireland holding up?"

Kerdik sighed. "I haven't been there in a couple weeks, but when I did stop in, it was bad. The Vampires are being caught, tortured and burned at the stake. An utter lack of consideration for what used to be their fellow man. The *Attelage* Vampires are treated no different than the *Farouche* Vampires, so I still will not tolerate Rosie being anywhere near Faîte. Even though Duke Lot is more discerning, and is merely locking up the *Farouche* Vampires, the *Attelage* are still treated as lepers in the district. They've started to form their own little faction inside Province 1. They occupy a smattering of houses on the outskirts of the western end of the region. They live there with their mates. It's actually quite a peaceful little colony. I think they're just so grateful to be alive that they don't want to cause trouble." Kerdik reached over and placed his hand atop mine, giving me a second to twist my wrist so I could grasp onto his fingers. "I've spoken to Urien, who sends his regards."

I'd wanted to ask about my father, but kept my mouth shut. It shouldn't matter how Urien was holding up; he didn't care how I was doing. A father shows up when his daughter's hurting. Mine sent a verbal sympathy card through his bestie.

I inhaled through my nose and did my best to think like a ruler, to push myself past my own pain of the moment so I could focus on the big picture. "You can tell King Urien that the Avalon Rose wishes Province 10 and its ruler the very best in this new age." I scrunched my nose. "That sounds queenly enough, right?"

Reyn's retort came back acerbic, which was a rare

occurrence for him. "Bastien, take Rosie upstairs. I have a few things to say, and she doesn't need to hear them."

Bastien didn't ask me my preference, but obeyed, escorting me around the corner to the stairs.

27

ANTONIO'S UNWELCOME OPINION

Instead of leading me up the steps, Bastien paused at the base. "Do you want to listen in, or do you want to do as Reyn said?"

I postured at being given a choice. "I think I deserve to be a part of a conversation that's about me. Can I squat here for a few? I can make it up the steps by myself if it gets to be too much."

"Sure, Daisy." Bastien lowered me to sit on the second stair, molding my fingers around my cane. He kissed my cheek and then trotted back to the living room, where the discussion had turned to shouting.

Reyn, of all people, was livid. "Urien sends his regards, does he? You can tell him we don't need his input, and that every effort he makes now is nearly two years too late. He *abandoned* that girl! He was afraid, so he cut off his own daughter over something she couldn't control. He didn't help her figure out how to bite Bastien without killing him. He didn't explain life to her when it turned on its head, yet again. He did nothing for her! What good is a father who abandons his child when she's been attacked? The Brother of Darkness attacked her, Master Kerdik, and Urien didn't even show up to confirm she was still breathing. He sends his regards? Do you have any idea what we've been through this last month and a half?"

Kerdik's reply was tart, but composed. "I would caution you not to yell at me. Your anger's with Urien, and I'll not rob you of it."

Reyn's volume didn't die down much. "Have you seen her arms and legs? She's covered in bruises! She can't walk down the hall without bumping into everything. She can't see her own mother. Do you know how much that kills Lane? She won't let Rosie know how torn up she is, but the second we get back to our house and close the doors, Lane can't stop crying. Rosie walks with a cane now! She's had to give up soccer, basketball, bowling, and she's even putting grad school on hold. Nearly everything she loved about her life is gone, but Urien sends his regards? Not even his regrets?" Reyn paused to sniff. "You tell him that we regret his entire being, and I sincerely hope he's unable to procreate ever again. If he tries to send another message through you, let him know that it won't be delivered. We're handling our situation with no help from him. We're taking care of his daughter, and she's doing as well as can be expected. Tonight was the first time she ventured outside our property, and she did beautifully."

Link blew a loud raspberry. "Are ye kidding? T'was a disaster. The lass wore more food than she ate, and was insulted at every turn. I'm surprised she's out of bed at all."

Since Bastien knew I could hear them, he defended me. "Like you've never made a bigger ass of yourself dozens of times over. Rosie doesn't have to be perfect; she just has to try to live her life. Reyn's right; she did that beautifully tonight."

"I agree," said Quinn, her voice mousy.

Antonio's voice cut through the landmine with all the finesse of a sledgehammer. "Link told me ye had to cut her noodles for her! She nearly had a complete breakdown, and couldn't manage to drink water without knocking it all over the place. This is no life for ye, Bastien. I see ye picking up the house every night, making sure there's nothing for her to trip over."

Bastien guffawed. "You're mad that I clean up my own house?"

"You're a warrior!" Antonio yelled. "You're not a house-maid. You're not a nanny. What are ye even doing here?"

Bastien's voice rose with incredulity. "Um, the same thing you are! There's no place for me in Faîte anymore."

"Ye mean there's no place for *her*. I never thought I'd see the day you'd follow a lass around, picking up after her and coddling her like ye do. You're just like Nicholai, losing your mind for a piece of arse. Women make men weak. A lass like Rosie? She's crippled ye, Bastien, only you're standing here, thanking your lucky stars tha she's carrying your balls around in her handbag."

Antonio's words felt like a swift punch to the gut, but I refused to break down. There was no shame in holding to the "in sickness and in health" part of your vows, but I felt the need to apologize to Bastien all over again. The worst part was that I agreed with Antonio – Bastien deserved a better life than this.

I heard the creak of the couch, and guessed Bastien had stood. "Are you standing in my house, eating my food, wearing my clothes, and calling me weak?"

"Tha's exactly what I'm doing, and ye need to hear it. Ye abandoned your country so ye could wet your cock and forget about your duties."

Link's indignation rose above the din. "Hey! Tha's enough, Antonio. If ye don't like the way Bastien lives, fine. You've said your piece. Ye can leave any time. Bastien's earned the right to choose whatever sort of life he wants. If he's happy here with Rosie, then ye shouldn't have nothing to say about it."

"I have plenty to say about an Untouchable throwing away his golden opportunity at life. You're chasing after a woman who can't even make it down the steps without falling!"

My heart raced when Bastien's anger rose to a visceral shout. "You're forgetting that my duty is to Rosie, not

Avalon. I'm her *Guardien*. I don't owe Avalon an ounce of my energy! They turned on me when I tried to leave the Queen's Army, or have you forgotten your own beating, and how you barely escaped?" I could practically picture the vein in Bastien's neck bulging, as it often did when he became enraged. "I owe Avalon nothing, old man! Rosie's never raised a hand to me. Why would I abandon her for a country that tried to kill me?"

"Whatever hold she's got over ye, it's messed with your mind. I wouldn't put it past her to have a little of her mammy's knack for witchcraft in her after all. If women could be Gancanagh, I'd peg her as one of those cursed creatures sure as the sun burns in the sky."

There were a few beats of pause, and then Bastien spoke, his voice quieter with bottled rage. "Rosie's saved my life on more than one occasion. I've had my time of fooling around. She's the one who dragged me out of a whorehouse and made me see what a mess my life had become. She's the one who got me sober. She forgave me after I slept with someone else. I can be patient while she figures out her new life."

"Make no mistake, brother. Her new life is going to be the thing that kills ye. Not fast, like a knife, but slowly, over the years. She'll wear ye down so tha ye wished your life meant something, instead of throwing everything away for a piece of arse tha's not even all that great."

The walls started to shake, and I knew Kerdik's feigned cool could only be expected to last for so long.

Reyn chimed in with, "You're out of line, Antonio. This is Bastien's home. You're a guest here. You've no right to cast judgment on a man who does a good job at loving his family. Just because you have no one doesn't mean the rest of the Brotherhood doesn't deserve to settle down. And I don't want to hear you talk about my daughter's ass."

"The keyword in tha was 'settle'," Antonio countered. "Bastien could have his pick of any lass he wants in Faîte."

Reyn was livid, even after the house stopped shaking. "Don't you get that he's already done it? He's picked, and his choice was Rosie."

"His choice might've been Rosie, but there's not much left of her now. She can't see, Bastien! Is this how you're going to spend the rest of your life? Picking up after a grown woman? Following her around like a lovesick puppy?"

"Tha's enough!" Link shouted. My monkey was finally fed up to the point of explosion. "I brought ye here to escape and rest up somewhere safe, not so ye could pass judgment on Bastien, who let ye stay in this world with him. The Brotherhood will hear about your attitude."

Antonio's retort had a cajoling jab to it. "Will they hear about your little blood whore, too? Don't think I can't hear ye murmur Quinn's name when you're rubbing one out."

Quinn yelped when the sound of fists hitting flesh interrupted the arguing. There was grunting and shouting, and Reyn yelling for the bulls to stop.

"You're finished," Kerdik ruled. Then I heard Antonio's muffled cries, and I knew Kerdik had intervened.

My pulse picked up at the note of danger that laced itself through the air. My heart always raced with dread when Kerdik was pushed too far. Antonio hadn't realized that every dig on Bastien could be said about Kerdik, who didn't tolerate criticism.

"Your mouth is sealed for the rest of the night to spare us from your insipid whining, all because you don't want to be alone without the Brotherhood to cling to. If they move on with their lives, then there's no one for you, is that right?" Kerdik scoffed. "Bastien can do as he wishes. He can take care of his wife, just as she takes care of him. You'll not insult Rosie in my presence. Bastien is wise to give up a life that would end his days prematurely, to spend his years with the woman he loves, and who's given up much for him. It's no mystery why you will never find this for yourself."

I heard Antonio's closed-mouth grunting, but only felt a ping of sadness for him. Then there were more fists, more brawling and tumbling about the living room. Something crashed, leaving me guessing at who was winning, and how many had been drawn into the duel.

When something metal cracked on something hard, I heard Antonio bellow a disoriented warble. Then the sound of his heavy body collapsed on the ground, ending the fight.

The metal thing fell to the hardwood floor. "What have I done?" Quinn said, afraid of herself.

"Tha's quite a swing you've got there. Good aim, too." Link sounded out of breath, but none of his swagger suffered.

"He'll have me killed. I attacked an Untouchable! I don't know what I was thinking. He punched ye, and I snapped!"

Link's voice was gentle, as if talking down a jumper. "Now, now. Antonio won't have ye killed, because ye didn't hit him with the frying pan, did ye? No, no. Bastien did."

"I did," Bastien concurred without hesitation. "You ran upstairs to go sit with Rosie. We all saw you leave when the fight started. I'm the one who knocked Antonio out."

"I should be put to death," she whispered, and I had to lean in to hear her. "Ye can't take the heat for me."

Bastien blew out a loud scoff. By that simple act of bravado, I knew he'd been hurt in the scuffle. "What heat? Antonio won't retaliate against me any more than he's already planning to. This was all between him and me. Link only got dragged in because he's on my side. And then you got thrown under the bus because you're attached to Link. Look at me, Quinn. This had nothing to do with you. Antonio's a pill. Always has been. He's the oldest Untouchable, so he treats us like we're his kids. He walks around like we've disappointed him by not living up to his rules."

Quinn's next words sounded muffled, like she was

talking into her hands or something. "Link, I'm so sorry! Please forgive me! I had no right to attack your friend. But he shouldn'ta hit ye!" Then I heard Quinn's soft weeping.

Link was gentle when he responded, and I was grateful he decided not to be a lunkhead. "Easy, love. Tha was right sexy."

"Don't make jokes!" Quinn cried.

"'T'was no joke. The only women who've ever fought for me was my mammy and Rosie. Tha was brave of ye."

"He... He shouldn'ta hit ye." Quinn still sounded scared.

"No. But I don't have to worry about tha now, do I. You'll take a frying pan to any lad who raises a hand to me." His voice turned measured and serious. "Are ye hurt?"

There was no answer, so I assumed she shook her head. I hoped she wasn't injured.

Bastien did Link a solid, and gave them both a push. "Link, why don't you take her up to her room? She looks a little shaken up. Plus, Antonio might wake up soon. It'll be a harder sell that Quinn was upstairs the whole time if she's down here when he comes to."

"Aye. Come here, love. Your old Link is alright. Didn't I say I'd always protect ye?"

Her crying picked up, and I guessed Link made a bold move and wrapped Quinn in his arms. I truly hoped that was the case. In my imagination, he would kiss her cheek, and then she would gasp and turn toward him. Link would lean in, and give her the first honest, passionate kiss she'd always dreamt of. She would gasp and then give in, kissing Link with everything in her, and turning him into a monogamous lovebug.

I wanted that for Link, and crossed my fingers in hopes that it came true.

28

QUINNY

ink and Quinn's footsteps came my way, so quick as I could, I gripped the edge of the stairwell and flung myself forward, skittering off the steps and tucking my body on the other side of the stairwell. I felt along the far side of the wall in the foyer, knowing they wouldn't see me unless they decided to go out for a walk down the street, instead of migrating upstairs.

"Ye know ye can't cry like tha. It makes me say stupid things. Mad warned ye I was no good with sensitive women." Their footsteps stopped just a yard from where I stood. I plastered my body to the wall that separated us and sucked in my stomach, hoping I wouldn't be seen. I heard the rustling of fabric, and when Link spoke next, his voice sounded like it was muffled, as if he was speaking into her hair while they hugged. "No one's going to lay a hand on ye, understand? I'm in the house, and I'll make sure you're safe. Didn't I tell ye I'd always watch over ye?"

"But who's going to watch over *ye*?" Quinn sniffled, crying into fabric. I hoped she was crying on his shoulder. "You're a good man, Link. Antonio hit ye hard. I was so scared for ye!"

Link paused, and in my imagination, he was fiddling with a lock of her hair. "Were ye scared because ye need my blood to live, or for another reason?"

Quinn stilled, her sobs stopping abruptly. "I don't know what ye mean."

My breath ceased when Link finally, finally, finally laid all his cards on the table. "Do ye fancy me, Quinn?"

I mime-squealed with glee. My heart raced on her behalf, and I cheered with everything in me for her to take that next step and be brave. Link needed someone like her. She was so good for him.

"I... I..." she stammered, and my heart plummeted that she was chickening out.

"Never mind. Forget I asked. I'm making ye uncomfortable. I'm no good around real ladies. Let's get ye upstairs."

Quinn's voice came out meek when she whispered, "Link, I shouldn't fancy ye."

Hope soared in my chest, like an eagle taking off without a thought of ever needing to come back down to earth.

I could hear the same hope in Link's voice, as well. There was a distinct smile in his reply, and I could practically see his grin oozing out a heaping helping of charm. "Now, who told ye tha? I think ye should pine for me morning, noon, and night."

"I'm a Vampire, Link. I'm an abomination. Ye should be with a woman ye could be proud to stand with."

All traces of Link's teasing deserted him. "I would be proud to stand with ye. Your ex-husband should have his balls cut off for talking to ye like tha. Ye aren't an abomination, Quinny. You're a fine lady. I'm the one who doesn't deserve to stand with someone as upstanding as ye."

I melted a little bit when he called her "Quinny". It was just so adorable.

"I... I... We shouldn't be talking like this. Someone might see us together, and they'll know!"

"What'll they know?"

"Tha I fancy ye! Tha I think about ye in ways I shouldn't." She sounded utterly distraught, and I could picture her hands wringing in angst.

"Kiss me, Quinn. I'm dying for it over here."

"Ye know I shouldn't! Ye deserve someone more..."

Link's voice took on an edge that made me rally. "I deserve the lass who takes a frying pan to the back of the head of anyone who attacks me." I heard a kiss to her cheek as she fretted some more. "Quinny?" Link uttered, low and breathy.

"We can't, Link!"

"Do ye think about me?"

"Ye know I do! But this isn't proper! I'm a good girl, and

I abided by the laws of the Faire Séparer. I didn't kiss Bram until our wedding day."

"Do ye want me to kiss ye here? What's the harm in a little peck?"

Her reply came back confused. "Ye want to kiss my hand? I don't know. I... people might see!"

"Forget about the world. What is it ye want?"

"I suppose... I mean, a kiss on the hand isn't too much a scandal, aye?"

"No scandal at all." I heard Link's lips pucker on the back of her hand. "Do ye want me to kiss ye here?"

Quinn's throaty gasp was a dead ringer for a good necking. Link wasn't pulling any punches. He knew the window where her guard was down was limited, so he pressed forward, declaring himself by claiming every inch of pure skin she gave him. He was an Untouchable, but she was the one who'd been elite in his eyes, and he was just the scoundrel to do away with the rules and go for what they both wanted.

"How about here, Quinny? Can I kiss your lips? I've wanted ye for so long. I've been good to ye." I heard his lips still moving on her neck. "Haven't I been a good lad?"

She let out a shiver and a light moan. Of all the things I wanted for Quinn, a good shiver and moan were in the top ten. Then she surprised me with coherent thought, though it was uttered to the tune of "tear my clothes off, you Untouchable beast." With all the sultriness of Sophia Loren, mingled with the sincerity and sweetness of an elementary school teacher, Quinn said, "You're the most noble, selfless, caring man I know."

I closed my eyes as my hand flitted to my heart, hoping the swell didn't somehow become audible. The kissing paused, and I visualized Link pulling back to look her in the eye. "I am?"

"Aye. There's no one I love more than ye."

As creepy as it might sound, I wanted to see – to have front row seats to the event of the year. I heard Link's lips crash on hers, swallowing her startled squeak. There was moaning, heavy breathing, bodies bumping against the wall, and love – total and utter love.

Blind as I was, I saw clearly what Faîte couldn't – that Quinn and Link were made for each other.

29

AN UNEXPECTED FRIENDSHIP

Quinn insisted they go upstairs, lest someone see Link kissing her. My grin practically split my face when I thought about Link having to pace himself for the sweet girl who could never be expected to survive passion from someone as uninhibited as Link.

I considered sneaking upstairs to my room, but overheard my name on Bastien's lips, so I froze in place in the foyer. "Rosie's not a complainer, so I have no idea how she's doing. So probably bad, I guess. She runs away and hides when she's upset, so I know she's not handling things as well as she'd like us to believe. Hold on. Reyn didn't shut the door all the way after he dragged Antonio out."

I heard the backdoor shut, and then Kerdik spoke. "I'm trusting you to keep her safe. Have there been any threats on her life as of late?"

"None other than the usual. A few more soldiers who

defected when Morgan was killed. Nothing I can't handle. My wards keep them off the property for the most part. Plus the vase of flowers you left her helps deter anyone coming around looking for trouble. It's not foolproof, but it helps. Link, Antonio and I've killed seven in the last two months, and I'm hoping that's all that were coming for her. They've slowed down, for sure."

My jaw dropped open as anxiety coursed through me. There hadn't been talk of any threats. No one told me a thing. As far as I knew, Kerdik was the only magical being who'd come from Narnia in a long time. I gripped my cane and remained stuck to the wall, facing the empty foyer. I was grateful to the wood floors for helping the sound to travel, so I could hear most of their conversation as they sat in the living room.

Bastien's voice held none of his usual contempt for Kerdik, but was almost conversational. "You want something to drink? I've got juice and water."

"Why not? I'll take some juice. This is the longest I've sat down in ages."

What the crap? Since when do the two of them shoot the breeze and lounge around together?

Bastien rummaged in the kitchen, and then paused in the hallway that led to the staircase, no doubt checking that I wasn't still lurking (which, of course, I was. Just on the other side of the stairwell). I heard the two cups clink together in a miniature toast when he settled back down in the living room. "I've got our property covered. You don't have to worry."

"She's unhappy." It was a borderline accusation from Kerdik that demanded Bastien explain himself.

"You can look in the mirror if you want someone to blame for that. She was on cloud nine when she graduated. Then she sleeps next to you, and she loses her sight. That one's not on me."

"Yes, well, I'm working on it."

"And what exactly does that entail? What sort of results have you gotten?"

"Don't pretend you understand the details of how hard I've been trying to fix it all. You know her blindness breaks me every bit as much as it does you."

"My wife can't see my face." He swallowed his juice loudly with a smack of his lips. "Fix it."

"You say that like it's possible. Like there's any way to best Dub. When a Brother of Destruction wants something, there's not much he won't do. I worry he's not done holding her hostage. When he realizes I'm not jumping for him, I'm afraid of what else he might do to Rosie."

There was a long pause in which I did not breathe. "Meaning?"

"Meaning there are worse things than being blind. At least she's seeing nothing. Dub can control what she sees. He can make her witness unthinkable things that would scar her for life. He's being merciful because he knows I..."

"You can say that you love her. I won't take a swing at you this time."

"Yes, well. Dub won't be merciful forever." Kerdik paused to take a drink. "I want you to keep her away from windows. Can you put bars on them without her noticing?"

"She's blind, not oblivious. She'd feel bars on the windows."

"Drat. Never mind. It probably wouldn't do much anyway."

"Any particular reason why?"

"Nothing I can't handle."

"You know, there's not a thing about that I don't need explained. Out with it."

Kerdik drew in a long breath. "I'm being paranoid. He wouldn't come after Rosie. He doesn't even know her."

"Who?"

"It doesn't matter. I'm just thinking about all my enemies, and hoping they don't turn their focus to Rosie. Allies are hard to come by these days, but I'm afraid they're necessary if I'm to make any real progress."

"You know I'm your ally. Come what may."

"Cheers, Bastien." I heard the two slap hands, but even in my wildest imagination, I couldn't make sense of that visual. "My trip to Common isn't just to see you all. I've got an old friend who lives in Common. Spoke to him just before coming here. Hopefully, given a couple hours to mull it over, I'll be able to persuade him away from his cushy life up here. I'm afraid I need help with all of this. This whole having a weak spot is new to me. Such an inconvenience it is to love her as I do, though I'm afraid there's nothing for it now."

Irritation rose in Bastien's tone. "Man, we're just trying to have a quiet life here, and it's like every time I turn around, something's trying to tear it all away. We left Faîte so we could live our lives, Kerdik. Whatever drama's going down that might swing our way, take care of it."

"I don't think I've ever hated and respected anyone as much as I do you."

Bastien chuckled. "You're not the first to tell me that, actually."

The two remained in the comfortable quiet until Kerdik broke the silence. "If I can't figure out how to undo her blindness, I'll do as Dub demands. I'll risk unleashing Carman so I can try my hand at killing her, along with the Brothers of Destruction. I promised you a life with her, and this doesn't count. I don't like seeing her upset."

My fists clenched, my jaw on edge that Kerdik would risk undoing Faîte on my behalf. That wasn't the right call, and we both knew it. I didn't want Dub to manipulate him, but that's exactly what was happening.

Bastien's relief was palpable as he shifted on the couch. "Good. Just don't tell her, whatever you do. She's bent on taking one for the team. I know you can figure out how to contain Carman so she doesn't get out and destroy Éireland."

"Your faith in me might turn out to be foolish, but thank you all the same. I'm working on it. In the meantime, keep Rosie away from the windows." After another long silence, Kerdik asked, "Are you two thinking of having children?"

Bastien took his time answering. I could picture him with his half-drained glass in his hand, laying back on the couch to feign ease. "All of that's been put on hold while we try to get a handle on the blindness thing. It's all I can do to get her out of the house for a few hours." He exhaled and shifted on the cushions. "Our date tonight went so bad, Kerdik. I don't know how to help her, other than to do a few things for her, which I know she hates. The whole thing sucks."

"When you do have that conversation, once life gets more normal, I'll make sure to recheck the protections around the property. I'll make the time to give your child a birth blessing, too."

Bastien sounded as taken aback as I was. "Thank you. I know Rosie would appreciate that. She loves that she can talk to animals. It's the only thing getting her through some days."

Kerdik's voice was measured and quiet. "For what it's worth, I want to hate you. I want to murder you every time I see your face. But I see that you're a good man, and it gives me peace knowing that she's loved while I try to fix Avalon."

"I know you're fixing it for her, and for what it's worth, I want to hate you, too. But I see how hard you're working to make her second life a safer one. Gives me a little peace to think that after I'm gone, she'll have someone who gets it all."

After a pause, the two men chuckled together as they drank. Some of the battles they'd fought were the same, and many of their anxieties mirrored each other. I loved them, and my shoulders relaxed when I heard them reach an understanding that somehow worked for them. Somewhere along the rocky road, they'd started to become friends.

30

THE THINGS WE NEED

My footsteps up the stairs were somewhat silent as I tried to sneak to my room. I smirked at Quinn's fretting over Link's tame advances that I could hear through the door, and then shut myself inside my bedroom. I had no use for lights, and finally stopped turning them on automatically, in hopes anything might help me see even a little bit.

It wasn't for another half an hour that Bastien sank into the mattress by my side. His arm wrapped around my middle, and hiked up my shirt to expose my belly. His hands moved slowly, and with measured pressure to let me know he was shaken up by the night, and needed comfort only I could give. "Are you hungry, Daisy?"

"Not really, but I can feed if you need me to."

His voice came back worried. "I think I do. I need you."

I shifted so I was underneath him, arching my back as

he undid the flannel and slid it off my arms. "Where do you want it?"

Bastien stroked a line down my breasts, squeezing and gently fondling the parts meant only for him. "Anywhere. The usual spot's fine. I'm too in my head, and I need to unwind."

"I feel you. I'm here." I leaned up on my elbows and rooted around for his meaty shoulder. It was already littered with bite marks, and felt bumpy from the many scars that made the formerly smooth skin feel like Braille. He kicked off his bottoms as my teeth locked onto my meal. The bite was quick, and I took only a few drops from him. My appetite was significantly diminished after the night's events, but I knew that sometimes Bastien needed to be needed, and that was how I could love him best. He had to be the only one who could provide for me. Though I'd bought our property and home with a couple of the family jewels, he still wanted to be the one to save the day for me. I respected that, and sucked on his shoulder, drawing out no more than half a teaspoon of blood that would tide me over for a day or two.

Bastien's hands were frantic as he tore my shorts and underwear down my legs. I knew that only I could calm him down like this, and cherished the intensity of our connection. Link was right; Bastien was addicted to me drinking his blood because I bit him directly. It sent euphoria through him that made our sex life more on the rough and acrobatic side than the old married couple side.

I had only been taking blood through him pricking his finger and dripping it into my tea for the past week. Judging by his frantic movements and impatient grunts, I guessed he was feeling the pangs of withdrawal, and needed a hit of the good stuff.

I had a thing for tattooed guys now, my preferences molding to what Bastien looked like. I wanted to study his tattoos, to ask what each one meant. Now that I couldn't see them, I wanted to imprint them in my brain somehow, worried they might soon fade from my memory. My fingers traced his pectorals while he took his time making sure we were both satiated.

By the end of it, we were both a sweaty, sticky mess of limbs that were too exhausted to get up and shower. Bastien fell asleep on top of me, murmuring his discontent every time I shifted to get a little breathing room. I kissed the top of his head, smirking at the fact that his favorite pillows were my breasts. His even breath teased my body, keeping me awake long after he passed out.

I hadn't had enough time with the animals to be sleepy enough yet, though I wasn't too far off. When I tried to get up to make myself some tea, Bastien held me closer. "No, no. Stay."

"I need to chat with Hugh Jackman some more, babe. I'm not tired enough to sleep yet."

"If you need me to tire you out, give me like, five more minutes. I'll be ready for round two by then." His perfect posterior humped up and down, grinding his pelvis to mine just to hear me moan.

"Go to sleep. I'll be back in a few." One kiss turned into seven, which turned into tangled sheets, panting and, let's face it, round two.

31

ELK AT THE DOOR

I was careful as I padded down the steps, using my cane to make sure I didn't crash into anything and wake the whole house.

"What're ye doing up?" Link's voice startled me, making me yelp.

My hand flew to my flannel, making sure I'd at least fastened the two buttons over my chest. "Couldn't sleep. You see Hugh Jackman around?"

"He's out in the yard. I saw him on one of my rounds."

I meandered to the kitchen, and Link met me halfway to offer his arm to steady me. "You're a good guy to watch the place for us like this. Thank you."

"It's nothing. Least I can do for ye putting us up for this long. It's been good for Quinn, to have someplace stable to rest her head. Sleeping in Faîte isn't as easy as it used to be. I understand why Kerdik came here when his body needed rest. It's just not safe to leave your body unguarded like tha. So many of the *Attelage* Vamps get garroted in their sleep."

"Yikes. Well, my home is your home for as long as you guys want to stay. Forever, in fact. I love having you both here." I moved around the perimeter of the counter, feeling my way toward the cupboard where we kept the tea.

"I can do tha. Sit down, wee Rose."

I grinned, letting him take my hand and lead me to a stool at the counter. "It's been a while since you called me that. It's my favorite nickname."

"I'll make a note of tha. What kind of tea do ye fancy tonight?"

"Whatever. I'm just too awake to sleep. How's Quinn doing?"

Link's movements were measured, and I could tell he was tempering his response. "She's tired. Master Kerdik makes her jumpy. I'm sure after ye and Bastien went at it the second time, she went right back to sleep."

"Dude, we are not that loud."

"Ye can't see it, but I just rolled my eyes at ye for telling such a blatant lie. Your first romp always sounds like animals in the springtime, and the second one usually sounds like you're murdering him. The nights ye go at it a third time, it sounds like two people running and panting, mixed with donkey noises." He breathed heavily to mock me, but my thighs clenched, wishing for round three.

"So, anything new with you?" I asked to change the subject.

"Oh, not much. Patrolling the property, like usual."

I desperately wanted him to confide in me about Quinn. I had so little going on in my life, and missed the more manageable ups and downs that had nothing to do with going blind. "How's Quinn? I know she gets anxious when Kerdik's around. Were you able to calm her down?" I hinted.

Link didn't answer at first, and I could tell he was debating how much to tell me.

"Link?"

"Quinn smells like fresh soap and peaches," he admitted in a quiet rush.

I grinned. "Is that so?" I pushed a little farther with, "I heard some distinct animal sounds in the stairwell earlier tonight. But I'm sure you wouldn't know anything about that."

Link turned on the stove with a few clicks for the kettle and whispered, "Don't say anything to anyone yet, but tha was us! I kissed Quinn, Rosie. I kissed her, and it was everything I've been imagining she might taste like. She's amazing, but I think the whole thing spooked her. We snogged like teenagers in her bedroom, but when I tried to move us to the bed, she freaked out. Then we had to talk about it for like, ten minutes. She's afraid she's not worthy or whatever."

I chuckled. "I hate to break it to you, but you're used to

an entirely different finish line on a date than she is. I think kissing might be the finish line for Quinn for quite some time. Enjoy that marathon, brother. She's worth the wait."

"Oh, I know. It's just taking some figuring out. She's so sweet and innocent. Then she goes and... I'm having a hard time getting a read on her. But boy, do I love studying everything about tha woman. Almost two years we've been together every single day, and it's finally happening!"

"Oh, Link! I'm so happy for you! She's amazing."

"Aye. And her lips? Grand, Rosie. Utterly grand."

Link was fantastic at girl-talk. We gabbed until my kettle sang, and he poured me my tea. The only thing that stopped the cuteness was when we heard a bump outside. My spine stiffened, until I rationalized the noise away. It was most likely one of the elk, trying to get in to say hello. "It's probably just one of the animals."

Link palmed my back, and I could hear the ring of his knife coming out of its sheath. The sound set my teeth on edge. I didn't want their brand of fighting in my world, but apparently it was necessary. "Aye. Stay right here." He banded my fingers around my cane. "I want ye to go back upstairs, now. Can ye make it without me?"

I wanted to protest harder that of course it was nothing out there, but prudence reminded me that Bastien had been shielding me from the knowledge that there had been seven attacks on the house already in the past two months.

Link can handle a rogue soldier. He's an Untouchable. There's nothing to be afraid of. Link won't let anyone nasty in the house.

I abandoned my tea and felt my way along the wall toward the staircase. My footsteps weren't so steady on a good day, and this was definitely not that. I heard the back-door creak open, and then a scuffle with plenty of muted grunts that made me curse my blindness. I should be helping Link, not sending him out to defend my home. My fist clenched around my stupid cane, but I obeyed, moving into the foyer to get to the stairs.

The backdoor creaked again, and heavy footsteps jogged toward me. "Quiet. I have to get ye out of here."

My spine stiffened that it was Antonio's voice, and not Link's. "Okay. Let me wake Bastien."

"He's already outside. Let's go."

My nose scrunched. "Huh? No, he's not. I left him in bed upstairs."

"He's outside, and he told me to take ye out of the house. Soldiers are here, so we have to move."

I gripped his forearm as fear made the hairs on the back of my neck stand on end. "What about Quinn?"

"They don't want her. It's only ye they're after."

"What the crap? Why?"

"Trust me, I have no idea why any man would want ye. This is taking too long!" Without asking permission, Antonio scooped me up in his arms and ran me out the side door that led to the garage. He took my cane and shoved it in the trunk.

Then he made my blood run cold when he laid me down in the trunk, shoving my legs inside when I started to resist.

"Antonio, stop! People don't ride in the trunk in Common! Put me in the backseat!"

Quicker than I could compensate, my hands were jerked behind me and zip-tied at the small of my back. I kicked, screamed and tried to worm my way out, but Antonio had all the advantages. He cupped his hand over my mouth to muffle my shouts of distress. "Ye know it has to be like this. Bastien will mourn, but he'll move on and come back to his life in Faîte. He doesn't belong here, following around a blind girl like he is."

There was no warning, no threat of violence – only the act itself. Antonio's concrete fist swung down and punched me square across the face, bashing his knuckles on the floor of the car. I howled in pain, but it was too late. Antonio shut the trunk, and a few seconds later, the car flew out of the garage.

I COULDN'T CALL KERDIK WITH MY HANDS TIED BEHIND MY back. I couldn't cry out for help with any hope that I might be heard and rescued. I didn't have my phone stuffed in my cotton shorts, or in Bastien's flannel. All I had was the fear that this might get ugly, and I had no recourse.

Antonio had no idea how to handle a car – not even an automatic sedan, like mine. He veered all over the road, making me seasick, and bashing my body against every inch of the hard shell of the trunk. He drove longer than I could keep track of the turns, and I guessed he'd made it to the freeway by now, since his speed leveled, and he didn't swing the car around as much.

There were too many emotions to pick just one, but one thing was for sure, I was in this alone – bound and blind. I wanted to cower. I wanted to lose my mind. I mean, really, this would be a fantastic time to check out, since reality was getting pretty grim. Instead, I practiced my deep breathing from yoga, and did my best to stop crying. There had to be a way out. There had to be a plan.

Something in the back of my mind sparked, and I remembered something about being able to kick out a taillight from inside a trunk. I set to work pushing my bare foot against what I hoped was the taillight. It was hard and solid, and without shoes, I winced with every kick. I talked myself through the discomfort like any good coach might. *It's only pain. What's a broken toe or two in comparison with your life?*

The taillight finally budged after a kick so hard, I knew something was off with my big toe. I didn't give myself time to assess the damage, but kicked once more, triumphant when the canister moved, and I felt a small waft of fresh air on my damaged foot. I bit my tongue through a scream, but that was the worst of it. I prayed with everything in me that a police officer would pull Antonio over – if not for his reckless driving, then for his busted-out light.

It was five whole minutes of feverish terror before I heard the siren wail. Elation made a cackle erupt from my mouth, sore as my face still was. "Suck on that, you prick!" I shouted, unsure if he could hear me.

Antonio sped up, but then coasted to a stop. Hope sprang in my chest that not Faîte, but Common, might be the one to save the day. Somehow, it felt like a point for my team. We had order. We had respect for the system. We had cops with guns.

After a quick scuffle, Common had one less cop. I bit my lip and sobbed when the officer cried out, and then hit the concrete. That was the moment at which I lost my mind. I screamed and flailed and kicked as best I could, letting the night know that despite life's best efforts to forever silence me, I would not go quietly.

32

FIGHTING IN THE DARK

Of all the things that sucked about Antonio, his driving was my largest complaint at the moment. The car swerved, and he didn't seem to understand how to gently compensate for the back two wheels, or how to slow down in anticipation of a turn. I really should've taught him to drive at some point. At this rate, he was going to get the both of us killed. Though, that would certainly cross "murder Antonio" off my list of things to do.

It was a quick bump that caught both of us off-guard, and a sharp turn that jerked a shriek from my sobbing lips. For the briefest of moments, I was weightless, soaring with the car, and then banging on all sides of the tight confines. I got the sensation that I was upside-down, and then slammed over and over with no purpose or mercy. My scream added an additional jolt of terror when the landing crunched with a metallic groan.

Smoky air that was filled with the stench of over-worked rubber was the first thing that hit me when the trunk popped open. Beneath the terror was the possibility of freedom, and the window of opportunity I didn't have time to question. I kicked the trunk as open as it would go, which wasn't all the way.

I couldn't sit up, but was able to roll ungracefully out of the back, scraping my hip on a jagged edge of metal I couldn't predict. I bit my lip through the agony, and thanked the slice on my flesh for the opportunity that made my escape route possible. My shoulder jarred painfully when I landed in the dirt. I couldn't tell where I was, only that the ground beneath me wasn't pavement. I hoped we weren't too far from civilization, and that some good Samaritan might see the carnage and come to my rescue.

I crawled toward the back right of the car, using the heat that wafted toward me as a barometer to help me find the tailpipe. It was the only thing I could think of, since I couldn't see the lid of the trunk to judge which parts were jagged enough to sever my bindings. I lowered myself to my knees and backed up to the tailpipe, wincing at the burn I got on my wrists several times before I was able to connect the smoldering metal with the half-inch-thick piece of plastic binding my wrists together.

I whimpered through the feeling of plastic melting into the sensitive flesh of my inner wrists, but kept my groanings to a minimum. I was afraid of waking Antonio, who I prayed had some sort of concussion – or spontaneous decapitation with an accompanying castration. I didn't know his state, and couldn't bring myself to investigate. The moment my bindings came loose, I nearly sobbed in relief. I ripped the melted plastic from my wrists, yelping at the sting I knew would come, and the blood that couldn't be helped. The agony made me dizzy – or perhaps that was the violence of the crash.

My shoulders protested any movement, though they should've been rejoicing at the newfound freedom. I'm not sure how long we'd been on the road. My arms were robotic and clumsy as I reached into the trunk and felt around for my cane. I felt drunk, my gait uncertain and my knees wobbly, but I knew I couldn't pass out yet. The cane I'd despised so often brought about a crash of relief when my fingers closed around it. The world was a dark, dark place that night, and the cane was my one token that allowed me to pretend that there was light shining down on my unsteady path.

My bare feet were hesitant to walk on the packed dirt. It was littered with errant prickly weeds and sharp rocks. I only made it a few yards before my toes were slick with my own blood. My head swam when the earth started tilting, and beneath the fog that was rapidly taking over, I knew I had to press the emergency button before it was too late. I palmed my heart with my right hand and moaned, "Kerdik, Kerdik, Kerdik!"

I made it seven more steps before I tripped over a large

stone that really had no business standing in my path. The smash to the ground gouged up my left knee, and smarted the heels of my hands.

The steps stumbling toward me weren't confident enough to be Kerdik's. My brain tapped into my last vestiges of fight, and caused my leg to kick behind me like a spooked donkey when Antonio's beefy hand wrapped around my ankle. His grip loosened just enough for me to roll onto my back and swing my cane up. The satisfying crack across Antonio's temple reverberated down my aching arms.

I'd never been a huge fan of vomit, but when it poured out of him a few feet from me, I loved the sound, and even the smell. The inside of Antonio's stomach stank of victory, and brought about a bloodlust in me that confirmed I'd come unhinged.

I scrambled to my feet, listening carefully to which direction the retching was coming from. I took calculated aim, and cracked my cane down on the nape of his neck. When that didn't seem brutal enough, I drew it up and bashed him again, this time on the back of his skull. Over and over, I whacked him, until he collapsed – I hoped in the pile of his own vomit.

I was supposed to be safe here. This was my time to live a violence-free life. I wasn't expecting to have to fight for that opportunity, but if that's what it came to, I knew my stubbornness wouldn't suffer me to sit this brawl out.

Tears rolled down my face, but I ignored them. I

ignored my conscience, and all that I held as good in the world. I ignored my bleeding feet that dragged across the dirt, back to the stone that I'd cursed earlier for tripping me. Now it was more beautiful than either of my bejeweled rings. I picked up the masterpiece, which weighed about as much as two bowling balls, though it was about the diameter of only one. Feeling around with my bloody toe, I found Antonio's lax jaw. With murder in my veins and darkness in my eyes, I brought the stone down hard, bashing him over and over until I felt the satisfying crack of bone that told me the shape of his skull was no more. In case I was mistaken, I reached down and felt his face – tracing over his misshapen jaw, the eye cavity, the broken nose, and the caved-in gap where his skull should have been bulbous.

It scared me that I exhaled with relief, and what that said about me.

For good measure, and because it felt like recompense for a life I was pissed at, I kept going. I took my fury out on Antonio's skull, bashing and mangling until I exhausted myself. Then I took a few breaths to steady my racing heart, and started in again, grunting my anger at my lot in life as I continued my murder of Antonio – whom I'd never raised my voice at in the entire time I'd known him. I'd tried my best to be kind, but my gentleness hadn't made a dent. My anger, though, I made sure that made its mark – denting his head until something slimy oozed over my fingers when I beat down too hard.

Brains. I'd felt this before. Demi, my boyfriend when I'd lived at my birth mother's castle in Avalon, had been beheaded to punish me. His cranium had been tossed down into the well I was abandoned to, and for that brief period of madness, Demi had been my very best friend. He'd acted as my priest, listening to my confessions in the well as his brains began to slowly liquefy and fall out all over me. I remembered the squish of Demi's beautiful mind, and the way his brain felt when bits of it dried and caked onto my bare arms and legs. I'd loved Demi, and didn't shy away from him, even when there was nothing left but atrophied mind matter.

I sobbed over Antonio, forsaking my weapon and feeling around for his hand. The fist that punched me was now limp and compliant. My lips trembled as I bowed my head in prayer. "Beyond the clouds there lies a home for the brave at heart to rest and roam. Your weapon's sure, your body best, but now you've earned a warrior's rest."

It wasn't for Antonio that I whispered the poem all warriors in Avalon were eulogized with. I performed the kindness for Bastien, who would most likely not forgive me for getting yet another of his friends killed. My cousin Roland had tried to murder me, so Madigan had carried out a long and gruesome torture before his inevitable demise. That had sent Bastien on a drinking binge where he'd slept with a prostitute in the throes of an epic drunk.

I'd sent him away after that.

Dread turned my blood cold when it dawned on me

that I couldn't send Bastien away if he cheated on me now. We were linked in too many ways to be able to be separated. Apart from our *Guardien* connection, I didn't know what would happen if I couldn't feed. Would I starve and die? Could I die from something like starvation? I didn't completely understand my partial immortality, which had plenty of conditions and stipulations. I needed to try to live without blood, just to make sure I could. If Bastien ever walked out on me, I had to find a way to survive without the sustenance he provided.

Then it hit me like a ton of bricks that if Bastien left, Link would go with him. I would lose both of them in one go, just like the last time. I hadn't pulled the trigger with Roland, but I'd caught the brunt of Bastien's bad decisions because of the loss. This time, however, it was *my* fingers that were coated in Antonio's blood and brains. The evidence was pretty damning.

All of that paled next to the fact that I couldn't get around all that well without a guide. Bastien would leave, and I would be alone in the dark.

33

KERDIK'S PRIZE

"*R*osie?! No! Rosie, say something!" Kerdik's footsteps caused simultaneous calm and fear to rise up in me, churning in my gut like bile. I was afraid to answer, lest I vomit all over his perfectly pressed white shirt. There were certain comforts about people who had borderline OCD when you were blind. Even though I couldn't see him, I could picture him perfectly, and trusted my image of him not to deviate from reality too much. He was most likely wearing his same crisp white dress shirt, chocolate-colored pressed pants and a charcoal vest – dapper and casual all at once.

"Is tha her?" a second, unfamiliar voice questioned. He had Link's brogue, but his voice wasn't as boisterous as my Lucky Charm. This dude's voice was slightly lower in pitch.

I was lying in the dirt, streaked in teary blood, red dripping from my knees, hands and feet as I cuddled the rock like it was my teddy bear. My cane was next to me, ready to be weaponized in case Antonio reanimated as a zombie and tried to eat my brains, to replace his own that I'd spilled.

You don't know. It could happen.

Kerdik ran to me, kneeling in the dirt and sullying his clothes for me. I don't know why I felt guilty about that, but it seemed self-flagellation was the mode I was stuck in. "Darling, talk to me. Are you alright? What hurts most? Say something, Rosie!"

My lower lip trembled, and fresh tears spilled over my cheekbones. "It w-w-was an accident," I whispered as he carefully sat me up. "Please don't be mad."

Kerdik scoffed. "I don't care about him. I care about you. If you wanted to take off his head so you could have something pretty to play with, I wouldn't bat an eye." He kissed my forehead, and somehow that act reminded me to breathe. Finally, my heart began to constrict in a gentler rhythm. "I need to see if you're alright, so I'm going to poke at you a bit, alright?"

"I didn't mean to," I confessed, scared that Kerdik might see the blackness my soul was now dipped in.

"You don't have to worry about any of it. Hold still and let me take a look at you." Then he called over his shoulder, "Lugh, can you do something with this body? I know Rosie's husband will want the carcass buried in Faîte."

"Seriously? There's not much left of him. Oh! He was an Untouchable. Tha can't be good."

Kerdik was tender, taking his time as he checked my pupils, fondled my neck, hissed at the burns on my wrists, and rotated my ankles to check their usefulness.

It was when he started washing my face, his fingers fluttering over the apples of my cheeks, that my spine released me from the terror my body had been stuck in. I slumped against him, but then jerked away, embarrassed. "I'm sorry. I'm ruining your clothes." My lower lip quivered, and another tear dribbled down my freshly washed face. "I ruined everything."

"You know I don't care about my clothes. You're all turned around. It's you I love, nothing else. Always my queen, always my queen." Kerdik shushed me, and proved his devotion to me over his need for perfection by sitting back on his butt, and pulling me onto his lap. "Take this rock, Lugh. She doesn't need to be holding it. Is that... Are those bits of Antonio's brain here? Oh, darling."

The stone was lifted from my lap by hands I didn't recognize. "Wow. Tha's a good shot. Bashed his brains in with this? He's not a slight lad, this one. I thought ye said she was blind."

"She is blind. But my prize doesn't surrender. She's a fighter, even when she's up against an Untouchable she can't see." His voice shone with pride at my dastardly deed, which only made the guilt strangle me more.

"I... I didn't mean to! Kerdik, I'm sorry!" I wailed,

cuddling into his warmth when he didn't pull away. I was covered in brains and blood, but I wasn't too much of a mess for him.

It's a good man, the one who stays with you when you're a mess.

Kerdik gently washed my hands, cleaning away the gore I'd caused. "What happened, darling? How is it you're so far from home?"

"Antonio j-jumped me! He stuffed me in the trunk and drove off. He killed a cop! Like, he just killed him!" I sniffled, holding on tight to Kerdik's shirt the moment he declared my hands clean. "He wanted Bastien to go back to Faîte. Jerk acted like Bastien was wasting his life, following a blind g-g-girl around!" My unspoken fears came bubbling out of me in my irrational state. "That's all I am, now! I'm the blind girl who holds her husband back. I clipped the eagle's wings. I made Bastien put down his sword so he could clean the house and make me tea. I'm a t-t-terrible person!" I sobbed. It became apparent that no matter how often Kerdik washed away my tears, only more would come.

Kerdik's reply was calm. "Did any of that come from Bastien?"

"No. That's what Antonio said. He was going to take me out somewhere remote and off me, so Faîte could have Bastien back." I explained that even after he crashed the car, Antonio had attacked me, and that was when I killed him.

"You did Antonio a kindness, ending him before I got here. Where did he hurt you?"

"Home," I begged quietly. "I just want to go home. Antonio attacked Link – I think he knocked Link out before he shoved me in the trunk. Link might be hurt."

Kerdik guided my head to lean on his shoulder. "How is it you've been in an accident, been attacked, you're bleeding all over, can't see or walk, but you're worried about Link?"

"Can you help me? I don't know where we are, or how to get back. I haven't heard any other cars this whole time."

"You're near a field, love. Of course I can take you home. Lugh, do you have the body?"

"Aye. Sturdy fella, this one. Next time, *I* get to rescue the damsel, and *ye* get to deal with the corpse." The candid way Lugh addressed Kerdik made it seem like they'd had years of comfortable back-and-forth as equals, which, I'll admit, surprised me.

"Deal." Kerdik kissed my trembling lips, taking advantage of the small window he had to be the man who loved me. "Don't worry, my darling. You'll be in your husband's arms in no time."

34

A LIFT FROM LUGH

I expected Lane to be upset. I expected Bastien to be close to tearing his hair out. I did not expect a slew of cop cars camped out on our property. Kerdik ported us to the street that led to our driveway, and grumbled as he described the scene to me from our distance. "I can't exactly show my face to your Commoners, but you can't walk. Lugh, you'll need to take her to her family. I'll port to Draper's basement after I deal with Antonio's body, alright? Come and get me when the dust settles."

I clung to Kerdik. "Who even is this guy? I don't want you to leave me with a stranger when I can't defend myself!"

Kerdik nuzzled my nose, which was the precursor to the sweet kiss he blessed me with. I tightened my arms around his neck. "Darling, this is Lugh. He's my oldest friend. We used to work together sometimes. He was a mortal Fae who was given an extended life, just as you were. He was Brìghde's pet long ago, but they fell out of favor with each other. He's been gone for quite some time, but with the darkness spilling all over Faîte, he's come out of the woodwork to help."

"Do you trust him?"

"Mostly," Kerdik answered swiftly.

I gaped at Kerdik. "Well, then obviously don't leave me with him!"

Lugh harrumphed. "Tha was ages ago, ye grumpy old codger. Man, do ye know how to hold a grudge."

Kerdik ignored Lugh. "I trust him to know how dangerous I am when trifled with. You're safe with Lugh."

I let out a tiny bleat of panic when Kerdik handed me off, and looped my fingers around my dangling cane. "I'm warning you both, I've hit my limit with being attacked tonight."

"Understood. Lugh won't harm you." Kerdik brushed my frazzled hair away from my forehead. "You did well, calling for me. I will always come when you ask. I'm glad you know I can be counted on."

I didn't say anything, but reached in the air for his face, exhaling when my fingers found his chin, and then his cheek. He let me pull him close, so I could kiss his soft lips without having to turn in Lugh's decently muscular arms.

For all of Kerdik's engrained violence, he was a gentle kisser. He was so careful with me, as if he thought one wrong move might spook me away. His tongue was seductive as it slid between the seam of my lips, parting them slightly. He hmmed contentedly when I pulled away.

"Thank you for coming to get me," I whispered. "I was so scared."

"You kissed me," he said, and I could picture his wistful smile. I hoped he had his hand on his heart, the way he did sometimes when he was moved. "It's always me kissing you, but you reached for me this time. You love me."

"I do."

There were a few beats of silence, and then Lugh grumbled with a good-natured tease to his tone, "The next time I'm holding a beautiful woman, ye won't be the lad kissing her. I'm putting my foot down on tha."

"The very next time," Kerdik promised. "Off you go."

Lugh hiked me higher in his arms and trudged off toward the house. He smelled like cigars and a little like sweat. "I'm Lugh, your slave for the evening." Then his voice switched to a higher pitch, so he could imitate me. "'Oh, nice to meet ye, Lugh. Thanks for carrying me all this way. Ye didn't have to.' Oh, it's no trouble. Any friend of Kerdik's is, well, usually only me. Welcome to the very small club."

I'm not sure how he managed to coax a smirk out of me, but a small show of levity birthed on my lips, letting me know I was still in there somewhere. "Thank you, Lugh. And thanks for carrying me. How about I cradle you in my arms the next time around?"

Lugh sniggered. "Tha sounds grand. But when it's my turn, I don't want it to be because some sodden lad tried to murder me. I want to be carried for no reason at all."

"Oh, you're no fun at all. Where's the adventure if there's not a little murder involved? I mean, not a lot of murder, but just a little." My jokes were terrible, but I was nervous.

"Aye. A little murder should warrant me getting myself a lass to carry me around, for sure. I've got a telemarketer who's just been hounding me. How about him?"

"But then how will you save ten percent on your car insurance?"

He chuckled again as he walked. "I didn't know ye would be fun. Guess I thought queens were proper."

"Newsflash, I'm not a real queen."

"You're the fake kind, then?"

I nodded, trying to joke through the ache in my bones. "I didn't know there were other half-immortals, like me. You and Brìghde, eh?"

"Aye." His voice was tight. "Tha was a long time ago."

I reached up and felt his face, searching for wrinkles or signs of aging. He had curvy lips, rounded cheekbones, and a dimple in his chin. "How old are you?"

"Sixty-two years. How old are ye? And what are ye doing?"

"I'm twenty-four. I'm still in my first life. You don't have wrinkles. Sorry. I can't see, so I was feeling your face."

"Aye. Tha's kind of the point."

"I guess I thought I might still age, just slower. Is that what's happening with you?"

"Do ye think Brìghde would want to screw me if I looked like a stooped old man? This double-long life thing? They do it as much for themselves as they do for us. Kerdik will want to have his fun with ye when ye two are finally together."

I factored in this information as he plodded forward. Though I was in the throes of an adrenaline crash, it was my one opportunity to converse with someone like me. I had so many questions. Everything else took a backseat. "You and Brìghde didn't work out?"

"Aye. Immortals are temperamental. No one's meant to live for tha long. Entitled prigs, the lot of them."

I wanted to defend Kerdik, but I knew part of him was an entitled jag sometimes. "Brìghde gave you an extra life, and then just let you walk away?"

"Tha's the grand thing about her stepping out on me. It was just good luck tha she turned me over for Kerdik a few decades ago. He did me a favor. I'm still grateful to him for it."

New light dawned on me. "You asked Kerdik to seduce Brìghde, who was your wife back then, so you could have an excuse to leave her."

Lugh shifted with discomfort that I'd connected the dots so quickly. "Aye. Best plan of my life. Kerdik was a good friend to do tha to help me out. Got me free from Brìghde's claim on me. So if ye were ever thinking of pulling the same thing on Kerdik, he already knows tha trick."

I guffawed. "I'm not going to try to get away from Kerdik. When it's our time to be together, that will be a good thing." I hissed when Lugh jostled me in his arms. "Oh, careful! My shoulder's not doing so hot. Or my legs. Or my head."

"Sorry. If ye plan on hurling, aim it away from me."

"I'll do my very best."

I was amazed that I'd just been in the throes of a fight to the death, yet now I was calmed enough to have a normal conversation with this stranger. That seemed to be the way with Lugh. He was easy to talk to, and seemed uncomplicated in a world of too many complications. I let the silence fall for a few steps before I spoke. "Kerdik never mentioned you."

"Aw, now doesn't tha make me feel cheery. Of course he didn't mention me. I'm the reason he can't have sex. Brìghde cursed him for sleeping with her, then ditching her, and giving me a good reason to leave, as well. She lost two lads in one go, and took it all out on him. Neither of us expected her to retaliate so harshly on him. Kerdik wasn't exactly my biggest fan after tha, but we get along well enough."

"Link and Mad never mentioned you, either."

"Makes sense. I've got no idea who they are. Ye forget. My time in Faîte was back before ye were born. I've been living in Common for a couple decades now. Best to give

Brìghde plenty of space." He hefted me higher in his arms. "Are ye ready for your homecoming?" He didn't wait for my obvious response, but instead greeted someone in a raised voice. "Oy, are ye missing something? I found this wee lass in a field. She claims to live here."

I heard the static of men and women talking into their radios, and people demanding Lugh hand me over – as if this was a hostage situation. Lane's tearful shrieks rose above the din, and I was immediately shuffled into her arms. "I knew you didn't leave us!" she shouted.

"Huh?"

"That stupid note! I knew it wasn't from you."

"What note?"

"The one on the counter that said you were tired of it all, so you were striking out on your own. I told Bastien you wouldn't leave him like that. I told him that you always sign something you have people write for you."

"Bastien thinks I left him?"

Cops, family and friends descended on me, barking out questions and freaking out over my injuries. A medic was summoned, and the cops took my statement while my legs and feet were disinfected, bandaged, and my vitals were checked. Quinn held my hand the entire time, and beneath all the cop jargon, I could hear her quiet sniffles.

I didn't know what I was allowed to say, so I stuck with the truth. "Antonio jumped me, stuffed me in the trunk of my car, and drove me out into a field to off me."

Lane's tears turned to fury as she whirled to yell at

someone. "You! You brought him here, and he attacked my baby!"

Link's voice was filled with regret. "Rosie, I'm sorry. I didn't know he would do tha. Someone with a phone needs to call Bastien. He's still out looking for ye with Reyn and Draper."

Lugh kept his mouth shut for the most part, answering only the bare minimum. It worried me that Lane had involved the police. So much of our life here was kept secret. Most of the people we lived with didn't have birth certificates, much less driver's licenses and the like.

It was a long time before the cops started to dissipate. A tow was called for my car, Lugh gave his statement, and the word on the street was that Antonio was still on the loose. Though by now, Kerdik had already stashed the body somewhere for safe keeping.

Hugh Jackman didn't feel like waiting for the coast to clear, but he was a good boy and bided his time until the cops and medics all left before he climbed onto my lap, nearly purring at the contact. He told me over and over again how frightened he'd been, and how much he'd missed me during our short separation.

When Bastien, Reyn and Draper came barreling in through the front door, my heart sang at the sound of Bastien's voice. "Rosie? Where is she?"

"Bastien, I'm in the living room!"

His heavy bootsteps thundered toward me. Without preamble, Hugh Jackman jumped off my lap, and I was hoisted up in my husband's beefy arms. "Did you leave that note, and run off with Antonio?"

"Of course I didn't! I wouldn't leave you." The whole explanation tumbled out of my mouth again, and I could feel Bastien's chest tightening at the news that his friend had betrayed us. Tears bled from my eyes as I trembled with anxiety that he might leave – that our marriage could balance so precariously like this. "I'm sorry, Bastien. I didn't mean to make Antonio so angry. Please believe me; I didn't want him to go off on me like that."

I expected him to bolt, as he'd done when Roland had tried to kill me. Instead, his feet remained fixed to the floor of our living room, inside the home we shared. "He wanted to kill you so I'd go back to Faîte?"

I nodded slowly. "That's what he said. He was pissed that you were stuck waiting on me. You're a warrior, and I domesticated you." I hit him with the brunt of it, wanting him to leave now if he was going to. I couldn't handle the limbo of wondering if my husband would stay with me or not. "I didn't plan the whole blindness thing, Bastien. I don't want you to have to wait on me. I'm so sorry that I'm doing this to you!"

Bastien paused, and then buried his nose in my hair. "Enough. Those are Antonio's issues, not mine. Those are the ideals of a single man. We took vows, Daisy. In sickness and in health. I'm not going anywhere."

"You're not?"

"Antonio really tried to kill you?"

I nodded. "I don't know how I keep ending up ruining your life. I'm so sorry!" I was stuck on apology mode, and couldn't bring myself to stop.

"Hey, you're not ruining anything. I'm just stunned, is all. I knew Antonio was having trouble accepting my life here, but I didn't know he'd up and kidnap you over it. This one's on me, babe. I should've listened to my gut. I'm sorry I let my guard down."

"I'm sorry you always have to be on your guard." I touched his features so I could feel if they were angry or not. My fingers flitted over his lashes, the smooth space between his eyebrows, and then his mouth.

Bastien took that as an invitation, and closed the gap between us to kiss me. He felt like home, and finally, I was back where I was meant to be.

35

THE HISTORY OF FAÎTE

My dreams had been pure darkness since I'd kicked Dub out weeks ago. But this time when I was sucked under, there was enough light that I could see the familiar black fog I'd know anywhere. The slick glitter stuck to the tiny hairs on my arms as I blinked at the sight of... well, anything. There was nothing before me except for the fog, but I was grateful for the break in the monotony. I could see my hands, wonders of beauty as they were, and the rest of my body, which was a sheer work of art that had been hidden from me. I didn't care that even in my dream I was as bandaged and bruised as I was in real life. I could see myself, and marveled at the sight.

When a basketball rolled to me, my eyes tracked the progress with lightning precision. I was able to see something orange and round. My heart raced with delight at the small victory. I picked up the ball and turned it over in my hands, memorizing the details and counting the strips of black in the orange. I hugged the basketball as if it was my precious bunny.

"I thought you could use a little happiness," Dub said, moving the fog out of his way as he walked toward me. It rolled out from him like a litter of puppies bounding a few feet out from where their master was.

I didn't speak, but moved toward him, studying his features with rapt fascination. It had been so long since I'd seen anyone that I didn't even care that the man I was finally looking at was one I didn't want to be around. I stood too close, observing every curve and crevice of his features. I could tell by his flared nostrils and furrowed eyebrows that he was wary of my reaction at coming face to face with him. "Hold still," I instructed quietly.

Though by now we both knew I couldn't hurt him, he flinched when I slowly raised my hand to touch his face. It was different, feeling someone's features when you could see them. I wanted to marry the two senses again – sight and touch. My fingers slid over the planes of his angular cheeks, memorizing them as if I cared about the man I was touching. There was an intimacy in the act of being this close, feeling his nervous breath on my nose. I didn't care about social norms at the moment. I cared that I could see. Whatever and whoever I saw would always be the most beautiful thing, simply because I could see them.

Dub closed his eyes after he trusted I wouldn't punch him, and simply allowed the contact to wash over his body.

His shoulders lowered, and as much as I needed to see and touch, it seemed he needed to be touched just as badly. It never dawned on me just how deprived of contact one might be in here. It was the simple things most people craved when pushed to their limits. I pried open his lips and touched the tip of his left incisor, testing the sharpness to compare it against my own. "Wha are oo oing?" he asked, unable to close his mouth as I peered at each tooth with rapt fascination.

"My teeth are sharper than yours. They didn't used to be this sharp. I want to look at teeth that are normal."

Dub leaned his neck back, so I didn't do something even weirder, like poke at his tongue. "I can hear everything around you when I'm tuning in. I heard Antonio, and the whole mess. I feel responsible for my part in it all, blinding you as I have. I thought you could use a little respite from the more harrowing aspects of your life."

"You're giving me back my sight?" I leaned up on my toes as I swelled with hope.

"No." At his verdict, I deflated, angst crushing me back to earth. Dub remained steadfast in his ruling, though his demeanor was decidedly less superior and a little gentler. "My word is my word. You'll see once more when Kerdik puts an end to my brothers. But in your dreams, I'll take away your blindness. At least you'll have something lovely to look at while you rest."

I sank back down until my heels touched the hard floor. My chin lowered as my heart broke in slow motion.

"Oh. Okay. Thanks, I guess. There's no negotiation room for the blindness, then?"

"None whatsoever."

I banded my arms around my stomach to hold myself together. I couldn't beat him up. I couldn't cajole him into somehow letting me see again when I was awake. There was nothing I could do but accept the small mercy he was offering. It wasn't enough to be an olive branch, but I wasn't in any position to turn up my nose at the offer. I kept my chin down and nodded glumly. "Okay."

He placed his hand on my shoulder. "Alright, then. What shall we see first?"

I shrugged, too caught in my melancholy and the wash of emotions that had led me to this state. "You can pick. Something nice. Something peaceful. Somewhere safe."

"Very well. I know just the place." He swept his right hand out to the fog, clearing whole clouds of it away. In the distance, I saw the Síocháin. The gold shimmering on the water was too much for my eyes to take in, unused to light as they were. I stumbled back and covered my face, ashamed that I had to cower from the brightness. Dub's arm coiled around my shoulders, and with an audible command, the overhead lights began to dim. "Sorry about that. Is it better now?"

I took my time blinking the world before me into focus. My gasp at the gold glimmer transported me from the fear of the night to a place where all of that was a distant memory. I didn't have to think about Antonio here. In fact, I didn't have to think about anything.

My feet moved of their own accord toward the lake. I hadn't seen anything so beautiful in months. The concrete gave way to sand, and the tiny granules glittered on my bandaged toes. I bent over to pick up a handful, and was caught off-guard again by how lovely my hands were. I hadn't seen them in so long. I had a few freckles near my right elbow that I never paid much mind. Now I knew there were seven. How could I not have known such a detail about my own skin? I sat down immediately and took inventory of my arms and legs, poring over every inch with all the fascination of an alien studying human life for the first time.

"Sight is a thing most people take for granted," Dub observed, sitting down beside me. He left a foot of space between us for propriety's sake. His black cape flowed out behind us, his hood pushed back across his shoulders. He had a long, narrow nose and high cheekbones. I wondered if he'd ever smiled, and what that might look like.

The mood and the setting were both so peaceful that my confessions started rolling off me without filter. "My body's changed so drastically since I learned about Faîte. Before you took my sight away, I would catch myself in the mirror and be confused every now and then. I didn't look like me. Maybe that's a good thing. People seem to like this version of me better, I guess."

"How different could you possibly have looked? Was your hair darker or something?"

I snorted, my eyes resting on my hands. "I had a hump and a lazy eye. Bad acne."

Dub scoffed. "You did not."

I quirked my eyebrow at his disbelief. "Why would I lie about that? Lane changed my appearance with some spell. My dad told her to take me away from my birth mother, Morgan le Fae. Lane took me to live in Common. She raised me without magic, or any of the wealthy castle life I was born into. She disguised my appearance so that anyone who came looking for me wouldn't recognize me right away. I look a lot like Morgan."

"I can see why you'd resent Lane for that. It's quite a loss to go from what I see now to a hump and a lazy eye."

I shrugged. "I don't know now. Lane's always been smarter than most people. When I wasn't pretty, I knew who my friends were, and people left me alone. Now there's attention. Some of it's nice, but so far a lot of it's been of the let's-molest-Rosie-or-lock-her-in-the-trunk variety. I don't think any of that would've happened if I still looked more like Cailleach than my own mother." I paused as I watched the gentle waves lap at the shore. "She told me that my greatest adventure wouldn't be Avalon, but that it would be with myself. I guess I didn't realize there'd be so many ups and downs along the way." My eyes cut sideways to him. "What about you? Where's your adventure with yourself taking you these days?"

"I think you're looking at it." He motioned out to the sea. Then, as if considering my question and not liking the answer that came to him, he cleared his throat. "You're right about Lane being smart. I never would've looked at it like that. One time, Carman put a hex on Dian so that he had warts all over his body. That didn't make him too easy on the eyes." He chuckled at the memory. "The blights didn't make Dian kind or humble, as you are. But then, perhaps that's the difference between you and them."

My expression twisted at the compliment. We'd only spent a handful of nights together, and he was talking like he knew me. I wasn't sure how I felt about his ability to listen in on everything I said during the waking hours.

I went back to studying my fingers, miracles as they were. "You call your mother by her first name. I do that, too." I paused to let the discomfort settle. "I'm sorry you don't get along with your mother."

"I'm sorry you had to murder yours to make the world a better place. Would that I had that knowledge back when I was roaming about Éireland. I might be in possession of the onyx stone myself, and then we wouldn't be in this mess."

"The mess you created for me," I reminded him.

"Yes, well. If my nephew comes through, you'll be free from my curse, and it'll all be an unpleasant memory."

"Really? Seems like the kind of thing you can use over and over again to get me or Kerdik to jump for you. As nice as this fieldtrip to the lake has been, I'll always have that hanging over my head."

Dub didn't deny it, and I didn't need him to. He considered my worry for what it was – the truth. "I can see how that would be troubling. I suppose you wouldn't trust me if I gave you my word that I wouldn't blind you again after this, would you?"

"I think it's sweet that you have concepts like 'trust' in your vocabulary. What a nice world that must be. It's good that after all you've seen and done, you still put value on the integrity of someone's word. I'm glad that optimistic part of you survived. Maybe there's hope for the rest of us after all."

I noticed Dub raising his eyebrow at me in my periphery. "But you don't trust my word?"

"I don't need promises. Trust doesn't mean all that much when an Untouchable turns on a woman in the Brotherhood in the dead of night. I'm just glad Kerdik found me before the cops did, covered in brains and bits of Antonio as I was."

"Ah, trust. Carman cursed my nephew. Did you know that?"

"What a crummy family tree you guys have."

"It's how he got his green skin. His father is a prideful one, and took to bragging about Kerdik all the live-long day. 'Kerdik's got magic like no one's seen before. Kerdik knows things without being taught.' Kerdik this, Kerdik that. Carman's the jealous type, and didn't relish the thought of Dother's son getting all of his attention. So she turned Kerdik's skin green, knowing that no matter how accomplished he was, no one would be able to look past his appearance to appreciate the boy beneath. As smart and gifted as Kerdik is, her plan was for him to die alone. So, not the same as Lane's plans for you, I guess, but similar actions."

My mouth fell open. "Are you serious? He hates his green skin! Carman did that to him? Why would she curse her own grandson?"

"Why would you expect anything different from a ruler like her?"

I frowned, my gaze shifting to the sea. "Well, joke's on her. I like Kerdik's green skin. I think it's sexy. It's one of the things that drew me to him in the beginning."

Dub's chest moved with silent laughter. "Forgive me. I've never heard anyone call my nephew 'sexy'. Oh, if only Kerdik were here to witness that. I think you might be the first to find him so attractive."

I scoffed. "He knows I think he's a hottie. I told him all the time when we were in Avalon together."

Dub's smile made him look younger when it was genuine, and not related to any kind of overlord type of plot. "I haven't known my nephew in many years, but I'm glad he's found you, even though your union seems to be delayed."

I shrugged. "The timing is what it is. I'm tired of defending my choices to people. Bastien, Kerdik and I are cool, and the list of people who need to weigh in on the subject ends there."

We watched the golden glinting atop the blue as the waves rocked the sea like it was trying to soothe a baby in a bassinet. The rocking lulled me, calming so many things that I needed to be soothed through.

"I heard the bit about your father. I know Kerdik had a friend named Urien a couple decades ago, but I've been trapped in the ring, so I'm not up on current events. Is that the same man? Kerdik's friend is your father?"

I nodded, my lips pursing against the vitriol and heartache I could never choose between when it came to my father. "Same dude."

"I don't understand why he can't differentiate between *Attelage* Vampires and the *Farouche* kind. Doesn't he know that your breed only feeds off of one source? They're not a danger to society."

"My dad doesn't love me," I said matter-of-factly. It didn't come out in a whine, but with the simplicity of the truth ringing across the sea. There was something about Dub's lack of a need to be pleasing to anyone that allowed me to be blunt with my hidden wounds. "I'm not sure what to do with that, so I've decided to do nothing with it."

"Is that possible?"

"It has to be. If I decide to be sad about it, I'll never stop crying. I wanted a dad for too long. I helped bring him back to consciousness, you know. Morgan poisoned him back when I was a baby. He was in a deep sleep for twenty-one years. I helped Kerdik bring him back to life. Things were great for a while, but then..." I couldn't bring myself to admit that I'd disappointed my dad by becoming what I was never supposed to be. "Wasn't meant to be, I guess. Doesn't matter. Morgan and Urien aren't my parents anymore. They didn't or don't want to be. So I have Lane, who's always wanted me, and Reyn, who tells total strangers that he's my father, as if I'm something to brag about." A small smile crossed my lips at how much I'd lucked out with the two of them putting their stamp on me.

"Reyn seems like a decent man."

"Decent is the perfect word for him. A gentleman if I ever knew one. I'm glad Lane ended up with someone so sweet and kind. He's good, you know? Like, deep down in his heart, there's a well of goodness. Can't complain that he gets to be my dad." I shot Dub a sideways smirk. "He's only eight years older than me, you know. He and Bastien were besties before I met them. Reyn ended up with Lane, and Bastien got me. Lane's forty. The guys are sandwiched in between our two ages. It's kind of funny."

Dub's eyebrows rose, and his lips curved into a small smile. "Is that so?"

"How about your dad?" I asked, trying my hand at switching the focus of the conversation.

"I don't have one. Carman was the first immortal. She created Faîte. She grew the three of us in her womb by dipping in the Síocháin that she conjured into being."

"Wow. I guess biology doesn't really matter much when there's mad amounts of magic involved. So then what?"

Dub leaned back on his elbows, addressing the ocean instead of telling the story of Faîte directly to me. "Carman created Faîte with animals and nature and mortals, but she was lonely for company that wasn't always dying around her, so she birthed me. I turned out to be quite the disappointment, so she brought forth Dother. Then Dother turned out to be a pill, so she gave birth to Dian."

"Gave up after Dian?"

"With good reason. Such violence you've never known. She couldn't control what abilities we were born with, but tried to with me. When I came into Faîte with the gift of darkness, she ruled that our magic might get stronger the more children she bore, but it only grew more volatile. Faîte was just Éireland back then, but she was tired of Dian and Dother, so she sent them off to create their own land."

"Wow. I didn't realize there were more nations than just Éireland and Avalon."

"There would've been, but Dother and Dian failed. They went through three countries that they built and collapsed before Carman stepped in. She made them stay in Éireland after that. Some time later, Kerdik was born. When he proved himself (after much unnecessary toil), Carman trusted Kerdik to create his own nation, which is how Avalon came to be. If there was ever anything that sealed Dother's disdain for his own son, it was when Kerdik did the impossible and earned Carman's favor."

"If they're tight now, then why is Kerdik afraid of letting Carman out of Cailleach's cane?"

"Because Kerdik is wise. Just because Carman sees potential in Kerdik doesn't mean she's less dangerous to Faîte. She could destroy Avalon on a whim, if she chose. If Kerdik somehow fell out of grace with her, all that he built and worked for could be gone. She's too temperamental to trust."

"Yikes. Makes my feud with Morgan seem so small by comparison."

"Yes, well, the stakes are higher with immortals. People don't understand that. They see the lengthy lifeline and think it must all be so glamorous. If Kerdik's nation fails, then he'll have failed, which is something Carman doesn't tolerate. Kerdik is much like his grandmother in that way."

I fished a stick from the golden sand and tossed it at him. "I notice you left yourself out of a lot of this little history lesson."

Dub fingered the stick, turning it over as if it might hold a secret of the universe. "Those who don't create or conquer are dismissed as lesser. Carman didn't care what I did, because I was of little use to her."

I hissed. "Dude, that sucks."

"It's not as bad as it sounds."

"Yes, it is. My mother saw me only as a tool to either

conquer or create, too. It was terrible. You don't have to pretend it's not."

Dub considered my offer to be a person when he'd been raised to be perfect. "I admit, when you speak your mind, sometimes I don't understand you." Then he lowered his voice to conceal his confession. "Yet other times, I'm afraid you're the only person who's ever understood me."

A small smirk played on my lips. "That's the thing about listening. It's my one decent magic trick." I stared out at the ocean, willing its calmness to center me. "Your adventure with yourself isn't over, Dub. There's still more to you that you haven't figured out yet."

"There again, I don't know what to say to that."

I shrugged, not needing a response.

Dub stared at me a few moments, and then returned his focus to his stick as he continued. "Dother and Dian were always competing for her favor, which left me to my own devices."

"Did you go off and create yourself a magical wonderland of your own?" I said, partly in jest.

"Something like that," he almost whispered, like he was uttering a long-buried secret.

I gave him an appraising look, and then clapped my hands. "Well done for being who you are, and doing what you wanted with your life. Some people spend all their lives trying to earn approval from parents or friends. They forget to be who they are, and then they become who they think everyone else wants them to be. Good for you, man. I bet your place is beautiful."

"I like it. Never had any complaints. I've never shown it to anyone, but still."

"Well, when this all blows over, if you're a good guy and Kerdik lets you out after he traps or kills your brothers, you should show me your Eden."

"You're being gracious. You don't know it's nice. It might be a craggy marsh, for all you know."

"You don't seem like a dude who skimps on the details. If you like it, then it's exactly as you wanted it to be. It's an extension of you. I'm guessing it was well thought out, and has lots of sounds and smells that are unique."

Dub's mouth fell open. "You can't know that."

I shrugged. "I can guess. You like the dark, which means you appreciate the other senses more than most."

There was a solid half minute of quiet that lulled us further into calm. "I can see why Kerdik is so taken with you. You see more than most. Yes, my place does have smells that don't exist in Faîte, and sounds that are unique." He lowered his voice, making it sound like a confession. "The grass sings."

My eyebrows raised. "Whoa, that's cool! Like, with little mouths?" I used my index finger, pretending it was a blade of grass, and started singing *Ice, Ice, Baby*.

Dub laughed – an actual laugh that shook his chest. "No, though that would be entertaining. No one's sung me a song in ages. Simply ages, my dear. The blades of grass don't have mouths. The wind blows across them, and they have nodules that catch the breeze and create music. I can sit on one end of a field and conduct quite the orchestra."

"That's awesome. Totally outside the box, D. I really like that."

"You know? I think you would. Perhaps one day I'll show you my world. Maybe you and Kerdik can borrow it as my wedding gift for your honeymoon."

I grinned as I looked down at my toes. "I wouldn't say no to that. Thanks, man." I reached out my hand, offering my friendship if he didn't want to be so alone anymore. "It wasn't so bad, getting to know you."

Dub's smile was humble, his chin lowered as he bowed his head in my direction. "It was nice to finally be known." He rested his hand atop mine, and somewhere in my dream, Dub and I started to become friends.

36

MY NAME IS BASTIEN

I bit down on my lip as I situated my shirt. I was pretty sure I'd put it on backwards again. *Darn these printed-on tags.*

Bastien's kiss to my neck tattoo was welcome, but still caught me off-guard. My knees went weak, and I bit off a gasp of desire that coursed through my veins at his simple touch. "You look great. It's time to go, babe. We don't want to be late."

"Maybe we should put this off another week. People are going to ask questions."

"They'll ask just as many next week. We haven't been to AA in months. It's time to get back to our routine."

I pinched the bridge of my nose, and though it didn't block out the world any more than usual, I squinched my eyes shut. My fingers were trembling, and I was holding myself back from pouncing on Bastien to take a gallon of blood from him.

Dub warned me this would happen. He told me I was welcome to try, but I'd only hurt myself with the attempt to stop drinking blood. "I'm never going to make it to my one-month chip."

"Yes, you are. Just think, by this time tomorrow, you'll be one week closer to your first thirty days. Six days without blood, babe. I'm so proud of you."

I wetted my lips and tugged at the collar of my shirt. My skin was dewy from the pangs of withdrawal that only seemed to get worse after day four. "Yeah? Well, you shouldn't be. I'm this close to either tearing your clothes off, or tearing into your jugular. It's not going so well over in Rosie Land."

"You're seriously up for more sex? How is that possible? Not to tap out of a good thing, but after five times this morning, I'll need a few before I can go again." Bastien cracked his knuckles – something he'd started doing around day three. It was hard on him not to be fed on, but he was managing the withdrawal with some amount of grace. Then again, he wasn't the one starving for sustenance. "Not for nothing, but I need these meetings, Ro. Ever since Antonio... It's hard for me not to want to check out and drink myself stupid. That was a hard hit to take."

I lowered my chin. "Have I told you how sorry I am for that yet today?"

"Yes, twice. And I told you both times that it wasn't your fault. You getting kidnapped was on me for not watching the house as well as I should've. I just didn't expect Antonio to..." He exhaled heavily, and I heard the weight he carried on a daily basis since I'd bashed his buddy's brains in. "It doesn't matter. Antonio forged that note," he said more to himself than to me. "You didn't bail on me, and I'm not bailing on you. We've got something good, finally. These meetings are going to help us not throw it all away."

I nodded, rubbing my forehead in chagrin. "This is embarrassing, but I can't tell if this shirt is on backwards or not. Can you check?"

Bastien's fingers slid over the back of my collar. The washed t-shirt was light blue, and hugged my curves without making me feel too exposed. When paired with comfy jeans that sat low on my hips, I felt as much like myself as was possible these days. "Shirt looks like it's on right, little Daisy. You don't have to be embarrassed about that."

When Bastien's knuckle grazed the nape of my neck, my libido flared to a ravenous level. I hissed, and let out a bleat of agony. "Okay, you can't touch me like that!" I leaned over and braced my hands on my knees, panting like a runner.

"Like what?"

"Like, at all. You have no idea what this feels like."

He paused, his voice careful. "You're sure you want to

shoot for the one-month chip? This isn't alcohol, Ro. You need blood to survive."

"No, I don't. Quinn does. She's mortal. I've got a double-long life, which means that if I don't drink blood, I can probably still live just as long. I just have to kick my addiction to you." Dub didn't think my logic was all that solid, but I didn't want to hear it. I was so over being a movie monster. I just wanted to be a normal girl again.

"That's a pretty steep 'probably'. You run this by Kerdik?"

"He's a little busy with Faîte to be bothering with dietary questions."

"Still, I feel like this is something he could help us with. I don't have a problem with you drinking from me. Have I ever complained?"

"I want us to be together because we're in love, not because we're addicted to each other." He touched my elbow, and I nearly fainted from lust overload. Everything in me tightened with a wave of hormones to rival the horniest teenaged boy. Fresh sweat beaded on my arms. "Oh! Bastien, you can't touch me like that! I'm serious, dude. I have to make it thirty days. I want that chip."

"I gotta say, I'm not loving this plan. How are we supposed to get anywhere if I'm not allowed to touch you? This seems like a giant step back for our marriage, if you ask me."

"Stop using your sexy voice!" My words came out with too much of a bark to be soft. I was on the edge, and wasn't handling it all that gracefully. *This is withdrawal*, I reminded myself. Marianne had described her withdrawal in detail, so I was well familiar with the lows. At least I didn't have the shakes, like she'd had to endure.

Bastien's chuckle did nothing to quell my attraction, which only fueled my level of irritability. "Sorry." Then he switched to Link's accent. "Would it help ye if I talked like tha? Let's go to AA, wee Rose."

My mouth filled with saliva, and I adjusted my bra strap. "Do not seduce me with sexy accents. I want my thirty-day chip, Bastien!"

His hand on my elbow sent electricity zipping through my whole body, lighting me afire with a tingly heat that disoriented me. I stumbled, banging my head on the doorjamb, and ricocheting to the other side of the frame, knocking my shoulder hard. "Oh! Daisy, I'm sorry. Breathe, now. Let's calm it all down for a second." He brought me in for a hug that did nothing to cool my libido. He kissed my forehead, and checked my shoulder for a mark.

"I'm so hungry!" I held my throbbing forehead and gritted my teeth through the gnawing in my gut.

"Well, you've been starving yourself for six days! Seriously, Ro. This is a bad idea."

I wanted to shout at him for not being supportive, but I bit my tongue to keep the acerbic words to myself. I gripped my stupid cane and tapped it to the floor, feeling my way down the hall at a snail's pace.

Bastien was near enough so I could inhale his intoxicating scent, but not so close that he might accidentally touch me and set me off again. He was careful on the drive, too, taking turns slowly and speaking softly to me. It was never more apparent that I didn't deserve him than when he responded to my venom with sweetness. I guess we really had grown.

The gasps and murmurs were expected, but each noise of shock still made me recoil. These people, except for the newcomers, had shared their stories with me. They'd listened patiently to my confessions that I couldn't make it more than three days without a drink. Though none of us hung out outside the meetings, there was a camaraderie about the group that made one of us going spontaneously blind something to whisper about.

Joseph, the facilitator, was the first to break the ice. "Bastien, Rosie, it's good to see you again. How are you, Rosie?"

It was the most diplomatic way anyone had asked about my blindness. "There've been a lot of changes. I had an accident, which is why I missed so many meetings. Kind of a life-changer. It's good to see you again, Joseph." I slapped my knee and fake-laughed. "'See you!' Get it? I can't actually see anything, because I'm blind now."

You could've heard a pin drop at my dumb joke. Only Bastien snickered, but that was probably because I'd made everything totally awkward.

"I'm so sorry, Rosie. Here, have a seat up front. Then you'll be able to hear everything more clearly." Joseph grabbed my hand and led me quicker than I was comfortable to the first row. My smile melted away, because I was afraid I might trip in front of everyone.

I waited until Bastien sidled up next to me. "I've got it from here. Thanks, man." I heard what sounded like the two of them shaking hands, and then exhaled when I felt Bastien's familiar grip on my elbow. He took my cane, and molded my hand to the back of the metal folding chair, and then moved my other hand to the lip of the seat, so I could feel what I was sitting down on. We'd learned so much in Vision Rehabilitation Therapy with our Mobility Instructor, but no matter how smoothly I completed the normal tasks, I could tell everyone was staring. I wondered if I sat more or less gracefully than a giraffe trying to sneak into a meeting. I managed to sit without falling on the ground on my butt, so, bonus points for me.

Bastien's arm around my shoulders steadied me, but didn't make me want to throw him down on the floor and have my filthy way with him any less. "Gum?" he offered, unwrapping a stick, so I had something to bite, aside from his flesh.

"Thanks." He popped the gum between my teeth, and then grazed my breast on the way down. His low, evil chuckle told me no one was in front of us, and he was happy to mess with me in a public setting, where I couldn't retaliate. "Oops. My mistake."

"I will straight up punch you in the penis if you don't knock it off."

He leaned in under the guise of telling me a secret, and bit down on my earlobe. "I want you so bad right now."

My nostrils flared and I froze, so I didn't accidentally tear his clothes off. I sucked in my lower lip, and reached over to grip his thigh harder than could be comfortable.

Joseph called the meeting to order just in time, moving to the front of the room. He did the usual introductions, and started off with our team mantra. It was your standard twelve-step program, but I never tired of it. People trying to better themselves, knowing the struggle might never be over, but striving to fight another day, and still another. People started sharing their struggles and triumphs they'd endured over the past week, and a few I didn't know told a little of what brought them there.

I didn't trust myself to go up to the podium and talk. Besides, I had nothing to report yet. Soon though, soon I'd be coming in with bells on, shouting from the rooftops that I'd gone a whole stinking month without my Bloody Mary. Bastien hated my new nickname for him, but I thought it was funny. My only regret was not thinking of it sooner.

Bastien leaned over and said quietly, "You alright here for a minute? I've got to do something."

"Sure."

I expected him to go make a phone call or something, but when I heard his bootsteps go forward instead of back toward the exit, I sat up straighter. Bastien cleared his throat and spoke into the mic. "My name is Bastien, and I'm an alcoholic."

My mouth fell open at the admission that I never expected to come from him. He never once got up to speak at these things. It never occurred to me that he might want to.

His low voice was hesitant, but he pushed through to the guts without preamble. "I've been coming to meetings for twenty-two months, and haven't had a drink in all that time, but lately I've been wanting to slip back into old habits. About two or so years ago, I was in a bad place. One of my closest friends attacked my wife – well, back then she was my girlfriend – and I didn't handle it too well. Roland was sentenced with the death penalty for all he did, and while I agreed with the verdict, it didn't make it any easier. So I ditched my girlfriend, who'd just been attacked, and went on a bender that lasted... I'm still not exactly sure. During that time, my Rosie was attacked again right in front of me, but I was too wasted to do anything about it."

I covered my mouth, stuffing my gasp back inside. I didn't know he still thought about that period, or even what he thought about it, beyond that he regretted our time apart. I was afraid to breathe too loud, lest the confession be cut short.

I heard the podium creak, and I knew he was nervously gripping the wooden sides. Bastien continued his confession, getting it all off his chest in a determined voice.

"Rosie and her brother tracked me down, and found me in a... I was with a prostitute. Probably more than one, if I'm being honest. Still not sure how many – I'd been there awhile. The whole thing's kind of fuzzy."

My eyes were wide. The fact that he was with one prostitute had been a hard blow. Admitting to the group that there may have been more? That was certainly news to me.

"I lost everything that day, and I wasn't even sober enough to realize it. She took me back after a long time of showing her that I'd gotten my act together. Every day, I know exactly how much I almost lost, and it keeps me honest." He paused, and I could tell something worse was still coming. "I haven't had a blackout drunk like that since, and I haven't touched alcohol in twenty-two months, but lately life's been getting hard, and sometimes I can feel myself slipping."

My heart tugged in my chest, wanting to be closer to him, to hold him through his confession – to somehow make the pain less excruciating. Instead, I listened, and let him get it all off his chest. Bastien's great adventure with himself wasn't over. In fact, parts of it might only be just beginning.

He cleared his throat three times, and I could feel the nerve rolling through him as he pressed onward with his public confession. "My wife had an accident, and she's blind now. We're not sure if it's permanent, or if she'll get her sight back next week. To say our life together has changed is an understatement. She's probably thinking I'm tapping out, and telling her this is too hard, but it's not. Taking care of her is what I love – the same way she takes care of me. What's hard is watching her struggle, and not being able to fix her eyes. What's impossible is seeing how hard she has to work now, when I fought with everything in me to give her a happy life." He cleared his throat again, gearing up for more. "A friend of mine, Antonio, died a month ago. It was one of those situations where you love him like a brother, but you're not surprised someone bashed his head in for the greater good. I guess I'm taking that one harder than expected."

I wanted to bolt out of the room, but knew I'd never make it out without falling, or running into a wall. He was making it sound flip, like the whole thing was hyperbole, but it wasn't. I'd bashed Antonio's head in. I was one of the reasons Bastien wanted to drink his problems away.

Only his problems would never go away, because I would be with him until his last breath.

THINGS WERE TENSE AS BASTIEN DROVE US HOME. "LOOK, I'm sorry I blurted everything out like that. Maybe I shouldn't have shared."

I shook my head. "I'm glad you talked. It sounded like you needed to say all that. I didn't know you felt yourself slipping."

"That was my way of telling you. I don't know why I thought it'd be easier in a group setting. I did it all wrong."

"No, babe. I get it. It was never going to sound perfect. You told me before you actually slipped, which is the important thing. How can I help?"

He sounded uncomfortable, and a little like he hated himself. "Maybe have Link clear out the alcohol from Draper's and Lane's houses for a while, just until I deal with the Antonio stuff."

"Of course. They only have beer in the house anyway. No one's going to miss that."

"Getting out more might help."

"Getting out? Like, as in, out of the house?"

"Yeah. We only ever go to Vision Rehabilitation Therapy, and now to AA. I need to be around people. Feel normal for a while."

I nodded, unsure how to say my piece delicately. "That's fine. You might not get 'normal' if I'm with you, though. My life is different now."

"I can deal with that, no problem. I just want us to have a life, is all. Staying cooped up like we've been isn't good for me. At some point, I need to go back to work."

I don't know why this hadn't dawned on me. "That makes total sense. Sure, Bastien. Call the foreman and go tomorrow. I can stay by the house with Link and Quinn."

"I'm not leaving you alone. Link was taken down, and you were abducted. Not out of my sight, Ro."

"Um, not to be all, blind people shouldn't build houses,

but you know, maybe blind people shouldn't be building houses. Especially ones who have never done that sort of thing before."

"Come with me and sit in the sun. Bring Quinn with you, if you want. You two can do your thing while Link and I build together. Or you can sit with Link while Quinn and I build together. Take your pick. I just know that I'm slipping, and this would help me."

I nodded, this time without hesitation. "Of course. Good for you for asking for what you need. We'll make it work."

Bastien's gusty exhale told me he'd been holding in asking for anything for himself for too long. I felt terrible that he'd been carrying all this around, afraid to talk to me about it. "Thanks. You're making this way easier than I thought it'd be."

"What can I say? I'm amazing."

Bastien chuckled, and reached over to hold my hand. "That, you are."

37

ROSIE THE LUSH

As the day faded into evening, my hunger was more and more insatiable. I went through a box of donuts (yes, twelve entire donuts), three heaping plates of Lane's macaroni with four kinds of cheese and Frosted Flakes on top (don't be a hater; the texture makes it grrrreat!), and half a pizza. When all of that was a drop in the bucket, I abandoned Bastien, Lane, Reyn, Lucas, Draper, Link and Quinn, and wandered out into our backyard. I stayed on the deck so Bastien wouldn't feel the need to get up off the couch to guard me. He could see me through the sliding glass door at the back of the den, where everyone was gathered to play Yahtzee. It was one of the few games I could still play, though someone read my dice for me and kept my score. So really, all I did was shake the canister and roll out the dice. They could spare me for a few.

I hugged my middle with sweaty and shaky arms, inhaling the fall weather that stung my nose and overwhelmed the senses that hadn't deserted me. I gripped the railing and called out to the birds, begging them for some company. I wanted to sleep hard tonight, to pass out through the pain of hunger that somehow felt worse than being starved in the well for twice as long. I'd taken to gnawing on my knuckles, but I'd bitten through four of them already. The taste of my own blood didn't do it for me like Bastien's did. My breath came in and out in panting grunts after a while. The birds flocked to me, chatting my ears off at the latest gossip. There were new bunnies born in the woods, and they were taking turns coming up with names to suggest to Ophelia, the mother.

I whined through my desire to push all the animals aside and run to Bastien just to open his veins. I whirled and walked to the sliding door, which I thought was two feet further away than it actually was. I smacked my nose right into the glass, ruining everyone's game as they scrambled to me and threw open the door.

"Lane, could you get some ice?" Bastien called, his fingers handling my face with care.

I was embarrassed that my family saw me succumb to such clumsiness. "I'm really fine, Bastien. Am I bleeding?"

"No, but you really banged yourself hard." He pinched my nose, feeling for a break. "I think it'll be okay."

Lane wrapped me in a hug, and pressed an ice pack to my nose. "Oh, babe. You alright?"

"Yeah. Misjudged the distance. Drape, I think I left something in your house. Could you help me find it?" I really hated that I was always ruining things. I'd totally put a stop to game night, reminding everyone that I was useless.

Draper was never annoyed by me. "Sure. I can run over and get whatever you need."

"Nah, I need some fresh air. Help a girl out?"

My brother's voice turned snooty. "Anything for a fine lady. Right this way, madam."

I breathed easier without people fawning over me. I hated being constantly vulnerable, and so prone to being pitied. Draper led me carefully to his house, after promising over and over to Bastien that he wouldn't leave me alone for a second. Nothing overbearing about that.

It was three hundred thirty-seven steps to Draper's place, and with every step, I wanted Bastien's blood more and more. It had gone beyond sex at this point. We'd made love four more times when we'd gotten back from AA, and it barely made a dent with how much I craved him. Every muscle in my body ached with dehydration and starvation, though I'd eaten and drank plenty. My body wouldn't be tricked. It was Bastien my stomach screamed for.

"What'd you leave here?" Draper asked after ushering me inside.

I tapped my thigh in an impatient rhythm. "My sanity. You got any vodka?"

Draper chuckled. "You know I do. I kept it hidden in a

safe spot, though, so Bastien doesn't know I have it. Blood cravings got you down?"

"More like got me keyed up. I can't calm down, Drape. I need to sleep, but the animals aren't wearing me out fast enough. I can't be near Bastien anymore. Every time I smell him, I'm an inch away from biting him."

"Would that be so bad? I mean, you're a Vampire, sis. I hear blood is one of those non-negotiables."

"I've got that double lifespan," I explained, fiddling with the hem of my shirt. "Maybe I don't need blood at all. It's a willpower thing. I'm sure of it."

"You look sickly," he observed with all the tact of a brother who didn't care about diplomacy, only results. "You should have some of his blood before it gets worse."

"I honestly don't see how it could get much worse. Vodka?"

"Sure. Sorry. I didn't pick up, so there are shoes and stuff here. Hold onto my hand." He led me past the foyer with careful steps, and into his kitchen. He hoisted me up and sat my butt on the countertop, making me feel like a little kid as my feet dangled. I was safe here. I could exhale for as long as I needed.

If only I could stop thinking about Bastien's blood, which was still calling to me.

I heard Draper set the bottle down next to me, and then he started rummaging around in the cupboard for shot glasses. I didn't need a tiny glass to slow me down. I unscrewed the bottle and started downing the fiery liquid straight from the source.

"Ho! Hold up, pumpkin. I've got glasses right here."

"Can't," I said between glugs. "Can't be awake anymore. Need to numb it." I drank more, wishing it tasted like Bastien. Bastien was my favorite drink, though vodka was coming in at a close second.

Draper wrestled the bottle away from me. "Take a breather, Ro. Seriously. You'll puke if you chug it like that. Or you'll make me puke. Either way, I don't feel like cleaning up vomit tonight."

"Do you have any rum?"

"Sure. Wait for a glass this time, you lush," he teased.

I heard a few plops of liquid into a glass, but trusted my aim and grabbed for the bottle instead. I ignored Draper's protest as I drank without stopping for as long as it took for him to arrest the rum from my grip. It was a few shots' worth, at least. I never drank much – just a beer here and there, and it usually took me all night to down it. This worked far quicker. Draper tried to talk me down for nearly ten minutes before he realized the only reason I came over here was to get stinking drunk. I wanted my thirty-day chip, damnit. Perhaps downing all the liquor in the world wasn't the best way to earn my sobriety souvenir, but it was my only option at this point.

When Draper was putting away the rum, I ganked the vodka again, drinking as quietly as I could while his back was turned. I could still feel the painful tug toward Bastien, but it was slightly less angsty than before the alcohol.

"Rosie, stop! This isn't healthy."

He took away the vodka, which set loose a pathetic moan from my lips. "I'm going crazy, Draper! I can't eat enough. All I want is him, and I don't want a marriage like that! I don't want to be a Vampire anymore! I'm tired of all of it!"

"Oh, pumpkin. I know. Deep breaths."

"Can I sleep here tonight? I can't be around him anymore. I'm afraid I'll bite him, and then I'll have to start all over again!"

"Sure. You can always crash at my place. I'll make up the guest bed for you. Wait here." He pecked my forehead and left the kitchen, thinking I wouldn't be able to stealthily make my way across the kitchen and locate the rest of the rum. He was dead wrong about that.

My brother carried me to bed that night, passed out and stone drunk in his arms. I slept without hunger pains or self-loathing. I slept without Bastien, which somehow made it feel like none of this was worth it.

38

THE MONSTER IN ME

I woke several times in the night gnashing my teeth, drenched in a cold sweat. I had the shakes now, like a full-blown addict who would punch her own mother for a fix. My bones ached deep down to the marrow, and try as I did to keep my pain to myself, I was unable to keep my agony trapped between my clenched teeth.

Fangs. I had fangs now. While Bastien swore he couldn't see a difference, I felt my two canines up top sharpen after I changed. I bit down into my pillow, which tasted nothing like Bastien. After I finished spitting out feathers into the room Draper had loaned me, I bit down on my knuckle, drawing blood, just so I had a poor representation to pretend I might be satiated. I wondered if André Roussimoff ever felt hunger of this magnitude. All the food in the world wasn't enough, and there was no amount of alcohol that might subdue the ravenous animal that was starting to take over.

The bedroom door creeked open, and I heard someone take a couple tentative steps inside. "Ro? I heard you crying. Are you... Oh! What happened?" Draper was at my side, brushing feathers off my face, which had stuck to the blood on my skin. "Why are you bleeding? It's not just from your tears. What's going on?"

"I want his blood!" I shouted, though there was no need for volume, since Draper was hovering over me. "It hurts, Draper! It hurts!"

"What hurts?"

"My bones! It feels like each one's in its own vice. And my teeth? It feels like they're ringing like a tuning fork! Like my teeth want to get to Bastien, and they know he's not in the house." I howled my pain into the night, writhing in the sheets. I was sweaty, bloody, and covered in feathers.

"Jeez, pumpkin. I'll go call him over. He'll be here in two minutes, I promise."

"No! I'm so close! I have to make it thirty days. How many days has it been? Twenty-seven? Twenty-eight?"

"It's one in the morning, which would make this seven whole days of insanity for you."

"No!" My arms flailed around, and while I'm sure it looked like I was being dramatic, the pain had warped me to the point where I felt deranged. "Make it stop!"

Draper opened my window to let the night air in. "Maybe some fresh air might help."

My cries reached my woodland friends, who rushed to my window to help. My room was on the first floor here, so not only birds, but rabbits, raccoons, and of course, Hugh Jackman came to my aid. They chanted for me to calm down, and vowed to avenge whatever it is that was twisting me so. When they asked me what I wanted, I screamed for Bastien, but then begged for them not to go get him. A few birds flew out anyway, while the rest of the creatures tucked themselves in around me.

Draper's cry of surprise was the only thing that paused my wailing. "What is it?"

"It's Bullwinkle. I just wasn't expecting him to poke his head through the window. Hey, buddy."

"Bullwinkle, Draper will let you in through the front door," I explained to them both. The woodland critters were sweet, but I needed something bigger. When Draper let Bullwinkle into the house, I waved him forward, so I could hug our elk's neck. I howled my pain into his thick, lightly furred skin, wetting his body with my blood. Hugh Jackman licked my torn knuckles, singing me a sad song to soothe my nerves, which were beyond repair. "Don't let me leave this bed," I begged them all. "I have to make it one month. I'm almost there! I have to make it thirty whole days."

"And what then?" Draper asked, his tone clipped.

My reply came out through gritted teeth. "Then I'll try

to make it sixty days!" I ran my fangs along Bullwinkle's neck. It was some predatory instinct that lured my teeth toward flesh.

"You can't do this for another day! This isn't withdrawal; this is starvation! You have to drink blood, Rosie!"

"Sweet girl, I love you. What can I do?" Bullwinkle asked.

"Just hold still." My voice had a low quality to it that I barely recognized. My logic flew out the window when my jaw opened wider, and my sharp incisors sunk through Bullwinkle's epidermis. The blood that flowed into my mouth wasn't Bastien's, but I pretended with my very best imagination that it was. I heard my feral grunting, and hoped that somehow this might satiate the canyon of ache in my stomach.

I heard Bullwinkle's frightened and confused bleat, followed by a string of, *"Rosie knows best. Rosie loves us. She would never hurt me. This must be what I need. I'm being blessed by my Queen."*

I sobbed over his skin, and finally tore myself away when it was clear Bullwinkle's blood wasn't doing it for me.

"Bullwinkle, go into the woods!" Draper yelled. "All of you, go back to the forest. Rosie's sick, and she doesn't know what she's doing!"

I screamed and writhed in the sheets, which were now wet with Bullwinkle's blood, and tangled about my sweaty legs. The monster inside of me hissed, baring my fangs at a bunny, who hopped across my stomach to get back outside. My hand reached out and snatched at the furball, ignoring its inner squeak of surprise. Before my conscience could stop me, I bit into her down-covered neck, slurping the small well of blood as she struggled against my punishing grip. I didn't mean to hold her so hard; I couldn't feel what my muscles were doing. Everything inside of me was seizing unnaturally. *"Please, no! My babies! My babies!"*

I wanted to jerk away, but the blood frenzy took over all rational thought. I drank until her cries grew languid, and finally Draper was able to wrestle her away from my shaking grip. "No! You don't want to do this!" He ran to the door and shouted to the animals – most of whom had escaped already. "Get Bastien!"

"No! I can do this! You don't believe in me! You want me to be weak, always dependent on one of you! I don't need anyone! You're trying to keep me like this!"

"Oh, baby girl. You're cracked. Completely out of your mind if you think that's what's going on. You just killed Ophelia! She had her babies this week! You took a mother away from her newborn babies because you won't admit that Vampires need blood!"

"I don't need anything!" I threw my shredded pillow at my brother, and felt feathers flying everywhere.

"You need to calm down! Bastien will be here soon."

Venom spewed from my lips before I could stop the awful words. "I hate you for calling him!"

Draper stopped, and spoke with a calm that made my

fury seem like child's play. "I'm going to ignore that, because you're clearly out of your mind. But I want you to remember that this is what you're fighting for. You're fighting to hate your brother so you can get a chip that means nothing! You're not an alcoholic! You're a Vampire, so deal with it!"

When I heard the front door open, I heard not just one set of boots, but two. "Daisy!" Bastien called through the house. "Honey, I'm here!"

My mouth filled with saliva at the sound of his voice. My back arched off the bed as my body reacted to the mere sound of my name on his lips. "No! I can't see you!"

Link's chastisement was swift. "Ye told me to keep ye away from her, mate. Get back to the house."

"I can't do this anymore!" Bastien moaned. "She's not the addict, I am! Daisy!"

"Bastien, you can't be here!" I called out, desperate and ashamed.

Draper's tone was grave, but firm. "We're in here, man. Do what you need to calm her down. This ends tonight."

Link gasped. "What happened to wee Ophelia?"

Draper stood in the hallway. "Rosie killed her because she's starving for blood. Get in here and do your thing, Bastien. I won't see my sister in this much pain."

"I didn't kill her!" I shouted, panicked. *Did I kill Ophelia?*

Bastien didn't need to be told twice. He barreled into

the room and tackled me backwards on the bed. "I'm here. I'm here."

"Get out!" I shrieked, kicking and thrashing beneath him. "I don't want to bite you!"

Bastien's body was bulky and heavy. All he had to do was sink down on me and stretch out, and I was pinned. "Bite me, Daisy. I need it. I need you. I can't hold out much longer." His whisper came out in a pained whine. "It hurts!"

"You're in pain?" I questioned, confused that it wasn't just me. I was deranged, for sure, but I didn't want Bastien to hurt.

He lightly humped me, grinding his pelvis to mine. "I need you to drink, babe. Every bone in my body aches right now. I even tried biting myself, but it didn't do anything."

"I tried that, too!"

"Bite me!" Bastien groaned, and I could hear the agony in his admission of need. He craved our weird connection almost as much as I did – it was anybody's guess who was more addicted.

"Bastien, ye have to get off her!"

Bastien somehow managed to cut a slice on the tip of his index finger, and then shoved it between my lips. "Taste me, sweetheart. I've always been yours."

The flavor of Bastien was like nothing I could ever experience outside of this terrifying connection we shared. My lips closed around his digit, and I sucked, pulling harder than his blood flow permitted. My tongue laved around his finger, sweeping up every errant drop as if it all belonged to me. Bastien did belong to me, and my heart was only his.

I whined when he removed his finger, and I smelled the sweet crimson near his shoulder now. My chin acted on its own, needing to drink more, now that I'd had my taste. "You're cut!" I whined.

"Not cut. I just smeared my blood on our favorite spot, so you could find it easier." Then he called over his shoulder, "I've got it from here, guys. Give us some privacy."

"For what? You both look deranged!" Draper probably only said that because I was exhaling in an angsty rhythm with my mouth wide open, and Bastien's body was moving sensually atop mine. What brother wouldn't want to see that?

Link clapped Draper on the shoulder. "They're about to mate like rabbits in your guest bedroom, brother. I don't think ye want to see tha."

I rooted around until I found the meat of my husband's right shoulder. My jaw opened wide, my fangs practically dripping with need. I tried only licking, but that didn't satisfy either of us. The second the door shut, Bastien cried out in anguish. "Rosie, I need you!"

My canines didn't pretend they had an ounce of decorum, but pierced with gusto. Bastien's blood released into my mouth, and both of us cried out with finally being given the sustenance we craved. I didn't mute my disgusting slurping noises, and Bastien didn't hesitate to reach his hand between us and fumble with his belt buckle. There was no sweetness when our bodies found each other, and no second thought in either of our minds as the rest of our clothes were shed in seconds. We'd made love hundreds of times in the year and a half we'd been married, but there was no gentleness this time. We were out of control, and desperate to be satisfied by the only one in the world who could take away the pain we felt at being separated. It wasn't just an emotional longing, but more a physical need now. We'd surpassed reason, and were purely animal as we made the bedframe creak in a telling rhythm.

I drank Bastien in as if I was afraid the restaurant might run out of the good stuff. I couldn't remember my reasons for abstaining, only that whatever they were, I didn't care about them anymore. I felt strong again, unafraid of the darkness that engulfed me, and unencumbered by hunger pangs. No thirty-day chip tasted as good as this.

I bit him again, deepening the cuts as Bastien thrusted for all he was worth. My body sang for him, I'm not sure how many times. He cried out in strangled victory, and then collapsed atop me, his body still managing to stir with need and longing. I don't know how he did it. "Rosie, hold on. Let me catch my breath."

I know he wanted me to stop drinking for a minute, but the blood was too good. I'd been without him for too long.

"Daisy, stop! It's too much."

Even if I'd wanted to stop, I'm not sure I could. I gripped him around the torso and locked my suddenly steady legs around his hips, securing him to me. I'd been hungry for so long, and he was just what I wanted.

"Wait! Hun, I can't... It's... My fingers are numb..." Bastien's fight to free himself was weakening as I drained more and more from him. I didn't want to hurt him, but I'd flipped a switch or something. I couldn't stop.

It wasn't until Bastien called out a terrified, "Link! Link, help me!"

Even when Link barreled through the door, I couldn't stop drinking. "Ah! Couldn't ye at least throw a sheet over your hairy arse? I didn't need to see tha."

"Make her stop!" Bastien groaned before his fight, along with his consciousness, went straight out of him. My husband fainted, but I couldn't slow down. I was scared for him, but that came second to the hunger. I drank beyond what any donor would be expected to give, stopping only when Link hefted Bastien off of me.

39

MY REQUEST OF LINK

I don't think Link counted on having to wrestle his bestie's naked wife when he came to Common to chill and hang for a few months. But as I hissed and fought to get more of Bastien, Link took charge without missing a beat. He wrapped the sheet around me and squashed me onto the mattress, smooshing the air out of me like a dying balloon. Draper dragged my naked and unconscious husband away, grunting at the bulk that was solid muscle. You didn't get to be Untouchable by luck; Bastien was huge.

My frenzy started to settle a little, the urges coming in waves now. I bit Link, sinking my teeth into the forearm that pinned me down, but he tasted all wrong. It was like craving a milkshake, and finally getting your tall, frothy glass, only to find the milk had gone sour. "Ah! I'm not going to taste right to ye, ye wee mongrel."

I screamed for Bastien a few more times, but as the minutes wore on that Link had to hold me in place, sense and reason started to trickle in. All fight died out of me, and self-loathing crushed what little had survived of my soul. Tears poured down my face, but I didn't have the wherewithal to be embarrassed by them. "I hurt him! He trusted me, and I hurt him!"

Link called over his shoulder, his pitch strained. "Draper, is Bastien's heart still beating?"

My brother's voice answered from down the hall. "Yeah. He's alright. Rousing a little now. Rosie, did you bite him anywhere besides his shoulder? I honestly can't tell where he's bleeding, and what's just smeared tears."

"Just his shoulder, I think." I managed to free one of my arms, so I could cover my face with one hand. "Oh, I'm not even sure if that's all! I lost control. For a second, I don't even think I knew who I was. I hurt him! I almost killed my husband!" I ran through a litany of options in my head. Panic made me want to run far away, so I couldn't hurt him anymore. He could go back to Faîte and fight with the Brotherhood.

"Well, now ye know ye can't fast off of blood like tha. Ye need to feed regularly, and this won't happen again."

My fingers were trembling with regret as I lifted my hand to fist the material of Link's collar. I gently lowered him, so I could whisper the only option that seemed feasible. "I need you to kill me, Link. Antonio was right; this is no life for Bastien."

"Stop it," Link hissed. "Don't talk like tha."

"I nearly murdered your best friend! I can't control this. I'm a danger to him. I'm not strong enough to leave him. Plus, I'd just end up attacking more people." A quiet sob rolled off my lips. "I murdered Ophelia! I bit Bullwinkle, and he thought he was being blessed by me! He didn't even fight back. He trusts me enough to let me hurt him, and I took advantage! I'm a terrible person!"

"Ye aren't a terrible person. You're a Vampire in denial tha ye need blood. You're daft, not terrible."

"Morgan was terrible, so I killed her." My logic felt solid. Erasing me seemed like the only option that might save Bastien.

Link rolled off of me, and then pulled me to sit up. He fixed the sheet around me like a gentleman, and then kissed my forehead. Link moved to the attached bathroom, turning on the faucet. He came back with a wet washcloth, and took his time dabbing at my face. "I don't know why these bloody tears scare me worse than ye losing control over your cravings."

I snorted. "It's because you have no idea how to handle a crying woman."

"Quinn doesn't cry anymore," he said in deference to the woman who had rapidly captured his heart.

I tilted my chin up when Link moved the rag to my neck. "Yes, she does. I hear her sometimes in the night."

Link paused his movements. "She does?"

I nodded. "She's a fish out of water everywhere she goes."

"I didn't know."

I felt a man's shirt flutter around my shoulders, but didn't smell Bastien's piney scent. I reached out and felt Link's bare chest as he fastened the buttons for me, giving me back a little of my modesty, so I felt like a person. He even went one further and found my underwear on the floor. He molded my fingers around the band, facing them the correct way so I could put on my underwear by myself.

"Thank you. Sorry you had to see me naked. Totally awkward."

"Don't think on it another second. You're my wife." Then Link chuckled. "Any time ye go attacking my mates, make it up to me by letting me 'just so have to' wrestle ye without your nickers on." We shared a little laugh, and then Link took my fingers and moved them to his lips. He always did that to warn me he was about to kiss me. It was sweet, and gave me a little say in the act. Link's lips didn't linger on mine, but sealed our tight bond with the acceptance and forgiveness I needed to feel. His forehead pressed to mine, and for a moment, the two of us simply breathed. "It worries me tha ye asked me to off ye like tha."

"I'm not trying to worry you. I'm trying to protect the man we both love."

"Not like tha, ye don't. You'll devastate him. He'd never be the same. Ye don't understand. Ye didn't know him long before he fell hard for ye."

"Hello, it took us forever to finally get together."

Link shifted on the mattress, and then drew me to his side, his arm around my shoulders to soothe me. "He never laughed before ye. I mean, never. He had exactly one facial expression, and it wasn't a smile. He didn't have a life. He holed himself up in tha cabin in the woods, and only came out when one of us made him. Reyn and Roland tried their best, but even tha didn't do much. If ye left him, he would go back to being tha man in the cabin in the woods. It's not an option." He rubbed my back in a circular motion. "Say it. Tell me ye know it's not an option."

I leaned my forehead into the crook of his neck. "Okay. It's not an option, then. I want to save him, not destroy everything good about him."

Link drew my fingers to his mouth, so he could kiss my knuckles before pressing my palm to his heart. "We need ye, Rosie. A bunch of angry, beaten-down ruffians don't do well without a woman to better themselves for. It's hard to find a fair lass who can deal with us."

"I bit you," I admitted. "I'm so sorry. I love you, Link. I never want to hurt you."

"Not for nothing, but I'm glad Quinn never bit me beyond tha first time. I'm already doing everything I can not to move too fast for her. Factoring in the level of intensity and addiction ye two have for each other because ye feed directly? I couldn't handle tha without spooking her."

"It's heady, that's for sure."

The front door banged open, making me stiffen. I

heard Link draw his knife. "Wait right here," he instructed, standing from the bed and moving soundlessly to the hallway. "Oh. Did Lane send ye over here?"

"Where is she?"

My chin lifted at the sound of Kerdik's voice. "I'm in here!"

"Before ye overreact, just be warned tha she..."

"What happened?" Kerdik bellowed. There was as much concern for my plight as there was accusation at Link for not keeping me from a roomful of bloodstains and ruined pillows.

"I'll leave ye to talk some sense into her. Rosie, I'll be with Bastien down the hall if ye need me."

40

THE DANGER OF DADDY DOTHER

It was a long time of talking Kerdik down, assuring him that *I* was the danger, and certainly wasn't in any peril that wasn't of my own making. Then there was the argument about me trying to live without blood, which he categorically vetoed. "That's ridiculous, Rosie. I don't have the patience to argue this further. Tell me you understand that Vampires need blood. Tell me you'll be more responsible about monitoring your food from here on out."

"You know, it feels a lot like you're bossing me, which I gotta say, I've never been a fan of. Did you come all this way to lecture me? Because if it's all the same to you, I'll pass. It's been a long night."

Kerdik exhaled, finally hitting the crest of his temper. He lowered himself to sit on the bed beside me after brushing off the bloody feathers. "I came because there's been a new development, and I wasn't sure what to do."

I reached around until I found his hand, stroking his knuckles with the pad of my thumb. "What's got you worried?"

"It seems Dother is after me." He didn't sound worried, more annoyed. "He's been trying to track me down, and I don't want him finding his way to you, or using you as bait to draw me in. I know it's coming, and I don't want to let him get a step ahead of me."

"Oh, jeez. Are you alright? Did he hurt you?" My hands felt around until they landed on his face. He was still while I traced his features, seeking out cuts he might not be telling me about. When there were no abrasions I could detect, I felt down his throat, across his shoulders, over the planes of his chest, and down around his sides. "Tell me what he did to you."

Kerdik's voice came back dipped in honey, sweetness dripping from the edges of his words. "You don't have to worry, darling. I can take care of myself just fine. I'm here as a precaution. Things are actually looking up. I've got so much of the dark magic wrangled; Avalon's doing better than she has been in a long time."

A smile brightened my face. "Are you serious? You mean this all might end at some point?"

"'Might' is the keyword there."

My hands moved to his face so I could feel his expression while we talked. "I knew you could do it. I've never doubted that you were capable of amazing things."

Kerdik slid me closer, and then lifted my legs to drape them over his lap. "You are a filthy mess, my darling, but still a sight for these sore eyes. How I've missed you." He traced a circle atop my knee, and coiled his other arm around my back to keep me close. "We need to leave," he whispered.

"What are you talking about?"

"I can't risk you being unprotected like this. Bastien's doing his best, but he doesn't have magic to protect three homes on as much land as you've got here. You're his princess, but you're my queen; I'll not gamble your safety any longer. You need to come with me so I can keep you safe."

"Um, I thought the plan was to keep me far away from Avalon and the whole drama. This is my life now, Kerdik. I live here."

"That may be true, but I know my father. I've embarrassed him. He won't tolerate my existence much longer."

I frowned. "Dub mentioned something like that. Carman liked you best, so Dother and Dian threw hissy fits about it, or something like that."

Kerdik narrowed his eyes at me. "I don't like you fraternizing with Dub. He can be wicked, just like the others."

"I don't have much of a choice, babe. He's in my head when I sleep. Dub's fine. We actually get along alright."

Kerdik muttered something under his breath. "Be that as it may, we need to leave."

"Where's safer than Common? Dother doesn't know where I am up here."

"Duke Lot's castle locks down like a fort. I've put probably too many charms on it to protect your childhood home from destruction. Plus, Duke Lot is actually proving himself to be worthy of ruling his people, so I've made sure he's safe in his home. I find I don't mind his company every now and again."

"Look at you, making friends. Good for you, K. Lot's a nice guy, for sure."

Kerdik kissed my cheek. "I need you to pack a bag."

I pursed my lips. "Did you run this by Lane? I'm thinking you'll get a big, fat no from her. Not for nothing, but I live here now. I'm not going back."

"I knew you'd be difficult about this. Very well, I'll pack a bag for you. Bastien, too."

Link's voice was too near for him to not have heard everything. He stepped in from the hallway, and I could picture his arms crossed over his chest. "Explain more than tha. If something's truly coming for Rosie, I need to know about it."

Kerdik sighed. "You can't handle Dother, Link. He's above you on every level. Though, I appreciate all you've done to watch the house for my fiancée."

"Aye. Untouchables take care of their own. Bastien and Rosie are my business. Where they go, I go."

I touched my heart, moved that he was so devoted to us. "I love you, too, Link."

Link was all business. "Tell me what we're up against."

Kerdik deflated, but consented to the third degree. "Dother targeted Urien because it's widely known that he's my friend." Before I could ask, Kerdik's thumb rubbed up and down my side to soothe me. "Your father's just fine. He's recovering nicely. But it's time I moved you."

My brows furrowed, and panic started to rise in my chest at the thought of being taken from my home yet again. "No! No, Kerdik. This is where I live. I can't imagine anyone gives a crap enough to gossip about you and me anymore, what with all the higher magic you've got swimming around out there. Dother probably doesn't know about us."

Kerdik shifted my legs so that they hung off the bed, permitting him to stand. He leaned over and kissed my forehead. "I'll pack you a bag. Anything in particular you need? Tell me now, because once we leave it'll be a long time before you're coming back."

Indignation rose up in me. "No! Stop it! I'm not leaving!"

Link ignored me and spoke only to Kerdik. "I can pack their things. Give me half an hour, and Quinn and I will be ready to go. Ye might want to explain it all to Lane, though. The family likes to vote together on this kind of thing."

"Lane's been through enough," Kerdik ruled. "I'll not

put her through relocating with the baby. She's fine here. Dother doesn't care about Lane. She'd be safer here."

"Well, ye won't make off with her daughter without explanation. She'd follow ye right into Avalon, thinking you've kidnapped her girl."

Kerdik let out a groan of frustration. "Fine. Rosie, where are your shorts?"

"I have no idea. Bastien threw them somewhere. Guys, seriously, I'm not going. I'm staying with my mom."

"Here they are. Step in, darling." I blushed at the mental image of Kerdik dressing me, but it was much easier than trying to find my own shorts in the mess. Then Kerdik looped my hand through the crook of his arm, and carefully led me out of the house and into the night.

41

THE FAMILY THAT STAYS TOGETHER

"No."

I imagined Kerdik throwing his hands up in frustration at Lane's obstinacy. "Are the two of you on some sort of loop? Rosie's not being given a choice. I'll take her there hogtied if I have to."

Quinn had helped me shower, dress and pack, and though Bastien was still sleeping off my attack, his bag was next to mine, Link's and Quinn's in the foyer. Kerdik explained yet again the urgency of my relocation, but Lane was operating out of fear, as I was. I sat on the couch next to Quinn, who held my hand. Link was on her other side, and every now and then, his arm that was around her shoulders reached out and squeezed my bicep for solidarity. I loved them, and in the midst of all the misfortune, I don't know how I got so lucky to have the two of them to share a couch with when life got hard.

By the time the sun came up, Bastien was awake. Convincing him was easier for Kerdik to do. After a quick shower, he was ready to go.

Lane was not quite as cooperative. Kerdik and Lane went back and forth for nearly an hour more before Lane started to ease up on the resistance. "I don't like this, Kerdik. Taking her to the world where someone who wants to kidnap her is living doesn't sound like a plan. It sounds like suicide."

"Leaving her out in the open like this is dangerous, and you know it. Bastien's told me how many of Morgan's soldiers have sneaked onto your property."

"We can handle our own!" She raised her voice, startling Lucas. No one ever yelled around Lucas; he was a sensitive baby.

I wanted to hold the sweet baby boy when he started wailing, but I was afraid I might accidentally step on him. "Come here, Lucas. Come to Aunt Rosie, sweetheart. Mommy's just scared, is all. No one's mad."

"I've got you, son," Reyn said, and I heard him sweep up his boy. "Kerdik, what assurances do we have that you'll return Rosie? Don't think I don't know you'd do anything to have her closer."

I could practically see Kerdik rolling his eyes. "Yes, so I can watch her marriage up close. Well spotted. I can't get enough of her fawning over another man. I'm taking her along with her husband because I love her, and she's not safe here any longer. Bastien only has *Guardien* magic to protect her with here in Common. He'll have access to his regular stores when he returns to Avalon. Do you object to any of that?"

Reyn didn't let up. "For how long? There doesn't seem to be an end to her blindness, which means you're nowhere near close to ending the madness. Dother isn't going to up and quit his quest of making your life miserable. How long is Rosie expected to stay locked up in Lot's castle?"

Kerdik was caught in a storm of frustration, meeting resistance everywhere he turned. "First off, the castle belongs to Rosie, so I'm merely returning her to her home. Second, as much as I'd love to snap my fingers and make all of this go away, finding an alternative puzzle piece takes time."

Draper was irate. "This is crazy. We've defended our property well enough. She should stay here."

Kerdik was firm, though not unkind. "She was abducted and nearly murdered by someone you let waltz in the door. And that was just Antonio. I'm talking about a Brother of Destruction."

Reyn bounced Lucas on his knee, but his tone was no less authoritative. "Actually how long, Kerdik. We need to know when we'll see our daughter again."

My heart always swooned when Reyn called me his daughter.

"Give me a year," Kerdik requested. He was quieter now, admitting that he didn't actually know when or if it would all end. "If she's not back in a year, then that would mean even *I* can't protect her, and she can die here, with her parents."

Somehow, after much back and forth, the terms were agreed upon, overruling my say in any of it. My mouth went dry as everyone said their goodbyes. I wanted to say something reassuring, but I was mute, unable to understand how my life was being taken and altered so drastically in a single night.

Lane's hug was too tight, but I didn't mind that my ribs couldn't expand to pull in a breath. It would be hard enough breathing without her after I left. Her words were choked out between sobs as she leaned in to speak into my ear. "I love you with a fierce love. Do whatever you can to come home to me. This is your home, okay? Your journey doesn't end in Avalon. We still have too many adventures in store for us."

"Okay, Mom."

Whenever I claimed her as my maternal lighthouse, her chest always puffed with pride. Tonight, however, it only made the tears flow more freely. "I'm your home," she said, jerking me tighter. "Say it."

"You're my home, Mom, and I'll come home safe to you when this is all over."

Her gentleness married with her mama bear protectiveness when she whispered the words that were branded on my heart. "Know who you are." She'd made sure the mantra stuck with me from a young age, and though I'd appreciated it then, now the promise felt like a fight that might require all I had in me.

I nodded into her shirt before I was drawn into Reyn's arms. His grip wasn't as tight, which meant I didn't feel as anchored to the ground. My worries started to climb until he whispered, "Never has there been a moment where I've not been proud of the woman you are. Becoming your father was the luckiest blessing of my life, apart from marrying your mother."

"I love you, Dad," I admitted, clinging to him to keep myself from a complete and total breakdown, which I'm guessing we didn't have time for.

"Never forget that we are your parents. We love you so much, Rosie. You belong here. You belong with us."

Though I knew as much, my chin started to quiver at the words that sang to my wounded soul. "Thanks, Dad. I think I needed to hear that."

When I was transferred to Draper's arms, neither my brother nor I spoke for several seconds. I sunk into his warm embrace, and listened to Reyn and Bastien hug so tightly that their words came out choked. "Be careful, brother. I mean, more than careful. Stay inside, and do all you can to come home to us. Bastien, I…" I couldn't swallow the lump in my throat when Reyn was audibly choked up. Finally, the floodgates broke, and Reyn spoke through his controlled sobs. "It's not right that I get to stay here, and you have to leave. I wouldn't have any of this if it wasn't for you. *You* pushed us harder to find Rosie, so we could locate Roland. *You* kept the team going when there was no chance of besting Morgan. *You* encouraged me to go for it with a Duchess who has always been so clearly out of my league. It's because you didn't quit that I now have a wife, a daughter and three sons." He let out a muffled noise of frustration, I'm guessing into Bastien's shoulder. "It's not right that I get to keep the life you gave me, but you have to go back into the lion's den. It's not fair! Why should I get four children, but you have none?"

Guilt pinged in my chest. It was normal for them to think about kids. They were in their thirties, and from a culture where women got pregnant just about as soon as they got married.

Bastien's reply was measured, and I could hear him bracing himself against his own breakdown. "You have this life because you're a good man. You deserve lots of kids, and a wife who can't stop smiling at you. I'd do it all over again even if I got nothing in the end, if only it would get you here. I love you, brother." He drew in several long, syncopated breaths. "I'll bring your daughter back. I won't let this family be broken."

"Bring yourself back, too," Reyn insisted. "I can't stand it when you throw yourself headfirst into danger. You can't do that when you're married. You have to think in the long-term. I'm scared that if I'm not there to remind you to be careful, that this will be the last time I see you."

Reyn's cries were muffled in Bastien's tight embrace, and I knew Bastien was a few seconds away from his own tears. He didn't like crying, much less with witnesses, so he kissed Reyn's cheek and released him. "I'll wait outside. I can't handle much more of this. I'm still a little weak."

Lane's mama bear voice was in full swing. "Oh, no, you don't. Sit right here and have a drink of water. Moms know best."

"That's the rumor, I hear." I heard Bastien chuckle as he obeyed, taking in a few swallows. "There. I'm all better now."

Lane's voice was quiet, but I could hear her clear as day. "I don't need to tell you to watch over her; you've proven that you're perfectly capable of that. So I'll just kiss your cheek and tell you that I couldn't have picked a more imperfect perfect guy for Rosie. I wouldn't change a thing about you, Bastien. Truly. I hope you know that you belong with us, that I'm your mother, and I love you." My heart warmed when she kissed his cheek.

"I love you, too, Mom. Take pictures, okay? I mean, like a picture every day of Lucas. I don't like that I won't see it all. And write everything down."

"Of course. Whatever you want, hun. Anything else?"

"Be safe. Sometimes you leave the door unlocked at

night. I come over and lock it for you, so no one breaks in. Bolt everything. I'm serious. I won't be here, and I'll worry if you don't promise me you'll protect yourself. When I come home, I want you all here."

"I promise my very best promise. I'll lock all the doors at night." I imagined her holding up her hand, as if she were swearing an oath in court. I heard Bastien playing with Lucas, and the bumpy cooing our baby cousin/brother/nephew did when Bastien bounced him on his knee.

"We should go," Kerdik reminded us.

I was still in Draper's arms, but neither of us had the guts to speak. I hadn't given Draper the choice of coming along. Though my brother was mad at me for the edict I wouldn't negotiate on, I didn't care. "I don't like this," Draper admitted, finally letting his worry out in a gust.

"You'll be safer the farther away from me you are."

"I don't care about safety. I care that we're apart."

"You still have your mom, and a dad who loves you."

Draper snorted a one-noted laugh whenever it dawned on us that Reyn was his father, though Reyn was around his own age. I guess it was kind of funny.

"Take care of them, okay? I... I'm no good at this kind of thing."

Draper gripped the nape of my neck, the sound of Lane's sobs still pinging our hearts even after Reyn had kissed Link and Quinn goodbye, told me he loved me once more, and ushered her back to their house with Lucas.

"Tell me that you'll do everything you can to come home in one piece."

"I'll come home to you, Draper."

"Tell me that I'm worrying over nothing, that you'll do everything you can to be bored in Avalon."

"I'll eat candy and sit on my butt all day long. I might even stuff your giant TV in my bag, so I can watch all my favorite shows."

I tried to do shtick, but he wasn't having it. He squeezed me tighter. "When you were a baby, you screamed if I wasn't there to sing you to sleep. I know it's ridiculous, but I've got this anxiety about you sleeping over there without me to watch over you."

My hand climbed up to touch his cheek. It was slick with silent tears, which made my heart beat unevenly. I didn't like it when Draper cried. "I'll be safe with Bastien."

He pressed his forehead to mine, and when my fingertips floated over his lashes, I could tell his eyes were closed. Softly, and just for me, he started singing the lullaby he'd sang for me when I'd been a baby. "Climb all the mountains, run off when you're grown, but for now, little girl, my song is your home."

I let out a foul curse word when my tears brimmed and started to spill. "Look what you did, Draper! Now I'm crying. I was doing so well, and then you had to go sing that stinking song." I stomped my foot in frustration, smearing the blood across my face with the back of my hand.

Kerdik turned me away from my brother and washed my face and hands. "It's time," he informed us both. "Look after the Duchess, Draper," he said, shaking my brother's hand. It was strange whenever Kerdik did something normal and showed respect to others, but he was learning, and I loved him for the effort.

"Yes, sir. Look after my sister."

"I promise." Then Kerdik moved me to stand next to Bastien, who coiled his arm around my hips. Kerdik held tight to my hand, and after Link hugged Draper, we huddled around Kerdik, each of us putting a hand on him in anticipation of porting to Avalon. Without immortal magic, we would've had to go down the well to the portal, but Kerdik had the direct route. He waited until Draper left the house before he said quietly, "Now, when we get to Avalon, I want you to stay low. Do whatever you can to keep your presence secret for now."

Bastien's voice was wary, his hand moving to the small of my back. "What are we about to walk into?"

Kerdik didn't answer, which somehow made it all feel far scarier than it had a few minutes ago. "This is our only option right now. We have to get her out of here."

Bastien drew me to his front, and then reached out to grip Kerdik's shoulder. "Whatever it takes. Let's do it." He pulled Kerdik in so I was sandwiched between them. It struck me afresh how unworthy I felt of such devotion on both their parts.

I closed my eyes as I clung to the men I loved, knowing

that when I opened my lashes again, Avalon would be my new home.

Love the book? Leave a review.
Otherwise I'll make Dub Rosie's new love interest.
(*Ick!* I just cringed)

42

BLIND GIRL

Here's a free preview of *Blind Girl*,
Book 9 in the *Faîte Falling* series.

"You don't sound like you're doing all that well," I observed.

Kerdik huffed through his response. "I'm amazing. Never been better."

I felt like a kid the night before exams. My stomach was in knots, and I had a guilty feeling I couldn't reconcile, even though I knew this wasn't a test, and very little was actually being expected of me. I placed my hand on Kerdik's back, hoping the simple touch might calm his breathing. He was bent over and clutching his knees still.

We'd made it from my living room in Common all the

way to Avalon in the span of a few seconds, but now we were in limbo while Kerdik recovered from the effort. We were in minute one million (or like, ten, but still), and I was itching to get to our safe house – or castle, I guess.

Bastien and Link were standing a few yards away, talking and planning about different ways to protect the castle once we arrived. Quinn was too afraid to stand near Kerdik, so my sweet friend stood on Link's other side, interjecting a question every now and then. This was her first trip to Avalon.

I stroked Kerdik's back to soothe his panting. "I'm thinking this is a bad time to ask if we're almost there."

"Which answer will pacify you? If you prefer I tell you we're almost there, then yes, in a mere moment you'll be strolling over your old drawbridge, and you'll be greeted by Duke Lot."

I glowered in Kerdik's direction. "You don't have to be a d-bag about it. It was just a question. It wasn't even a question. It was an almost-question."

"Well, then I'm *almost* irritated with you. Do you think it's easy to port four people, plus all their gear across whole planes of existence?"

I didn't miss a beat with my tart, "yes."

Kerdik paused, and then started laughing at my frank demeanor. "I suppose I should be used to your mouth by now, but I can't decide whether I want to kiss it or be cross with it."

"How about neither," Bastien said, his tone a little

gruff. I was glad he was upright, and that I hadn't accidentally killed him when my Vampire tendencies took over. I was bonded to my husband by more than just vows. I'm an *Attelage* Vampire, and he's my mate, so if I didn't feed off of him regularly, my cravings went bonkers. Apparently, just shy of seven days of starving myself was when I checked out of Rosie Land, and went to Crazy Town. At the first drop of his sweet blood that broke my fast, I couldn't stop myself, and took way too much. Link had to launch Bastien off of me to save his life. That's the danger of marrying a delicious man. Unfortunately, we hadn't been granted the space to talk about the incident, so I hadn't been able to apologize properly. I was ashamed of myself, and certain he wouldn't be able to trust me for a while.

I held onto Kerdik's hand until he was ready to stand up straight. He pulled me to his side so he could lean on me. "You're using too much magic these days," I observed of his heavy limbs. "Any chance of you cutting back at all?"

Kerdik blew out a raspberry, which meant he was dragging more than he wanted to admit. "I'm fine. Never better. Just had to catch my breath."

"Wouldn't it have been easier to port us directly into the castle?" Bastien inquired. "We've still got a ways to walk. I thought the goal was stealth."

"It still is. You're forgetting who's in charge. I can't port into the castle because of my own charms set up to ward against such things." Kerdik fumbled with a buckle, though I couldn't tell what the metallic clang belonged to. "I brought the invisibility cloaks Cailleach gave you two to wear. No one cares if these two are here." I'm guessing that last bit was directed at Link and Quinn.

"Oh, sweet! I totally forgot about that. When you see Cailleach again, give her a big, sloppy kiss from me. Old girl is a great gift-giver." I held out my hand, hoping Kerdik would set the cloak in my palm. That's the problem with being blind; you have no idea what everyone's doing around you, so there's a lot of guesswork involved in normal day-to-day exchanges.

Instead of handing me the cloak, Kerdik slid his palm against mine, interlocking our fingers. "We're hidden for now. The trees are quite thick."

"Where are we?" I hated asking things that everybody knew but me. It made me feel stupid. I could smell pine and air that was crisp with the thrill of autumn. The ground beneath me was soft grass with a few crunchy leaves, but other than that, I wanted a clearer picture.

"Forgive me. We're in Avalon, in the woods near the back of the castle. We're still a solid ten-minute walk away, though it's all on the back of the property, so as not to draw attention to Link, Quinn and me."

Bastien moved to my side and wrapped his arm around my back, tucking me tight to his body so I didn't trip over the uneven terrain. I breathed anew at the contact I'd been too ashamed to ask for. I wanted to be near him, but I knew I didn't deserve the privilege. I'd attacked my own husband, seeing him more as food than as my partner. I was a horrible person, yet Bastien didn't seem too put off. "Here, put the cloak on me. I'm taller. Link, take the second one for you and Quinn. No one's after you two, but news of an Untouchable in town spreads fast." He lightly shoved my face into his armpit. "How's the air, babe?"

I pretended to gag, but truthfully, I loved Bastien's oaky smell. "Totally rancid!"

Bastien tied the cloak around his neck so that we both vanished from view. We walked in-step through the woods, though our progress was slow. Walking across a flat surface was more difficult than people often realize. My cane did its best to tap along the grass and seek out problematic roots. That, paired with Bastien's keen eyes might've been enough, but after the third time I tripped, he ruled that me simply walking wasn't safe. "Oh, the joys of being the weakest link," I muttered as I clicked my telescoping cane down to a mere eight inches.

"You can carry me when I go blind, if that makes you feel any better." Bastien scooped me up in his arms, making me feel small and incapable, though I know that wasn't his intent. He loved me, and did his best to make sure I didn't do a Three Stooges faceplant along the way.

"I used to be able to keep up with you warriors," I mumbled, disheartened.

"You still can. This is only temporary."

"You keep telling yourself that, pal."

Bastien's arms tightened around me. "Come on, Daisy. We can't lose hope. Everything's going to be alright. I've got you."

My sullen expression softened, and I relaxed in his arms, letting him cradle me to his chest as he walked steadily forward. "Well, what could be better than that?" I rested my head against his thick shoulder, marveling at the muscle beneath. "Are you sure you should be exerting yourself like this? You lost a lot of blood last night."

"I'm doing just fine. I can't believe I actually fainted. *Now* who's the damsel in distress?"

"I'm really sorry I hurt you. I didn't mean to take so much blood. I completely lost control."

"I have that effect on women."

My fist bunched the material of his shirt to get a little closer to my ultimate source of comfort. "You should be mad at me. You should be furious. I hurt you. If Link hadn't been there, I'm scared to think at what might've happened."

Bastien paused to kiss my lips, letting the others trail ahead. "But he was there, and you did stop. Now we know that you can't fast off of blood anymore. Problem solved."

"Aren't you afraid of me?"

Bastien's chest vibrated with silent mirth. "Oh, absolutely. You're the most terrifying queen I've ever known." He pinched my thigh. "Do you want me to be scared?"

"No, but I... Bastien, I'm so very sorry. And don't forgive me. Somehow that just makes what I did seem even worse."

"I'm not worried, and I'm not upset."

I swallowed a lump in my throat. "I could've killed you."

Bastien was silent for a few beats. "But you didn't, so we don't have to be upset about that. If you had killed me, boy, would I have had a thing or two to say about it."

I snorted, and then kissed his scruffy cheek. I absolutely adored his perma-five o'clock shadow, and rubbed my nose up and down it just to get a little closer. "You're precious to me, and I was careless with you. I won't put you in danger like that again. I won't try to go off blood like that."

"Music to my ears. You know, if you're feeling this guilty, I've got a few ideas as to how you can make it up to me." He proceeded to whisper a litany of filthy things into my ear, making the heat rise in my cheeks, and my body curl into his like a needy kitten.

"I think all of that can be arranged, once we get settled."

Link's brogue interrupted our forest flirting. "We're moving into the open now, so stay close by, Bastien. Quinn, let's walk next to Bastien, so if something comes at us, he can leave Rosie with ye, and help me fend it off."

"What exactly are we worried might attack us on the castle grounds?" I asked quietly.

Kerdik's voice was quiet as well, so I knew Link wasn't being paranoid. "*Farouche* Vampires, or any number of disgruntled Dullahan. There are two groups of headless horsemen now. One are mostly harmless. They actually help Duke Lot by gathering up the decapitated Vampires. The other group is more vigilante. Not quite so forgiving of the townsfolk who turned on those affected by the higher magic. They ride on horseback, and whenever a Dullahan stops riding, someone dies."

"Yikes." My spine tingled with the threat of the ominous. "Um, guys? Are we still in the forest?"

"We are," Quinn replied. "We'll be out soon enough."

"I don't hear any animals. Like, none at all." With my birth blessing, I could not only hear the chirping and movements of animals, but I could talk to them, too. Usually they flocked to me for the chance to finally be heard, but I couldn't hear a single cheep.

Everyone stopped moving, and for a moment, I wondered if we'd all stopped breathing at the same time.

I should've known we were in the calm before the storm. I should've known the storm would do its best to suck all of us under. I stiffened at the footfalls that were too heavy to be a critter, and too erratic to be a person.

"Behind us!" I warned, but it was too late. Link cried out at the collision that I couldn't see, and hadn't been able to prevent. His cry pierced my heart and made my blood freeze in my veins. If whatever it was could take Link by surprise, then we were all in trouble.

. . .

Start Book 9 in the *Faîte Falling* series,
and read <u>Blind Girl</u> today!

ABOUT THE AUTHOR

USA Today bestselling author Mary E. Twomey lives in Michigan with her three adorable children. She enjoys reading, writing, vegetarian cooking, and telling her children fantastic stories about wombats.

While she loves writing fantasy, dystopian, and paranormal tales for her readers, Mary also writes romance under the name Tuesday Embers, and cozy mysteries under the name Molly Maple.

Visit her online at www.maryetwomey.com, and sign up for her newsletter, so you never miss a new release.

www.ingramcontent.com/pod-product-compliance
Lightning Source LLC
Chambersburg PA
CBHW010316100726
47906CB00006B/1012